Summer Unscripted

Also by Jen Klein

Shuffle, Repeat

Summer Unscripted

·JEN KLEIN·

Random House 🏠 New York

Text copyright © 2017 by Jen Klein
Jacket illustrations and hand lettering copyright © 2017 by Sarah Coleman
Jacket photograph of couple copyright © Shutterstock/TijanaM; other boy copyright © Getty Images/ViewStock; dock copyright © Shutterstock/Elovich; water copyright © Shutterstock/Anthony Benger

All rights reserved. Published in the United States by
Random House Children's Books, a division of
Penguin Random House LLC, New York.

Random House and the colophon are registered trademarks of
Penguin Random House LLC.

Visit us on the Web! randomhouseteens.com

Educators and librarians, for a variety of teaching tools,
visit us at RHTeachersLibrarians.com

Library of Congress Cataloging-in-Publication Data is available upon request.

ISBN 978-1-5247-0004-1 (trade) — ISBN 978-1-5247-0006-5 (ebook)

Printed in the United States of America
10 9 8 7 6 5 4 3 2 1
First Edition

Random House Children's Books supports the
First Amendment and celebrates the right to read.

For y'all.
You know who.

Summer
Unscripted

Chapter 1

When the lightning strikes, I'm a bored rose between two snoring thorns. The thorns are my best friends, Marin and Sarah, who are crashed out on either side of me, and the lightning is #nofilter-perfect Tuck Brady, sauntering across the stage of our high school auditorium. I—Rainie Langdon, the bored rose—am planted in row J. It's not a place where one usually encounters lightning.

But it's the final week of the school year, which at Dobbs High means roughly a zillion mandatory assemblies designed to highlight talent in every discipline. Sarah delivered a science lecture on Monday. Marin was part of the art show on Tuesday. Now here it is Thursday—and, true to form, I have yet to set foot on the stage.

Today's festival of shame is theater, which means the entire junior class has earned the endless joy of slumping in a too-warm auditorium while drama kid after drama kid trots onto the stage to deliver handcrafted monologues intended to punch us right in the angst.

It's the worst.

Until Tuck.

He clears his throat, runs his fingers through his golden-blond hair, and turns to the audience. More specifically, he turns to *me*. Across the rows of disinterested classmates, through the dim lighting of the auditorium, Tuck Brady's sky-on-a-sunny-spring-day eyes lock right onto mine.

Which can't really be happening, because that would be crazy. If Tuck and I happen to run into each other out in the real world—say, at a gas station or a hot-dog stand—we definitely say hello, and that's definitely it. When we see each other in the halls or the cafeteria at school, we generally don't even make eye contact, because he's too busy with his drama-head friends or his soccer friends or his music friends, and I'm too busy gabbing with Marin and Sarah. What I'm saying is—we do *not* run in the same circles, so there's no way he's looking at me.

Yet . . . he is.

I've tuned out the last six hundred monologues, so I have no idea how different this one is, but it must be different because . . .

Because Tuck isn't just talking *to* me.

He's talking *about* me.

"You're a canoe," Tuck says to me (and, presumably, the rest of the auditorium). "You're floating. Aimless. You're drifting. Getting knocked askew by the waves of speedboats rocketing past you. They all know where they're going. They all have a plan. But you . . . you don't."

I glance at Sarah. She's a speedboat with big plans. Neurosurgery plans. She's got her next fifteen years mapped out to the minute. Then there's Marin. She's spent every summer since eighth grade at a different art program and already knows she's doing undergrad at Pratt, and Glasgow for her master's. Me, however . . .

Tuck is right. I'm a canoe. No effing idea where I'm going. Nary a paddle to be found.

"Floating is easier." Tuck's gaze drifts to the balcony overhead, and I slowly relax. I was right the first time. Tuck is just being an actor, and I'm just being my usual: the girl without a country. "You don't have to be brave if you're not the one steering. It's the current making choices, not you."

Tuck's eyes suddenly dart back to my own. He sends a smile blazing across the seats at me, and—because I can't believe what I'm seeing—I throw out both elbows. They connect solid with my friends. Marin only waves a hand at me and huffs a little, flopping her head to the other side and going right back to sleep, but Sarah bolts awake. "What?" she asks too loudly.

Several people shush her. One of them is me. I point at the stage, and Sarah swivels her head to look at Tuck. Who is looking at me. Looking back at him.

I am not used to all this looking.

"It wouldn't be so scary if you had a road map, if you could see the signs." Tuck shifts his weight and continues his monologue. "Then you would just *know* what path to take. You wouldn't have to guess. You wouldn't have to be terrified of going in the wrong direction. I get it."

By extension—I extrapolate—Tuck Brady gets *me.*

Something clicks inside me. It's a door opening, a door that has always been locked. Behind it is something desperate and wild and free, some buried part of me that wants to get out, that wants to experiment, to *risk* . . .

And, let's be honest, that wouldn't mind kissing Tuck Brady. God, that boy is hot.

"But sometimes you can't see the path until after you've walked it. The signs are there, but you don't know where to look yet." Tuck gazes down at me from the stage. "So take a chance."

Sarah nudges me. "I think he's—"

"I know," I tell her. "Hush."

"Risk it." This time, Tuck takes a step forward. Toward me. Toward the future. Toward . . . dare I say it . . . *our* future? "If we're not alone, maybe it won't be so scary." He stretches his hand out. Slowly, slowly, like he might actually be able to reach all the way out to my row and touch me. I straighten in my seat, leaning forward, starting to rise . . .

"Rainie." Sarah grabs my wrist, keeping me in my uncomfortable auditorium chair on planet Earth. "Don't make it weird."

I don't know how I could possibly be the one making it weird when Tuck is currently doing the weirdest thing that anyone has ever done, but I settle back down. It must be right, because Tuck flashes a grin at me—a blinding-white, heart-stopping grin—before walking offstage to half-assed applause from 99 percent of the audience, and to thunderous, palm-stinging, whole-assed applause from the last percent. Otherwise known as me.

Crash.

Lightning.

• • •

I'm in a daze as I follow Sarah past a row of lockers, past a group of freshmen playing cards in a corner, and past a steamy couple just rounding second base. Basically, the entire school is treading water until the week is over. We reach the art room—a place where we clearly do not belong—and plop our lunches onto a table. Marin looks up from a sketchbook she's drawing in: an indication that she clearly *does* belong. "Reminder about the condiments." Marin gives us each a stern look. "Keep it on your fries, not the supplies."

Sarah drips ketchup over her paper envelope of French fries. "Buzzkill."

I flick Marin on the arm. "Yeah, one mustard finger-painting incident and suddenly it's all TSA in here."

Marin flicks me back. "Behave," she says as I reach toward Sarah's envelope. Sarah swats at my hand but allows me to take a fry.

We eat in silence for a moment: Marin because she's still sketching, Sarah because she's trying to power through her fries before I snag the rest of them, me because I'm trying to decide if fate just stepped in to have its way with me or if I'm hallucinating. Was Tuck talking to me from that stage? Surely it didn't happen.

But what if it did?

"Dude, quit." The world snaps back into focus, and I realize I've been staring straight at Marin, my mouth open with a half-chewed fry inside. Marin looks at Sarah. "Why is Rainie doing . . . that?"

Sarah shrugs. "There was a weird thing in the assembly, and now she's tripping about it."

"I'm not tripping about anything," I inform them both. Even though I am 100 percent tripping about all the things.

"I didn't see anything weird." Marin erases something in her sketchbook.

"You were asleep," Sarah and I say together.

Sarah nudges me. "Tell her."

"No."

"Then I will." Sarah leans toward Marin. "Tuck Brady couldn't take his eyes off Rainie. It was like the end of *The Jungle Book,* when Mowgli follows the girl into the village."

"It was not like that," I say, even though it completely was. "And Tuck has a girlfriend."

"Not anymore." Marin flicks a thick red braid back from her face. "He broke up with Olivia."

"Why? When?" Sarah looks as surprised as I feel. Tuck and Olivia are one of those perfectly iconic high school couples: hot artsy drama boy with hot artsy artist girl. Does this mean Tuck is now an actual option?

"I don't know. Maybe a couple weeks ago?" Marin shrugs. "Olivia thinks there's another chick, but Tuck said there's not. Who knows."

"I'm telling you, he's Mowgli." Sarah gives me a pointed look. "And you're the girl with a water bucket on your head."

I roll my eyes at her. Marin flips her sketchbook to a blank page and slides it across the table at me. "Here, do you want to draw your feelings?" She's making fun of the life coach who spent a week at school earlier this year, trying to get everyone to identify their dreams and goals.

"I can't draw," I tell her. "Especially dreams and goals."

Because I don't know what mine are. I never have.

Marin gives me a look that I think is supposed to be supportive. "You took that one art class, remember?" She reconsiders. "I guess, technically speaking, you only took *half* of the class. But you weren't bad."

"I was bad," I tell her.

"You were better than Sarah, and she stuck it out until the end. Here." Marin shoves the sketchbook at Sarah. "Show Rainie what a bad little artist you are."

Sarah draws a stick figure giving the finger and holds it up toward Marin.

"See?" says Marin. "She sucks."

Sarah pokes out her tongue at Marin. I don't do or say anything. I'm too confused.

• • •

I've just reached my locker after algebra (specifically, after an algebra test on which I'm fairly certain I scored my old dependable grade of C). I'm twirling the combination lock when Sarah slams against the locker beside mine. "You're going to rupture something," I tell her.

"You're going to love me," she says.

"I already love you."

"Love me more." She leans in, bringing her voice down. "The drama kids are having a party tonight."

"The drama kids are always having a party." I'm being flippant, but the ramifications are already spinning through my head. Recently single boy plus music plus alcohol. These are the ingredients of a zillion successful high school love stories. "Where?"

"Wendell's house. His parents are in the Poconos for their anniversary." Sarah pokes me in the arm. "I've never hooked up with a drama boy."

I glance over at Sarah's flawless complexion and gorgeous Indian features, so different from my boring look: dirty-blond hair, blue eyes, pale skin with a smattering of freckles. She will have no problem finding a drama boy . . . or any boy, for that matter.

"I'm in."

• • •

As it turns out, Marin doesn't have Friday plans either, although she draws the line at hooking up with drama boys. "I only like slam poet boys and tennis boys," she reminds us. "Or the occasional rockabilly girl."

Marin has very specific tastes.

When the three of us get to the party, Wendell is hanging out on his big wraparound front porch with a couple of other kids. He doesn't look surprised to see us approaching through the cloud of clove-scented smoke that surrounds him. He throws a peace sign at Sarah. "Slumming it?"

"More like a change of pace," Sarah tells him.

He jerks a thumb toward the house. "There's a pony keg in the downstairs bathroom."

We thank him and head in. On the way, I nudge Sarah. "Wendell is cute, if you don't mind the cigarettes."

"I mind."

Inside, the party isn't raging, but it's not dead either. A couple dozen people mill about, talking and drinking. It looks like Wendell's anniversary-celebrating parents have a shot at getting their house returned to them in decent shape, which is better than I can say for the parents of the cheerleader whose party we crashed a few weeks ago.

Reggae music plays from a speaker, and an underclassman sits cross-legged on the floor with a guitar, strumming along. Ella Reynolds kneels beside him with a set of bongos that she's not so much playing as tapping. Ella and I used to be best friends, but we stopped hanging out in middle school, when I "lost focus" (the guidance counselor's words, not mine) and Ella started turning into the type of girl who knelt on the floor with bongos.

When Ella sees us, she pushes the bongos off her lap and rises to greet us. "What are you doing, slumming it?" she asks me with a grin.

Sarah rolls her eyes. "I thought you guys were supposed to be all original." Marin elbows her in the ribs, and Sarah throws up her hands. "What?"

"Sorry," I tell Ella. "They don't get out much."

Sarah throws me a look of mock anger. "We'll get drinks."

She drags Marin toward the back of the house, presumably in the direction of the famed downstairs bathroom.

Ella takes in my outfit—short dress, tall boots, mascara— which makes me realize I probably overdressed for this particular occasion. The cheerleaders may have been too wild for my taste, but at least I understood their party. You want a boy, you show some skin.

"So, really." Ella cocks her head to one side. "What are you doing here?"

I shrug (what else am I going to do?). "First summer weekend. Seemed like fun—"

I stop because Ella's eyes have slid past me and narrowed. I turn to follow her gaze to the front door, where James Dean is entering the room. I mean, James Dean if he was young and artsy and Latino.

And also alive.

The guy is tall—even taller than I am now in my three-inch heels—with light bronze skin and dark brown eyes. Despite the warm June air, he wears jeans and a black jacket over a white T-shirt. As I watch, he reaches up and tucks a strand of his choppy black hair behind one ear.

I give a subtle tug to my hemline. On second thought, maybe this is too much skin.

Beside me, Ella makes a disgusted sound under her breath. "Do you know him?" I ask her.

"Yeah, unfortunately." She throws a fake smile at him. "My ex. Milo Cabrera. Goes to North. I don't know why he's here."

I remember Ella's very first boyfriend: a shy sixth grader who later moved out of state. Fine, but nothing to write home about. This Milo guy, however . . . well, let's just say Ella has leveled up since sixth grade. Like, *all* the levels.

I kinda want to keep staring at him, except suddenly Tuck Brady is sauntering into the room. He's also wearing jeans and a white T-shirt, so maybe there's some sort of drama-boy dress code I've never noticed before. He walks over to Milo, and they do a handshake-into-a-one-armed-hug routine.

Ella makes another one of her sounds. "Of course. Tuck. God, get some new friends." She turns to look at me. "Well, now we've made eye contact, so I have to say hello or I'm the asshole. Come on."

She strikes out across the room and I follow. We reach the boys just as Milo is asking Tuck a question: "How'd your thing go today?"

"Awesome." Tuck raises a fist to bump Milo's. "Totally connected onstage." He turns to look at me and I swear that his sky-blue eyes deepen to the color of the ocean. "You were there. What did you think?"

Of course I was there. I was *there.*

I tell Tuck the truth—"It was amazing"—and am rewarded with the world's most perfect smile. It makes me want to say it again, just to keep him smiling at me, but his ocean eyes are already sliding to Ella.

"Ella-bella?"

She purses her lips, considering. "Your monologue was good.

It was *really* good, don't get me wrong . . . but I liked the one you did in class better. It felt more authentic."

I wish I felt "more authentic," because I'm not really sure how to contribute to this conversation. Instead, I give my hemline another tiny tug. It gets Tuck's attention, and those eyes turn back to me. "Sorry, this is Rainie," he tells Milo. "She goes to our school."

Milo and I exchange "heys" and head bobs before I focus on Tuck again. "You guys had to write the monologues yourselves, right?"

"I mean . . . yeah." Tuck looks embarrassed. "Was it too much? Was it over the top?"

Before I can answer, Milo clears his throat. "I'm gonna grab a drink. Anyone want anything?"

"I'm good," Tuck and I say at the same time. I take it as a sign that we have indeed been brought together by fate. Ella apparently takes it as a sign that no one else wants a beer.

"I'll get my own," she says, and heads away with Milo. She's being my wingwoman without even knowing it.

It leaves Tuck and me standing in the middle of the party while an R&B song I don't know blares from the speakers. Nearby, several people start dancing. Thank God, Tuck isn't one of them. He gazes down at me. "It's hard, you know?" It takes me a second to remember he's still talking about his monologue. "To expose yourself like that."

I understand. I understand so hard I want to kiss him or cry or scream into a pillow. I never expose myself. Not in a *real* way. I don't want to be seen. Not as raw truth. It's way easier to skitter over the surface of everything like a light, flat stone on water. Never sinking, but never ending up anywhere important. "It's the hardest thing I can imagine."

"Hey, Rain." He looks at me like he's trying to decipher something. Like he's trying to decipher *me*. "How come we've never hung out?"

"Because you do all the things and I . . . don't." I guess I'm going with awkward honesty, then.

"You've always been here, though. I've seen you around, but I've never . . . *seen* you." He cocks his head, still trying to figure me out. "I don't know why I've never seen you."

"You saw me today." Unless I was hallucinating, that is.

"Yeah." Tuck takes a step closer. "I walked onto the stage and looked out, and everything was a blur except you. You came into focus and . . . I don't know. You were like an anchor."

I frown. Anchors are big and heavy and, I assume, rusted from all the salt water. They're hardly sexy.

"Senior year," Tuck says. "We are going to hang out."

But that's forever away.

He reaches out and runs a fingertip down my arm, so lightly it tickles. I keep looking at him while people dance around us, and the music shifts to a pop song from the eighties, and the smell of cloves wafts in from the front porch.

"What are you doing this summer?" It comes out of my mouth in a whisper.

"Olympus."

My heart sinks. That's a university town in the Appalachian Mountains, a couple hours north of Dobbs. My grandparents took me once to look at the autumn leaves (yes, looking at leaves is a thing in North Carolina), and Ella's older sister, Annette, goes to school there. That's the sum total of the information I possess about Olympus. "Why?"

"I'm playing Paris."

"The city?" It pops out of my mouth before I really think it through, and Tuck laughs.

"The Greek prince who carried off Helen and started the Trojan War."

And now I remember: Olympus is home to a theater of the same name. A musical about Greek mythology plays there every summer. "Are you the lead?"

"Yeah, and it's not an easy role. I'm kinda freaked out about it." I wish I remembered more of the myths I'd read as a child. "It's a risk, you know?" Again, I nod along. Again, I pretend. "The whole summer will be a risk."

"I get it." Not a total lie, but not the truth either. I flash back to his monologue, parroting back his own words. "You have to take a chance."

"Exactly." Tuck sets his hands on my shoulders. They're warm through the thin fabric of my dress. "Thank you for being there today. For listening to it." His eyes are pleading, but I don't understand what he's asking for. "You *did* listen to all of it, right?"

"Yes," I assure him. "I listened to the whole thing."

"I meant it," he tells me. "I meant all of it."

I hearken back to the assembly, to the look on Tuck Brady's

face as he stared right into my eyes. And to the last sentence he said.

"If we're not alone, maybe it won't be so scary." Even though the sentence floats out of my mouth in a whisper, it echoes loud in my ears. Tuck smiles at me in a way that is maybe grateful, maybe relieved.

"Good." Tuck's thumbs caress my shoulders. "You heard me."

"I did," I breathe, and this time I'm not lying.

Tuck leans forward and brushes my cheek with his lips. "Take a risk," he says into my ear, and then he swings away into the party.

I watch him go, beaming. Because—for the first time in my life—I have a road map. I know what I need to do. At this moment, I would follow Tuck Brady to the moon and back, but I don't have to.

The only place I have to go . . . is Olympus.

Chapter 2

Given my track record, I suppose my parents' reaction shouldn't have surprised me. Still, as we glare at one another over a platter of my dad's famous slow-cooked pork ribs and my mom's much-less-famous canned corn and pre-baked rolls, I feel blindsided. "But you're on the board of the state arts council," I say to my father. "You have to know someone at the theater."

"Not happening," he replies between bites.

"Mom." I turn to my mother, who has been known to cave more easily. "You have friends at the university. You can do something."

Mom and Dad exchange glances. Actually, what they exchange is more like the parental version of an eye roll.

"Remind me." My mother sets down her fork. "When you joined Science Olympiad, how much of the periodic table did you memorize?"

"I was in eighth grade." Defensiveness creeps into my voice. "How am I supposed to remember that?"

She turns to my father. "Barry?"

"Zirconium rings a bell." He glances at me. "Riddle me this, Rainster: Why'd you stop running track?"

"Because I hated sweating!" I fling my hands into the air. "And we had record humidity last year!"

"Except you'd already dropped soccer for the sweating thing the year before that," Mom reminds me.

"Ooh, remember sculpting class?" Dad looks almost gleeful. "Done in two lessons."

I protest—"That teacher was a jerk"—but no one seems to care . . . or even hear me.

"Ballet," says Mom.

"Journalism," says Dad.

"Fencing!"

"Photography!"

"Buddhism!"

They say the last one together and then burst into gales of laughter. It's just rude. I shove my chair back from the table and storm toward my room. I can't win here.

"We love you," Mom calls from her seat.

"A lot," calls Dad.

"Sure," I mumble under my breath.

Whatever.

• • •

The Olympus website is easy to find but difficult to navigate. It's mostly cluttered with photos from past performances of the summer musical, which is called *Zeus!*

Yes, the exclamation point is part of the title.

After several minutes of poking around, I find a section on auditions and job interviews, but they were done months ago. I scroll through photos of last summer's show and quickly find one of Tuck. He's dressed in a toga, standing with one foot propped up on a rock. He appears to be staring off into the sunset, and he's holding a spear in one hand.

It's pretty hot.

Tuck is in a whole bunch of pictures, and so are two other familiar faces. There's Milo Cabrera—Ella's ex-boyfriend from Wendell's party—and Ella herself. I find her name in a digital image of last year's program. Apparently she was an "intern." When I scroll down the list, I notice there's another Reynolds in the program: Robert Reynolds, the company manager. Now that I see it in writing, I do remember something about Ella having a relative who works at the show.

Ella and I might not be true *friends* anymore, but we aren't enemies either. At least, I don't think so.

There's only one way to find out.

• • •

Monday morning, I start stalking Ella online. Monday afternoon, my diligence is rewarded when she checks into the public library. Luckily, Dobbs is small, and I make it to the library in eight minutes flat.

Ella is in the back, behind a row of Victorian romances, making out with Bradley Ruiz. At my arrival, they spring apart.

"Do you mind?" says Bradley.

"Not cool." It takes me a second to realize Ella is talking to Bradley, not to me. "It's a public arena. Literature is for everyone." She waves her hand at the books. "Have at, Rainie."

"Actually, I'm glad I ran into you. Do you have a second?" The surprise washes over Ella's face and quickly disappears. I glance at Bradley. "In private."

Ella gives Bradley a shrug, and he wipes a smudge of red lipstick from his chin. "See you."

We watch him walk away before I turn back to Ella. "I didn't know you guys were dating."

"We're not. I'm just taking him for a test drive to see if we have chemistry. I want a good scene partner for senior play auditions in the fall." She plops onto the floor and—after a second of hesitation—I do the same. She turns her dark-lined gray eyes to me. "You're not a summer library girl, so this isn't a happy accident. What's up?"

"We don't hang out anymore." Since I'm already busted, I might as well start with the obvious. "So I recognize this is going to be a big ask. A *really* big ask."

"You want to tell your parents you're staying at my house overnight or something? Fine."

"No." I look at Ella, so different from me with her thick fringe of brown bangs shot through with black streaks, with her deliberately ratty jeans and screen-printed T-shirt. "It's bigger than that. And weirder than that." I take a deep breath and plunge in. "I want to be at *Zeus!* this summer. I don't know how to get in, and I'm not qualified to do anything, but I promise I will work really hard and—" I stop because Ella is staring at me like I've turned into a tomato. "I know it sounds crazy."

"It does."

She seems amused, not pissed, so I soldier on. "You have a relative at the theater."

"Uncle Rob."

"Right, Uncle Rob!" The words stream out of my mouth faster and faster, making less and less sense. "Maybe he needs someone to answer phones? Lead tours? Or pass out programs and walk people to their seats?"

Ella bursts out laughing. "Wait. Let me get this straight. You think you're qualified to lead tours around a theater dedicated to Greek mythology?"

"No . . ." I shake my head, color rising to my cheeks. "But I can learn. I'll do anything—I don't care. I just have to be there. *Please, Ella.*"

At the sound of her name, Ella stops laughing. She sits back against the shelf, folding her arms over her chest, and stares at me long enough to make me feel uncomfortable. "What is this really about?"

I stare back at her—this girl who used to be my friend—and decide to throw myself on her mercy. "Don't tell anyone."

She holds up a pinkie finger. "Scout's honor."

I link pinkies with her, very certain that it is not at all the symbol of the Scouts, neither boys nor girls. "There's a guy." Ella opens her mouth, and I jerk my hand away from hers, covering my face. "Please don't laugh again."

"I'm not laughing." I feel her hand on my arm, and I pull my fingers away from my face. She peers into my eyes. "Just . . . Tuck Brady? Really?"

The heat in my cheeks deepens enough that now she'd be justified in thinking I'd turned into a tomato. "How do you know it's him?"

"He's the only guy at our school who spends his summers there." Ella makes a face. "It's so predictable. He's so . . . *obvious.*"

"I'm sorry." And I am, but not for the reasons Ella probably thinks. I'm sorry because *I'm* obvious and *I'm* predictable. Because I'm not at all interesting or specific like the drama kids, like Marin, like Sarah.

Because I'm just mediocre me. Nothing special, no talent, no big plans.

No plans at all.

Except for Tuck.

"It's fine." Ella shakes her head. "I don't get it—what you see in him—but whatever. I'm a sucker for a star-crossed love story." She hops to her feet and juts a hand down. I take it hesitantly, and she pulls me to my feet. "I'll see what I can do."

With that, she spins and takes off, vanishing between the rows of books. I stand there, wondering what exactly Ella Reynolds can do.

• • •

Dad plops a tub of ice cream onto the table and sits across from me, clattering two spoons between us. "Rocky Road," he tells me. "For when your road is rocky."

"That's not a thing," I inform him, but I grab a spoon anyway.

He peels off the lid and takes a scoop before shoving the tub toward me. "I bet you could get a summer job at the geology museum."

My brow furrows on its own. "We have a geology museum?"

"On Main Street, between the Christian bookstore and the Reiki studio."

"I don't want to work there."

"It's easier to get the job you want when you already have a job."

"That doesn't make sense."

"It's the way the world works. When a potential employer sees that you already have a job, you suddenly look more interesting because someone else already wanted you." Dad shrugs. "Human nature."

We take several bites of ice cream in silence. When the home phone rings, it startles us both.

"We still have that?" Dad says.

It's Ella. She skips the pleasantries. "Can you hold a rake?"

"Yes." I don't know what that has to do with a job, but I don't care. I just need to get to Olympus.

"Are you allergic to latex?"

"No." *Where is this going?*

"Are you comfortable in front of people?" This time I pause, and Ella clears her throat. "I'll rephrase. Can you handle standing around onstage as part of a crowd six nights a week?"

Actually, that sounds mildly horrifying. "Is there maybe something I can do *behind* the scenes?"

"Look, I went to bat for you." Ella's voice hardens. "Either you want the job, or I have to tell my uncle you got hit by a bus."

I definitely don't want to get hit by a bus, even if it's a fictional bus. And I *do* want the job. Or at least I want proximity to Tuck, even if the thought of being in front of an audience fills me with dread.

There are no other options.

So I say yes.

"Great," says Ella. "Rehearsals start next week."

Chapter 3

The next day, I get mixed reactions from my best friends. Sarah says it's awesome, but Marin thinks I'm insane. In fact, she takes me to our local coffee shop to voice her concerns.

"Explain your job," she demands over the rim of her chai latte.

"It's called an actor-technician. I'll wear a costume and stand around in crowd scenes. I might move a prop or two."

Marin *thunk*s her cup down and casts a glance around as if looking for other patrons to share her shock. Sometimes Marin is more dramatic than the drama kids. "But you don't act," she says. "You don't . . . is there a verb associated with 'technician'?"

"Ella says it's easy."

"No offense to Ella—I know you used to be friends and all—but she's hardly a shining beacon of normalcy. What's easy to her is going to be craziness to you."

I stir my cappuccino, starting to feel defensive. "It's not Cirque du Soleil. It's an outdoor drama. It's *mythological.*"

Marin gives a huff that sends her red bangs dancing from her forehead. "Have you ever seen it?"

"I've heard about it," I tell Marin. "It's supposed to be amazing. It's like Broadway in the mountains."

"You mean a freak show in the sticks." Marin picks up her cup again. "Have you thought about working at that geology museum downtown?"

• • •

Six days later, one of my suitcases is scrunched between Ella and me in the rear bench seat of her parents' minivan. The other suitcases are in the trunk of my own convertible, which is behind us and being driven by my father, with my mother riding shotgun. All the parents thought it would be fun for "the kids to ride together."

Clearly, none of the parents asked the "kids."

We're halfway to Olympus and my legs are starting to feel cramped when Ella finally takes off her headphones and turns to me. "I didn't think you'd go through with it." I can't tell if she's impressed or disappointed, so I just nod. "What did your friends think?"

"Sarah thinks it's cool."

Ella's eyes narrow. "What about Marin?"

"Marin thinks it's cool too." Not exactly the truth, but Ella doesn't need to know that.

"Wonders never cease," says Ella.

Or maybe Ella *does* know I'm lying . . .

We drive for another hour up through the Appalachians, winding beneath the canopies of red maple, and alongside the white-flowering dogwoods, and over bridges across mountain lakes scattered with lily pads. Even though every mile is prettier than the last, each one tightens the knot in my stomach. I'm second-guessing every decision that led me to this point, especially the one about not giving Tuck a heads-up. On that, Sarah and Marin were in agreement, but for different reasons. Sarah didn't want it to seem like I was asking his permission. Marin thought it would make me look like a stalker. "Better to just show up and let him ask why you're there," she said.

"But then what do I say?" I asked.

"You fell in love with theater, you wanted to hang out with Ella, whatever. It won't matter. The deed will be done."

Now, however, I'm wondering if not telling Tuck was a stupid move.

We finally arrive at my new summer home. It's located on Crestline Drive, in a large gray block of an apartment building. Ella's parents' van sidles past the patchy-grassed lawn out front and into the cracked-asphalt parking lot in the back. "Here we are!" Mr. Reynolds chirps, turning off the engine.

Ella shoulders her canvas messenger bag. "This is our stop." She climbs out ahead of me.

I look through the van's window. A giant black dumpster graces the rear of the concrete apartment building. Someone has spray-painted what might be gang symbols on its side. On the second floor, where Ella's sister Annette lives, a wooden deck runs along the entire building. At various intervals, I see the following: five half-melted candles and three ashtrays on the top rail, two dangly wind chimes, a long-haired brunette talking on her cell phone, a guy playing what I think is a banjo, and a giant tie-dyed sheet apparently being used as a privacy screen.

It looks like a camp for wayward hippies.

Mr. Reynolds slings the strap of Ella's duffel bag over his shoulder and then heads toward the building with Mrs. Reynolds. "This is Annette's third year here," he calls back to us. "She loves it."

We make our way up to the deck, where Mrs. Reynolds knocks on the door to apartment number eighteen. Only a second passes before it flies open and Annette leaps out with hugs for everyone, including my parents and me. "Oh my gosh, you're all grown up!" she exclaims as she pulls back from our one-sided embrace.

I stare at her. Annette used to babysit me when I was little. My parents loved her because she was so strict. Even on the occasions when Annette brought Ella with her so we could play, she always made us go to sleep exactly at bedtime, and she never sneaked us candy, like the other sitters. She was nice enough, but she wasn't exactly *fun* . . . which I'm pretty sure is why my parents agreed to let me stay in Olympus for the summer: because hard-core Annette would be in charge.

The Annette of my memories was also rather plain. She didn't use makeup, her hair was always in a ponytail, and she wore dark-rimmed glasses that tried to be artsy but were more librarian. Current Annette still doesn't wear makeup, but she also doesn't have glasses or a ponytail. Her hair—the same light brown as Ella's—is now long and straight, with sideswept bangs.

She's . . . pretty. Hard-core, no-candy, bedtime-tyrant Annette is now pretty.

"Well, I am sixteen," I tell her.

"Of course you are." Annette gives me a patient smile. "It's just that it's been a long time."

Thankfully, the inside of Annette's—I mean, *our*—apartment is nicer than the exterior led me to believe. Daisy-patterned curtains cover the windows. There are cobalt-blue throw pillows arranged neatly on the sofa and papasan chair in the living room to our right. A bamboo coffee table holds a set of glass coasters that match the pillows. The walls are hung with framed pressed flowers . . . and also with a calendar featuring a bald man in his underwear eating spaghetti. Annette laughs when she catches me looking at it. "The guys at the restaurant where I work made those. Aren't they funny?"

None of the parents bat an eye, so I lean closer and flip through it. Yep, twelve photos of squishy dudes playing with pasta. Hawt.

I'm starting to feel better about the living situation until we delve further into the apartment. Namely, the bedrooms. Mine is small—which I'd expected—but it also has two twin beds that make the floor space extra cramped. I heft a suitcase onto the bed by the door. Might as well use it as extra storage space, since the closet and the dresser are also tiny—

"That's cool." Ella slings her duffel bag onto the far bed. "I'd rather be by the windows."

"We're sharing a room?" Ella's eyebrows shoot up, making me instantly regret the question. Yes, I am aware that many people the world over share rooms, but I've never been one of them. I am an only child, which means that I was expelled from the womb and immediately put into my own bassinet. I've always had solo space. Always.

Ella gives me a funny look. "Did you think you'd share with Annette?"

Actually, I thought *she* would share with Annette—since they're siblings and all—but I don't say it. I only shake my head and go back to the main living area.

Annette brings out iced tea for everyone, and we all sit around for a while, being extraordinarily polite, while she goes over the house rules: no parties, no boys, no alcohol (apparently Tyrant Annette isn't dead after all), and we have to come right home after the show every night. We're less than a mile from the theater, and it's well lit the entire way, so we can walk or I can drive us. Dad gives Mom a nervous glance at that information, but she squeezes his hand and he settles back against the cobalt pillows.

"Rainie, keep your cell phone on you at all times," Mom reminds me.

"Should we get her pepper spray?" Dad asks. Ella smirks at his question.

The parents hang out for a little longer. My dad wants to take everyone out to lunch, but the Reynoldses say they need to get back down the mountain because Ella and Annette's little sister has a soccer game.

As Ella's parents are getting ready to go, mine pull me out onto the wooden deck. "Shall we go over the final points of the Great Negotiation?" My father is referring to the series of discussions I'd endured before receiving my parents' stamp of approval on my summer plans.

"Please, no."

"It's like joining a sports team." Mom brushes an imaginary strand of hair out of my eyes, which is something she does when she wants to touch me but doesn't know how it will be received. "People are counting on you."

"You have to follow through," Dad says. "The whole summer."

"I know." Because we've been over it. A lot.

"Also, it's the key to continuing to own a car for your senior year." Dad makes a face that I think is supposed to be hard-ass. "No follow-through, no car."

"I get it," I tell him. "I'll stay here and be a part of the team."

"We know you can have a productive summer," Mom says. "We know you can be successful."

"And by 'be successful,' we mean 'finish.'" Dad swoops me into a hug. "We'll miss you."

Against all sense, my throat tightens. I allow Dad to hold me a second longer than I normally would before I pull away.

"Have a good time in Europe," I tell them both.

Twenty minutes later, Ella and I watch from the deck as the Reynoldses' van cruises through the parking lot and disappears around the building, taking all four of our parents in it. "Bye," Ella says, and I'm surprised to hear it come out in a strangled whisper. I'm about to ask if she's okay, but instead we're both simultaneously startled and silenced by the sound of Annette's voice in the apartment behind us. It's not the calm, authoritative tone I've known since my childhood—the one saying, "No, you cannot have another drink of water, go back to bed." Instead, it's a loud war whoop followed by one word delivered in a deafening screech:

"Biiiiiiiiiiiiiitches!"

Ella and I whirl as Annette careens through the doorway. She has one open bottle of beer in her left hand, and two in her right. On her face is a giant, victorious grin. She slaloms over and hands a bottle to each of us. "I have three words for y'all." She performs a little dance move that is half hip-shake and half shimmy. "You. Are. Welcome."

Chapter 4

Without any parents around to witness them, Annette's *true* rules are a lot less tyrannical: "Be quiet when I'm asleep, and don't steal my booze."

Ella doesn't seem fazed at all by her sister's remarkable change of attitude, but I'm shocked. Pleasantly so.

However, by the time the next morning's sunlight is peeking between the plastic vertical blinds of the bedroom I now share with Ella, I'm more than ready to get out. The apartment's walls are already closing in on me. It doesn't help that I'm exhausted after a night of sleeping only in fits and starts. Not a great way to start the summer with Tuck.

I pull on the clothes I chose last night—jeans and a tank top for a deliberately casual look—and slide my feet into raspberry Havaianas. I spend twenty minutes trying to pull my hair into a ponytail with just the right amount of escaped tendrils before giving up and letting it hang in curly waves down my back. Maybe I'll catch a break and it'll turn out that Tuck loves chicks with messy hair.

By eight o'clock, I've strolled up Nine Muses Street—which

is what substitutes for a downtown area in Olympus—and am pushing open the door to Barney's Bagelry. A little bell heralds my entrance with a *ching-ching*. I walk past a bulletin board filled with advertisements for room shares and art shows and mountain-bike rentals. I order a steaming mug of coffee from a young bearded guy wearing a baseball cap with *Lug Nut* embroidered on it.

The vibe in Olympus is really confusing.

On the rear wall is a set of swinging saloon doors. A small hand-lettered sign beside it says *Gallery and More Seating*, but I decide not to go exploring. I also eschew the handful of stools and tables in this room, instead settling into a vinyl beanbag in the corner. I set my mug on the conveniently located—but weird—carved stump beside me so I can have my hands free to dork around the *Zeus!* website on my iPad. I click on a photo and stare at the toga-clad Tuck that fills my screen. Muscles, hair, spear? Check, check, check. Clues to how he will react to my appearance in Olympus?

Nothing.

It all happened so fast that I haven't had time to formulate a plan. Do I greet Tuck with a hello? A hug? An *extended* hug? I swipe Toga Tuck away so I can scan through his other pictures when—

"Hey, I took those."

—a male voice comes from behind me. As I scramble to close out of the site, I register someone plopping into the nearest beanbag. Long jean-covered legs stretch out, and a black Chuck Taylor bumps my foot. "Sorry," the guy says. "I didn't mean to interrupt—" He stops because I've gotten my iPad shut down and now we're staring at each other. "I know you."

He does, and I know him too. It's Ella's dark-haired ex-boyfriend, who, now that I'm seeing him in broad daylight, looks even hotter than he did the first time I met him.

"Rainie." I nod to him. "Wendell's party."

He grins at me. "Blue dress."

I'm startled into a pause, oddly touched that this random boy remembers what I was wearing two weeks ago. Although . . .

"It was gray." Okay, so he only *kinda* remembers the dress.

But apparently he remembers *me*.

"Milo." He extends a hand over the stump that our coffee mugs are now sharing. "What are you doing here?"

I shake his hand, realizing he's asking about the town, not the coffee shop. "I'm working at the theater."

"Cool!" He lights up. "Another Dobbsian in Olympus— I like it. What's your gig?"

"Um." I scramble to remember my job title. "Actor-technician."

"Very formal." He cocks his head. "You're not a drama girl, are you?" My answer must be broadcast all over my face, because he grins. "Then why did you come here?"

"I just . . ." I think fast. "I *want* to be a drama girl."

This time, Milo laughs out loud. "Just like that? You heard a clarion call to the stage?"

It does sound a little silly.

"Sort of," I tell him. "Our school does this thing where

the theater class has to write and perform their own mono-logues."

"Oh yeah?" Milo looks interested, so I forge ahead with my story that is partially true but also partially a lie (again, depending on how you look at it).

"Yeah. They were really good this year. Everyone loved them." I don't mention Sarah or Marin or their snoring. "One of the monologues really got to me."

Milo pulls his knees up to his body and wraps his long arms around them. "That's cool."

"Yeah, and then I started thinking about all the perfor-mances I've seen at our school. How fun it seems, how the the-ater kids are all bonded." Milo is nodding along, which makes me decide I might as well go for broke. "My friends and I went to Wendell's party, and everyone was really nice—" (mostly true) "and normal—" (not at all true) "and friendly" (unclear, since I didn't talk to anyone else once Tuck arrived). "So there was no clarion or anything, but Ella said she could hook me up, and I wanted to check it out. To be a part of it . . ." I trail off, looking at Milo looking at me. "What?"

"Nothing." He shakes his head. "I just like your reasoning, that's all." He takes a sip from his mug—which, from the smell, I can tell is hot chocolate—and sets it back down. "What was the monologue about?"

"Huh?" Of course I know what he's asking, but I'm buying time. Not sure how to answer when my interpretation of it—the reason I feel like Tuck understands me—is all about what a hot mess I am. That's not something I'm going to admit to a cute stranger.

"The one that made you pay attention." Milo cocks his head again, smiling at me. "*That* monologue."

"I couldn't really do it justice in an explanation," I tell him. "But you should ask Tuck Brady about it. I bet he'd let you read it."

"Good for Tuck. He was freaking out about that piece." Milo rises to his feet, slinging a camera strap across his shoulder. "I'm walking over. You wanna come with? I will be so kind as to regale you with pro tips."

"Pro tips?"

"So you know which way to go when someone says 'exit stage left.' "

"Yes, please." I shove my iPad into my backpack and scramble up. "I would *love* to not look like a complete fraud."

• • •

Nine Muses Street is adjacent to Blue Ridge University—where Annette is a student—and is strewn with stores selling incense and herbal tea and clothing made out of hemp. Milo points out a green-awninged restaurant called McKay's as the gathering place of choice for *Zeus!* company members. "Decent food and, apparently, cheap drinks if you have a fake ID."

"Do you have one?"

"Please." He shoots me a sideways glance. "A Mexican American guy in the South? I like to stay on the right side of the law."

"Fair." I don't have a fake either. I've never needed one at house parties or to snag an occasional taste of something from my parents' liquor cabinet when Sarah and Marin are over. Plus, I'm not a big drinker. I don't love the idea of potentially doing something stupid in front of other people. "So this isn't your first year at Olympus?"

"Nope, my seventeenth."

"What?!"

"Turn right, here." Milo guides me around a corner and onto a busier street lined with fast-food places and campus parking-lot entrances. "I was six weeks old the first time my mom carried me onstage. She and Dad met selling refreshments at a summer stock theater in Roanoke when they were kids. They fell in love with it, and now we spend summers here. It's like this weird working family vacation. Mom's in the front office, and Dad helps build the set." Milo hits the pedestrian button at the intersection by the big *Blue Ridge University* sign that graces the front of the college campus. "You know, I should warn you that not everyone might think it's cute, how you don't know anything about theater."

He thinks I'm cute?

"The auditions and callbacks and interviews—they're kind of a big deal. You might not want to mention that Ella got you in the back door." As we cross the street, Milo pulls a purple bandanna out of his back pocket and ties it onto his head, do-rag-style, shoving pieces of his black hair under it. It makes me realize that I'm starting to get sticky warm. It's going to be a hot, humid day. It also makes me realize that—

"You look like a pirate," I tell him, and then immediately wish I hadn't, because it seems odd, somehow. Because—

"A lot of people think pirates are hot."

Because that's why.

Milo grins down at me. "I'll take it."

To be fair, it's not a wrong assessment.

He gestures to the long sidewalk in front of us . . . the one that slants up at almost a forty-five-degree angle. "Almost there."

"You've got to be kidding me." If I feel sticky now, I'm going to be disgusting by the time I actually start the first day of my job. Also, my breath is coming harder than I'd like it to.

I'm a mess.

"You'll get used to it." Milo nudges me. "Altitude."

I certainly hope that's the case, because by the time we reach the Olympus Theater parking lot, ringed with thick oak trees and dotted with cars, I feel like I ran a marathon. Forget messy chicks. I hope Tuck has a thing for vile, sweaty slimeballs.

Dammit.

I turn to Milo, again going with a half-truth. "I maybe don't want to be gross for my first day on the job."

"I don't think you're gross."

For no reason, I flush when he says it.

"Is there a ladies' room?"

"On the other side." Milo points at a long, low brown building, in front of which stands a line of people waiting before a folding table. "When you're done, sign in at the table. See you in there."

He turns and lopes away. Belatedly, I call after him. "Thank you!"

I do the best I can in the bathroom with a sink, a cloudy mirror, and some paper towels, but I'm still not in prime condition when I come out and join the line. A couple of minutes later, I'm standing before the folding table, where a lady with gray curly pigtails checks names off a list on a clipboard. She hands me a packet of papers, I sign a form, and—just like that—I'm a company member of *Zeus!*

A wooden sign at the entrance to the amphitheater says it seats 2,200 people. Standing at the top of all those seats, I believe that number. Wide concrete stairs lead down between the rows and rows of curved aluminum benches. Way below, the stage is more like a slice of Appalachian nature than a location for dramatic performances. There's no floor—it's just dirt—and the whole area is surrounded by rhododendrons and sugar maples and stone retaining walls. It looks like a huge picnic area on the Blue Ridge Parkway . . . if you wanted to eat a sandwich while 2,200 people watched, that is.

A group is gathered on the audience benches closest to the stage. I start down the stairs, walking slowly so I can get a good look, but I don't see Tuck . . . or even Ella or Milo. Instead, they're a bunch of strangers who will be my coworkers for the summer. Who I need to fit in with.

As I get closer, one thing becomes painfully apparent: it's not going to be easy.

One guy is sitting off by himself, thwacking at the strings of a little wooden instrument shaped like a trapezoid. Another seems to be asleep with his bare feet (*ew!*) perched on the back of the seat in front of him. Two girls are facing each other, playing some sort of hand-clapping game I vaguely recognize from my childhood. A whole crowd of older teens (college students, maybe?) stand around in a circle, laughing and talking. As I get closer, one of them—a blond in a miniskirt—suddenly screams "Trust fall!" and flings herself backward into the circle. Lucky for her, the others have catlike reflexes and, en masse, catch her before her head can crack open on the aluminum seating.

Apparently, I gasp aloud, because from behind me I hear a voice say, "That's just Gretchen." It's Ella. She's scowling at me. "And BTW, WTF?"

"Huh?"

She rolls her eyes. "By the way, what the—"

"Yeah, I know what it means. Why are you saying it?"

"Where were you?"

"Oh. Downtown." Whoops. Ella *did* pull strings to get me here, after all. I'm sure she doesn't want me showing up late and mucking up her good theatrical name. "Don't worry, I'm always on time."

"Not worried. I just thought we'd drive up together." She rustles through her own packet of papers. "But you walked, so that's cool."

Except it doesn't *sound* like it's cool. . . .

"I'm sorry," I tell her.

But Ella only repeats herself. "It's cool."

To make things even more awkward, that's when Milo plops

down on my other side, handing me a cold can of soda. "To help with the altitude." He opens his own and then leans forward to wave at Ella. "Hi."

He sounds friendly enough, but Ella only nods.

Nothing else is said and no other gestures are made, yet somehow the tension deepens, and I get it: whatever Milo is or isn't to Ella, he's still her property. Just like this entire theater is her property. And I'm here as Ella's guest, so I need to watch my manners.

I hand the soda back to Milo. "I'm good. Thanks." I ignore the flash of confusion that crosses his face before I turn away, shutting him out.

I also ignore my own flash of guilt. After all, the guy was nice to me all morning.

A new influx of "company members" (I'm starting to learn the language here) tromps down the concrete stairs. I crane my head to see if Tuck is in their midst, but no such luck. The reason I'm here is still nowhere to be seen.

There's a series of clicks from beside me. Milo has unsheathed his camera and is taking shots of our coworkers' arrivals. I remember what he said when he first showed up at the coffee shop, that he'd taken the photo of Toga Tuck on the Olympus website. "Are you the photographer too?" I ask him.

"Yep. They keep me around because I'm cheap." He pulls the camera away from his face long enough to give me a quick smile. "Actually, I'm free." He nudges Ella. "You. You're not an intern anymore, are you?"

"Nope. A/T." I don't have to turn my head to catalog her

frosty look. "I've grown since last summer. I'm not interested in the same things."

Surely her double meaning is as obvious to Milo as it is to me, but he doesn't let on. "A promotion, awesome!" He sounds like he really means it. "You deserve it."

"Thanks." There's a pause before Ella asks the question that she *has* to ask in order to be remotely polite. "Are you an A/T again?"

It occurs to me that had I also been remotely polite, I would have asked the same question when Milo and I were walking to the theater.

"No," Milo tells her. "Supporting."

Ella frowns. "Who'd you get?"

"Achilles." Milo sounds almost apologetic. "I guess they figured I've been here my whole life, maybe they can toss me a couple of lines and a heroic death."

Ella's frown deepens. "Do you even *want* those lines? I thought you were a photographer or something."

Milo only shrugs. I'm about to ask him about his photography when there's a blond blur in my peripheral vision. It's Tuck loping down the cement stairs. He's every bit as radiant as he was at school. Maybe even more so, because now the sun blazes his hair into golden fire and his T-shirt is bright, bright white against his tan skin.

He already looks like a Greek god.

I straighten on the aluminum bench, tossing my hair back from my face. I might be a sweaty mess, but with any luck, maybe it isn't obvious upon first glance. I watch as Tuck descends the last few steps to reach the group of people closest to the stage. He sits down next to the trust-fall girl, Gretchen. She beams at him and tilts her face up to his. It's the classic "kiss me" move, but surely that's not what she's doing because—

Nope. It's *exactly* what she's doing. Because now Tuck is kissing her. Passionately. Lengthily. Meaningfully.

I am a block of ice, but apparently Ella is not, because, beside me, she sucks in a great gasp of air. I don't look at her. I can't.

I am frozen.

Chapter 5

"Move," I tell Ella, who is standing between me and the bathroom exit.

"No." She shakes her head vehemently. "You're not leaving."

"You are not the boss of me," I retort, because apparently I've lost maturity along with my dignity. "This is not what I signed up for."

"Uh, yes, it is. You literally signed a literal contract to work here for the summer."

"Not in blood!" I decide to try appealing to her sense of compassion. "You know why I came. I can't stay if Tuck is with that Gretchen girl. It's humiliating."

Ella's frown softens. "Look, you have no idea how long those two will last. It's a new thing. It's not like they're married."

"So I'm supposed to—what? Sit around and wait for them to break up? That sounds like fun."

"Or you could try actually *having* fun." Ella's scowl is back. "This is a great place, you know. Your life doesn't have to be about chasing some stupid boy."

Now, that's just rude.

"I'm not *chasing*. I thought he was a *sign*." I make a move, but Ella shifts her weight, still blocking me. "Let me go!"

"No." Ella folds her arms. "Typical Rainie, bailing out on me like always."

"But it has nothing to do with you!" After all, it's not like it's Ella's theater. "So there's one less person standing around in crowd scenes, big deal."

"I went out on a limb for you. I thought you would be here—actually *be* here. You can't just leave."

"I have to." My eyes brim over with tears, and I start to wipe them away but change my mind. Perhaps the sight of my sorrow will convince Ella. "It's too hard to stay."

Ella stares at me for a long beat, then raises her hands, taking a step away from the door. "Okay, fine. Go for it." I'm about to thank her, but Ella keeps talking, her words clipped and hard. "But you should know that I'll tell Tuck why you came and why you left, so enjoy that when our senior year starts."

My mouth drops open. "What?"

"You think it's humiliating now." Ella shrugs. "Wait until all of Dobbs High knows how you chased a boy into the mountains and then ran home. Funny story. Everyone will get a kick out of it."

Rage boils up my chest and neck into my face, staining my cheeks. "That is the shittiest—"

"No, you're the shittiest." Ella glares at me. "If you walk away, that is."

I shake my head, trapped. "You need to get a life."

"You came here to get a life." Ella opens the door. "You should get on that." She steps out of the bathroom.

"You're blackmailing me!" I yell after her as the door starts to swing shut. Ella only raises her hands in a dramatic shrug, continuing on toward the theater entrance. The door closes and I stand there, alone in the bathroom, staring at it. What is Ella talking about, "bailing out"? I bail out on *things,* not *people.*

But this time, it looks like I'm not allowed to do either.

When I rejoin my coworkers—this time sitting on the other side of Milo, away from Ella—a gorgeous twentysomething with nearly black skin and a mane of red-gold hair is speaking from the middle of the stage. "Nikki Bray," Milo tells me. "Production stage manager."

Nikki is telling us a list of rules about the two weeks of rehearsals that will be followed by two months of performances. To me—trying not to look at Tuck and Gretchen cuddled together—it might as well be two millennia followed by two eons.

Finally, Nikki introduces the longtime director of *Zeus!,* Del Shelby. He's tiny and wrinkled and pale, but his shirt and jeans and boots are all black. So is his giant cowboy hat. He looks like a vampire who accidentally wandered into an old western movie.

Del Shelby welcomes us to the thirty-ninth year of *Zeus!,* which is apparently also the thirty-ninth year that the "brilliant master thespian" Hugh Hadley has played the title role. From the first row of seats, a bearded gentleman with silver hair gives a wave to the group. "Looking forward to thirty-nine more!" he calls out to a round of applause.

Milo nudges me. "Started as an actor-tech," he murmurs. "Dare to dream."

Ella shoots Milo a dirty look, which changes to one of compassion when it slides to me. I narrow my eyes at her. She doesn't get to act like she's my friend when she's in the middle of blackmailing me.

Onstage, Del talks about the history of the theater, and then Nikki has more things to say about showing up on time, and finally everyone is excused until tomorrow: the first official day of rehearsals. I shove my packet into my backpack and am about to make a break for it when Milo reaches past me to tap Ella's shoulder.

"Hey, you guys coming to McKay's tonight?"

She shrugs. "Is there a thing?"

"First night before rehearsal. Always a thing."

"Then maybe." Ella glances at me. "Last summer, I had to live with Uncle Rob. He wasn't so hot on me going to things."

I bid a hasty farewell to Milo—which Ella also does because she clearly doesn't like him—and escape up the concrete steps, Ella right behind me. We cross the parking lot and make it all the way down the long street before I'm able to get words out between my clenched teeth. "I really don't want to be near you right now."

Ella nods, placid. "And yet I'm your only friend here, so you're kind of stuck with me."

I disagree with her definition of "friend," but still—she's kind of got me there. We cross the street and walk another two blocks before I pull Ella to a halt. "There's no foreseeable way that Gretchen is also an actor-technician, is there?"

"Sorry." Ella shakes her head. "Helen of Troy."

"What."

Ella's look of sympathy deepens. "Also known as Paris of Troy's lover."

"No, really. You have *got* to be kidding me." The summer of following through and falling in love has turned into the summer of absolute suck. I'm a failure. Tuck wasn't asking for me to come here. He was speaking . . . I don't know, metaphorically or theatrically or some crap.

I'm worse than a failure. I'm an idiot.

We're making our way up Crestline Drive when Ella breaks the silence again. "Do you want to be cheered up?"

"No." But by the time we've trudged up the stairs and are on our splintered wooden deck, I've changed my mind. "Fine. Cheer me up." I add the word "blackmailer" only in my head.

"They won't last." Ella unlocks the apartment door and I follow her inside. We plop down on opposite ends of the living room sofa. "Gretchen doesn't do Forever Love. She doesn't even do One-Whole-Season Love. They'll break up by the end of the summer, and Tuck will be back at school for senior year, totally single. In the meantime, you'll get to know each other."

"You mean while I'm actor-teching and he's sucking face with Gretchen?"

"No, backstage. Between scenes. Before the show. At the parties. That's how it works." Ella tucks her legs up under her splash-patterned wrap dress and gazes at me. "I know you're pissed, but I'm telling you, it's good here. We all end up . . . kinda on the same team."

Yeah, maybe if you know how to play the game in the first place.

"Trust me, if you two started off as a couple, there's no way you'd end the summer together." Ella cocks her head so her chin-length hair swings against her face. "Summer stock theater is not a hotbed of long-term relationships."

"Milo's parents met at a theater in Roanoke." I don't know why I say it; I guess I'm trying to defend my adherence to my own pain. Ella's face hardens and I hasten to explain. "I ran into him downtown and we walked to Olympus together."

"Interesting." Ella unfolds from the sofa, heading toward the bedroom. "Let me know if you want to go to McKay's tonight with your blackmailing ex–best friend."

"Who wouldn't want that?" I yell after her, but she doesn't respond to my sarcasm.

Although no part of me wants to go hang out with a bunch of people I don't know—not to mention one person I'm super pissed at—I eventually come to the conclusion that it's better to get to the Tuck meeting sooner rather than later. He's going to be surprised to see me, and I'll have to explain it, and I hate everything about it, and . . . I just want to get it over with.

That evening, I walk into the bedroom right as Ella is pulling her dress off over her head. "Sorry!" I back out fast.

"Don't be silly," Ella calls from the other side of the door. "Come back." I hesitate but then do as she says. She's wearing a pale pink bra and a pair of faded-blue boy shorts. "Leave it open. Only girls live here."

Other than the occasional guy who's remotely interested me enough to persuade me to remove any clothing, I haven't changed in front of anyone since we were all forced to do so during ninth-grade PE. Because—why would I?

I open my closet so I'll have somewhere to look. It's not like we are *actually* in a locker room, after all. Here, doors are an option. I scan the random assortment of clothes I packed for a summer that doesn't exist. What *do* you wear to see the boy who's breaking your heart? I turn back to Ella. "Are you wearing a dress?"

"It's a small-town bar," Ella replies. "Not the senior prom."

Uh, she just wore a dress to the first company meeting. Was *that* the senior prom?

As it turns out, we both go casual. My shorts are denim and my tank is black, and I've paired them with some of my favorite Havaianas—the teal ones. Ella, however, is in zebra-print shorts and a gray camo tee. She's also wearing big, glittery star earrings and scuffed orange cowboy boots with chunky heels that raise her so that she's only a couple of inches shorter than I am. I would look like a Texan hooker in all that, but somehow Ella manages to pull it off.

I drive us the few blocks to Nine Muses, and we find parking next to a tea store advertising free henna tattoos. Ella and I head toward the main street, where I point out the green awning. "Yeah, I've been here before," she reminds me.

The inside of the building—which is decorated in neon beer signs and old movie posters—is already packed with *Zeus!*

company members of all ages. I recognize some by their faces and some only by the theater T-shirts they're wearing.

"Damn it." Ella snaps her fingers. "I forgot about the discount. You get fifteen percent off if you wear the shirt."

I follow her past the bar and through the booths to a busy side room. Here, Christmas lights line the ceiling, illuminating dozens of people weaving between a pool table, a dartboard, a jukebox, and a scattering of high round tables with stools. Off to the left, a man in a *Luck o' the Irish* T-shirt stands behind a bar. Above him hangs a wooden sign that proclaims *Bar menu and alcohol-free drinks ONLY.*

As we enter, a leggy girl in a halter top and sequined miniskirt leans low over the table to shoot. She completely misses the cue ball, instead jabbing her stick into a stripe and sending it into a side pocket. She straightens with a fist pump—"Do I win?"—and we see that, of course, it's Gretchen.

Which means that Tuck is right there to catch her by the waist and spin her around into his arms. And kiss her. A lot.

Before I can do anything, Ella's hand is on my elbow and she's propelling me to the bar. "A Roy Rogers. Um, two," she tells the bartender, who is either Irish or just enamored of the clothing. As he starts pouring, I give her a look.

"Roy Rogers? Are we children?"

Ella shrugs. "If your options are a soda *with* cherry syrup or a soda *without* cherry syrup, why would you ever choose without?"

She has a point.

The bartender slides the drinks to us, and Ella drops a bill on the counter. She turns to me, raising her glass. "To forgiveness."

"I'm not ready to forgive you," I tell her.

"You will be," she says. "You need a friend here."

I roll my eyes but allow her to clink her glass against mine. "To the tortured hellscape that is my life."

"That's the spirit." We take sips, and then Ella leads me to an unclaimed table, where we hike ourselves onto stools. She looks at me over the rim of her drink. "You know, this may be a blessing in disguise."

"What, did you get the bartender to sneak some alcohol in there?" Ella must be drunk, because there is nothing about this summer that could be considered a blessing.

"No, but they say it's better to get to know someone as a friend first."

"You know who says that?" I'm not in the mood to be cheered up, especially by Ella. "Sad people. Lonely people. Delusional people who can't see what's right in front of their eyes."

And what's right in front of my eyes is Tuck getting some congratulatory tongue from Gretchen after sinking a corner shot.

"Whatever happens is what's meant to happen," Ella informs me.

"Thanks, Socrates." I'm still mad, but I do recognize that, in her own way, Ella is trying to help. After all, it's been several years since we've talked about anything important. In fact, maybe we never did. I skim through my childhood memories of Ella—sleepovers, stealing Annette's clothes, water-balloon fights—and can't dredge up anything that seems like Deep

Conversation. I guess we were too young, because it seems like I didn't start talking about real things until Marin and Sarah and I were all hanging out.

"You're welcome, Eeyore." Ella grins at me, and I manage a weak smile in return. "You need to say hello to him."

"I know."

"And then you need to flirt with another boy."

"What?"

"Oldest trick in the book." Ella makes what must be her version of a wise face. "Boys like a chase."

"Yeah, except I'm the one doing the chasing."

"That's my point. Don't be that girl." Ella hops down off her stool, taking her glass with her. "Come on. I'll distract Gretchen."

"Wait, how?"

"Observe." Ella winks at me. "Learn." I don't want to do either, but it doesn't look like I have much of a choice, so I follow her over to the pool table, where she steps directly between Tuck and Gretchen. "Hi, guys."

"Hey!" Tuck slings an arm over her shoulders and squeezes her in a sideways hug. "Dobbs represent!"

Gretchen nods at her—"Ella, right? Good to see you"—before her eyes slide over to me. She assesses, confirms we don't know each other, sticks out a hand. "I'm Gretchen."

Because it's what one does, I shake her hand and manage to get my name out between tight lips. "Rainie Langdon."

Which is when Tuck realizes it's me standing there with them. His eyes widen, and he steps forward to engulf me in a hug. "Dude, what are you doing here? You come up to visit

Ella?" I don't answer, because I'm too aware that I'm encircled by Tuck's magical, muscled arms right in front of his girlfriend. I squeeze back just long enough to make it weird, and then I pull away. Tuck turns to Gretchen. "Rainie goes to my school."

I open my mouth to babble some sort of explanation that doesn't make me sound like a deranged stalker, but Ella beats me to the punch. "Rainie's a company member. I convinced her to come up for the summer, see what it's all about." Before anyone can comment, she turns to Gretchen. "I desperately need your help. I heard you're the expert on a certain life skill."

"What?" Gretchen looks flattered. She allows Ella to pull her away toward the bar, leaving me alone with Tuck. His bright blue eyes are lit up and happy as he looks down at me, which makes me think that maybe I don't need to murder Ella in her sleep after all.

"Why didn't you tell me you were coming?"

"I didn't decide until last week." At least that's the truth.

"Cool." Tuck reaches out and slides a finger along my bare arm. "You're gonna love it." He's smiling into my eyes like I'm the only girl in the room—no, on the *planet*—and I suddenly have a hard time believing we'd be having this interaction if Gretchen were still here.

"I hope so," I tell him.

Tuck's smile deepens. "I'm glad you're here. It's a good surprise."

The moment is real enough and complete enough that it's totally, 100 percent okay when Milo arrives, carrying a basket of fries. "Hey, you came." He holds the fries toward me.

"So did you." I take one and watch as he and Tuck do their fist-bump thing.

"By yourself?"

"Ella's over there." Tuck answers for me, gesturing toward the bar. "Learning an important life skill from my girlfriend."

Girlfriend, ugh.

Both Milo and I turn to look at Ella and Gretchen, who—by all appearances—are in the middle of a silent standoff at the bar. They're perfectly still, staring at each other. Their mouths move like they're chewing. Or, more accurately, like they're cows chewing their cuds.

"I don't get it," Milo says.

"Look closer," Tuck says.

I zero in on Gretchen's glass, filled with red liquid. . . .

No, not liquid. Cherries. Gretchen's glass is full of cherries. Which means—

"Oh." Milo nods. "Her stem thing."

Yup. Tuck's Helen-of-Troy girlfriend is teaching my roommate how to tie cherry stems in knots with her tongue. Fantastic.

"Impressive, right?" says Tuck.

"It's something," says Milo. "You guys wanna play darts?"

"Nah," says Tuck. "I'm kinda into the cherry lesson."

Even though I'd like to continue letting Tuck smile at me and touch my arms, I'd rather perish in a fiery explosion than watch him watch his girlfriend demonstrate her fruit-based oral-sex technique. "I'll play," I tell Milo, snagging another fry from his basket.

Milo and I find an empty board in the corner, near a

conveniently located wooden shelf, where we stash his fries and my drink. "Are you any good?" he asks.

"Not at all. You?"

"Nope." Milo plucks darts from where they're jabbed along the perimeter of the board and waves the handful in my direction. "You can go first."

I throw three darts, two of which hit the board but miss the circle, and then Milo does the same. As he collects the darts, I search for a conversation starter that doesn't have anything to do with Tuck, and land on the one thing we have in common: *Zeus!* "So what's the deal with Achilles?"

Milo gives me a wry smile. "Did Ella tell you I don't deserve the part?"

"No." I make a mental note to ask Ella what actually happened between the two of them. "I just don't know anything about the character."

"You haven't read the script?"

"We just got it this morning, and it's not like I have to talk." It sounds defensive even in my own ears.

"I hate to break this to you." Milo hands me the darts. "But you'll have a line."

"That wasn't part of the deal." No way am I making a speech in that giant amphitheater.

Milo looks amused at my visible horror. "It's just a line. All the actor-techs get one."

"Did Ella have to do it last year?" I can't explain my rising panic, the fact that I already don't know what I'm doing here, that I can't speak the language, that I don't belong. Not to mention the fact that Ella didn't mention this little detail.

What else hasn't she told me?

"Yeah. So did I." Milo shrugs again. "It'll be in a crowd scene, probably only a few words." I stare at him, not sure how to handle the information, and he points to the darts clenched in my hand. "Don't shoot the messenger."

I don't. Instead, I turn back to the target, letting the darts fly fast, one after another. Two land outside the circle. The third misses the board completely, striking the wall and clattering harmlessly to the floor. I start to step back so Milo can take my place, but he's standing behind me and I bump right into him. "Sorry."

I move to the side, but he doesn't come forward. Instead, he stays right where he is, looking down at me. "You're actually freaked out, aren't you?"

"I mean . . . I didn't think I'd have to talk. I thought I'd blend in." Milo cocks his head, assessing me. The moment lasts longer than feels comfortable. "What?" It comes out a little rudely.

"Nothing. You just don't seem like the blending-in type, that's all." He turns to the board, and this time all three of his arrows *zing-zing-zing* right into the target circle. He looks back to me, his dark brown eyes scanning my face. "Would you feel better if I told you my line from last year?"

"Probably not."

"Suit yourself." He lopes forward to get the darts, and I

change my mind as he's pulling them out (and collecting my stray from the floor).

"Okay, go ahead."

"Are you sure?" Milo spins around. "Maybe I shouldn't. It's really impressive. You'll probably get all intimidated by my acting ability."

"I'll try to keep it together." I fold my arms in front of my body, realizing that, oddly, I'm looking forward to it.

"Hold on." Milo sets the darts on the shelf and then shakes out his hands. He runs his fingers through the choppy strands of his crow-black hair. He rolls his shoulders. He tilts his head one way, then the other, like he's cracking his neck.

"What are you doing?"

"Warming up. You'll learn about it." He stretches one arm over his head, then the other. He starts what I assume are vocal exercises. "Puh-buh, puh-buh, puh-buh."

"Oh good God." I try to make an impatient face, but a smile creeps into it despite myself. "Just tell me the line."

"All right, but don't say I didn't warn you." Milo strikes a pose like the statue of a famous general, or perhaps an underwear model. He takes a breath, and then, in a deep, loud voice, he intones, "The yolk's on you, Pollux!"

I wait, eyebrows raised, as Milo stays frozen with one hand held high. A full ten seconds later he still hasn't moved, and I realize that was the entire line. I hasten to applaud.

"Thank you, thank you," he says, bowing.

Through my laughter, I find words. "What does that even mean?"

"Oh, you'll see." He swipes the darts off the shelf and trots back. "It's a pivotal moment in the stellar melodrama that is *Zeus!*"

"I can hardly wait." We smile at each other and—just as I realize that, for a few minutes at least, I forgot about Tuck—I hear Ella's voice behind me.

"I'm ready to go."

I turn to find her standing with her hands on her hips, a reminder of the less-than-stellar melodrama that I'm currently starring in. I shake away my sudden flash of guilt. Blackmail is a crime. Talking to a boy is not.

I mean, talking to a *person.*

Even if he's not Tuck.

Even if he's Ella's ex.

"Sure." I hand the darts back to Milo. "Thanks for the game."

"My pleasure." He nods at my roommate. "Hi, Ella."

"Hey." She doesn't make eye contact with him, only turns and heads for the exit.

I glance at Milo and edge my shoulders up in the tiniest shrug before following Ella between the tables and stools and people to the door. But then—for no discernable reason—I pause and look back. Milo is standing right where I left him, by the dartboard. Watching me.

He raises a hand in farewell and I respond the same way.

Then I flee.

Chapter 6

I stick close to Ella as we begin the morning backstage tour of Olympus. Even though at least half of the company members have worked here before, Nikki insists that the entire cast and crew—all eighty-eight people—take the tour so everyone can be reminded of the rules along the way.

Nikki is very big on rules.

Ella and I lag toward the rear of the group as we all trek down from our seats. Then, to what I know must be Ella's great chagrin, Milo falls into step with us. "Hi, guys."

His arrival secretly fills me with delight: partially because it annoys Ella and partially because . . .

Actually, I'm not sure why.

"Morning," I tell him.

Ella only nods.

As we congregate at the center of the stage, Nikki informs us that it was built forty years ago and is a half acre in size. Gretchen pipes up from somewhere in the middle of the crowd: "It's not the size of the stage, y'all. It's what you do with it."

A guy in a Florida Gators cap lets out a bark of laughter. "Not exactly a compliment for Paris."

"Shut up, Logan," Gretchen says, and now I can see her standing with Tuck by her side.

As giggles ripple across the crowd, Tuck gives a good-natured shrug. "I know what to do with it."

He pulls Gretchen into a kiss, and I make a small retching noise before I think to stop myself. Ella elbows me in the ribs at the same time that Milo says, "Tell me about it."

Oh yeah. Milo's here too. Whoops.

"Okay, enough." Nikki glares everyone into submission. "Get it out of your system and let's be professional. Even the newest of you should know that backstage is this way."

She strikes out toward the edge of the stage, where there's an opening between two groupings of boulders. They look like actual rocks to me, but maybe they're fake. After all, my greatest summer takeaway so far is that I have no sense of when things are real and when they are not.

Milo nudges me. "Stage left. House right."

"Huh?"

"This way is left if you're onstage." Ella elaborates, throwing a dirty look at Milo. "It's right if you're in the house, where the audience sits."

Even the directions here don't make sense.

We all follow Nikki around the side to a long, low, roofed wooden deck that runs along the back of the stage. There are "dressing rooms" at each end of it—with quotation marks because the dressing rooms are more like grubby middle-school locker rooms. With all the other females, I traipse into the women's, where we see a center island of lockers surrounded by yellow benches. I find my name on a locker two down from Ella's.

Off to the side is what looks like a communal shower: one small room with drains on the floor and several spigots coming out of the walls. I don't know why anyone would choose to shower right out in the open instead of just waiting until they get home, but, as we all know, theater people are weird.

We leave our dressing room and follow Nikki down the wooden deck. One side is open to the outdoors, with only a low railing separating us from a tangle of trees and vines. The other—the back side of the stage—is a wall hung with framed *Zeus!* programs from summers gone by. There are also two corkboards. One is empty, but the other is covered in information: a rehearsal schedule on yellow paper, a weekly menu on blue paper, a sign-in sheet on white paper. Nikki points to the last one, explaining that we need to sign in every time we come to the theater. There's a pause while everyone is silent, and then Nikki gives us a collective look. "That means now."

There's a rush for the sheet.

"When you're done, report to the stage-left wings if you did not submit a cast photo online," Nikki calls out. "And, no, I don't care that you haven't primped."

I'm waiting to sign my name when I feel a hand on my shoulder. I turn and come face to face with the brilliant master thespian

Mr. Hugh Hadley . . . otherwise known as Zeus. He nods at me, his eyes crinkling up at the corners. "Got your script?"

"Pardon me?" The man's been acting in the play for thirty-eight years. Surely he knows his lines by now.

"So I can sign it for you." He smiles, and the eye wrinkles intensify. "I figure you're new—you should get an autograph."

"Uh, sure." I open my backpack and fumble for my script. Hugh Hadley pulls a pen from somewhere within his khaki bomber jacket and scribbles what I assume is his signature across the front page of my script.

"Wait till I'm dead before you sell that." He pokes me in the arm. "It'll be worth more."

"Thank you?" I don't mean it to come out as a question, but it does.

Because of my encounter with the brilliant master thespian, I'm one of the last people to sign in, which means that when I round the corner to the left side of the stage, Milo is putting his camera away. "Oops, sorry," he says when he sees me. "Thought Paul was the last one." He points to a spot between two fake (real?) boulders. "Right there."

I go as directed and wait while he fiddles with his camera. "What do I do?" I ask him.

"Look at me and smile." The smile Milo flashes at me is so genuine and warm that it's impossible not to return. "Exactly." He raises his camera and I freeze, my arms dangling awkwardly at my sides. Milo lowers the camera. "You don't have to pose. Just be normal."

Not exactly my strong suit. Besides, I wasn't *posing*. I was *paralyzed* . . . but I guess he wouldn't know that.

Milo prepares to take the picture, and I cross my arms, but again he pauses. "Do the first smile again."

I try, but even I can tell it's coming out weird. "Sorry," I tell him. "I'm not good at this."

"It's okay." Milo raises the camera. "Stinky diaper."

"What?" I hear the series of clicks and know he just got my startled expression. "Please don't use those."

"My mom teaches second-grade Sunday school," Milo says from behind the lens. "I help take pictures of the kids when they're doing crafts or they have a performance. Saying something gross always makes them smile. I like to mix it up. Sometimes I go with 'smelly socks.'"

I laugh and Milo gets the shot. He pulls the camera away from his face and looks at the screen. "Perfect," he says with great satisfaction.

I suddenly realize I'm still smiling.

Milo and I catch up to the rest of the backstage tour in time to see the counter where we can buy discount meals on show nights, the pyrotechnics staging area (off-limits to everyone but the pyro crew), and the path that leads up to the parking lot so we don't have to walk through the theater.

Finally we're back onstage, theoretically doing the thing that we were all hired to do: make a play. It starts with Nikki calling out the names of the actor-technicians, one by one. The first one called (not me, thank the heavens) is Paul Longman, an African American dude with a shaved head and a nice smile. Paul steps to the front of our crowd so that Del Shelby can stare at him. After a moment, Del whispers to Nikki, and she scribbles something in her binder before waving Paul back to the crowd. As she calls the next name, Ella whispers in my ear. "He's picking lines for people to say."

"I hope I don't get the yolk one," I whisper back, and immediately wish I hadn't because Ella's expression darkens.

"How do you know about that?"

I shake my head because Nikki—who apparently has bionic hearing—is shooting us a disapproving look.

Six or seven more people—including Ella—are called before Nikki gets to me. When I step forward, it feels like Del stares at me for a very, very long time. Or maybe it's just that I'm out of whack from stress and doing everything wrong and not understanding what anyone's saying.

After the delightful stepping-and-standing-and-staring portion of the day is over, we start "blocking scenes." This means we all wait around, withering in the heat, while Del and Nikki confer endlessly before telling us where to stand and when to move.

In the first scene of the play, my job is to mill about with all the other chorus members as we sing a song to set the stage (as it were) for our audience. When Nikki points me to a spot in front of one of the boulders, I'm surprised to find Milo beside me. "I thought you had a real part."

"Achilles doesn't show up until the end," Milo explains. "In theory, it's a promotion. In practice, I'm a glorified actor-tech."

I'm oddly comforted by the thought that Milo will be around in the crowd scenes. "So you still might say your yolk thing?"

"God, I hope not. I'm happy to stand in the back and sway in a line."

From what I can tell, we'll all be doing a lot of that. I take a small step toward Milo. "Where are all the main characters?"

Truthfully, I'm asking about Tuck, but Milo doesn't need to know that. "Paris and Helen don't show up for a little while, but Zeus is in the first scene. Kind of."

"What do you mean, 'kind of'?" I know I'm new to theater, but common sense dictates that you're either in or you're out.

"Little secret about Zeus." Milo edges closer and brings his mouth near my ear. "He's not really the star of the show."

I jerk back so I can stare at Milo. "But it's called *Zeus!*"

"You know the title, well done." Milo grins at me. "And Zeus *was* the star when the show first started, when it was all about the mighty Olympian gods, but not anymore. He's too old. The play has been rewritten a dozen times since the beginning."

"That makes no sense. Why don't they just fire him and bring in someone new? Why bother rewriting the play?"

"Because Hugh's history with the theater is part of the draw. People love that he's been doing the same role for a billion years, that they can say they saw the original. . . ."

He falls silent, and I follow his gaze to Del and Nikki. They're looking toward the back of the stage. Waiting. Finally, Nikki opens her mouth. "Mr. Hadley?" she calls. "We're ready for you."

A moment later, Hugh Hadley appears on the floating walkway that runs the length of the stage. "You ready for me?" he calls back to Nikki.

"We're ready for you," she says again, and watches as Hugh Hadley (I'm having a difficult time calling him just "Hugh," even to myself) slowly walks out. He stops in the middle of the walkway to look at the actress who is coming across the stage. She's one of the college kids, and I think her name is Katrina.

Milo bends slightly at the waist, speaking to me in the barest of whispers. "That character is Leda. During the show, she'll do ballet. Watch, Zeus is about to fall in love with her."

Sure enough, Hugh Hadley sets his hand over his heart in a way that is just as dramatic as Milo's delivery of the yolk line for me last night. Hugh—as Zeus—says one word: "Leda!" And then he shuffles off across the walkway.

"Boom," Milo whispers. "In love."

If only it were that easy.

The day drags on and on, and I never find out my line because apparently I don't speak during the first half of the show. However, Ella receives hers, which—just to double down on her annoyance with Milo, me, and life in general—is Milo's yolk line from last year. "Are you kidding me?" she says under her breath when Nikki assigns it to her.

"What was that?" Nikki calls across the stage.

"Nothing!" Ella calls back.

Nikki is a little bit scary.

Ella's line is in the second scene, after two giant, human-sized eggs crack open so that Helen and Pollux can be born. I nudge Milo. "Wait, are they chickens?" It's a legitimate question—we're not in costume yet, so anyone could be dressed as anything in the actual performance—but Milo bursts out laughing

- 67 -

and has to stifle his amusement when Nikki's head swings in his direction.

"You really need to read the script," he tells me. I flip through my pages but don't see anything in the lines to explain why two of the main characters are being *hatched.* Milo points over my shoulder to a page of music. "Here. The chorus sings what's happening."

I skim the lyrics—which I guess I'll eventually have to memorize—and discover that Helen and Pollux are half mortals, half gods. Their mother is Leda—the ballet dancer from the first scene—and their father is, of course, Zeus himself. So Tuck's girlfriend is not only his romantic lead but also a half goddess. In even worse news, the last line in the song—which I'll be singing with everyone else—is about her beauty.

Perfect.

Specifically, the line is *"She is the most beautiful woman on earth."*

Then the actor-tech Paul steps forward and jerks a thumb toward Pollux. "He . . . is not."

Pollux—played by Logan, the Gators fan—slumps in fake dismay as the chorus proclaims that Helen will be given in matrimony to King Menelaus of Sparta. "Wait, what about me?" he says, ending the question with a squawk.

I lean toward Milo so I can whisper: "He *sounds* like a chicken."

Milo grins but doesn't answer. He points to Ella, who steps forward to deliver her—previously Milo's—line. "The yolk's on you, Pollux!"

Her delivery is halfhearted at best, which earns her a beck-oning from Del. As Ella sags and heads over to talk to him, Nikki calls for a twenty-minute break. People scatter, and I zero in on Tuck, who is sitting in the front row of the amphitheater, poking around on his phone. Gretchen is nowhere in sight, so I sit down next to him. "Must be nice, nothing until Scene Four."

"Maybe a little boring." Tuck slides his phone away and turns to look at me. Out here in the direct sunlight, his sky-blue eyes are even bluer. "But it's better now that you're here. Do you like it?"

I like you. Does that count?

"It's cool."

"You know what's cool?" He gazes at me the same way he did during our high school's assembly: like he's looking into my soul. "You. Coming here was very cool of you."

"Yeah?"

"Yeah. And brave."

So if there's one thing Tuck and I have done, it's perfect the art of the monosyllabic conversation. If only I understood what it meant . . .

• • •

That night, Ella and I are in our apartment, alone. She's standing by the living room wall, flipping through Annette's restaurant calendar while I peruse the contents of the kitchen cabinets that have been designated as ours. We have to be back at the theater at eight tomorrow morning—an hour before the principals and supporting cast, by the way—which isn't very far off. I'm not sure I want to use up any of that time making dinner. "Do you want to order pizza?" I ask Ella. She might be the fren-iest fren-emy I've ever had, but I'm stuck living with her and I'm starving. I can put our differences aside for dinner.

She doesn't answer. She's gazing at one of the photos—October, featuring a dude in overalls attaching spaghetti to the top of a jack-o'-lantern, like its hair. "Would you sleep with any of these guys?" she asks. "Look at this douchebag." She flips to December, which has a photo of a young man poking his head out of a giant gift box. He's wearing a red Christmas hat and holding a plate of what looks like fettuccine. "Who could take that seriously? Who could have sex with that?"

Not me, that's for sure. Of course, I've never had sex with anyone, so trying to picture doing it with a stranger from a weird pasta calendar is not within the capabilities of my imagination. Although I'd sort of like to do it before graduation, I've never been tempted. The closest I came was last year with a guy from the baseball team, but even that wasn't *that* close.

I wonder if Ella's ever done it. I don't remember noticing any serious boyfriends of hers over the past few years, but—to be fair—I don't remember noticing much about her at all. Now, as I look at that weird calendar, an unbidden thought floats to my mind: Did she have sex with Milo?

I shake it away. Although I want to know what happened between the two of them, I don't want to ask about it now. Not when we've just been talking about sex.

"Is Annette dating one of them?" I ask.

"That's what I'm wondering." Ella flips back through the

calendar. "She didn't come home last night, and when I texted her this morning, she said she'd stayed at a friend's house."

"Really?" I had been so concerned about getting to the theater early to maybe run into Tuck before rehearsal (which didn't happen) that I didn't even pay attention to Annette's whereabouts. "You think it's someone from work?"

"She spends an awful lot of time partying with the restaurant people."

I look back at the calendar. "I hope it's not the one in the box."

"Me too." Abruptly, Ella drops the pages so that the calendar flips back to the present month. "How about macaroni and cheese? I'll make it."

"Deal," I tell her.

• • •

The reason actor-technicians have to arrive at Olympus an hour earlier than everyone else is not a glamorous one. It's our job to rake the stage. Actual rakes, which we use to rake the actual dirt—like we're *farmers*—so when people come onstage barefoot, they won't stub their toes on rocks or anything. The worst part is that while I'm lugging my rake around with Ella and Paul and everyone else, Tuck and Gretchen show up early to practice their lines. They're sitting halfway up in the amphitheater seats as I'm working. I can't hear what they say, but they're starting their day with a clear view of my menial labor. When they're not gazing into each other's eyes, that is.

Bleh.

The rest of the cast and crew (aka everyone who's *not* an actor-tech) arrive as Ella and I are returning our rakes to their place: a rustic wooden closet by the women's dressing room. Milo—who is wearing a plain black T-shirt that makes his eyes look even darker than usual—waves as he walks by on the wooden deck.

I would wave back, but Ella is with me, and it feels weird to be friendly with Milo in front of her. Except then she waves back at him, so maybe he was never waving at me in the first place.

Before we start rehearsal, Nikki calls a girls-only meeting for performers (which, technically speaking, is what I am). We gather in a huddle beside the possibly fake boulders by the side of the stage, where Nikki informs us that tomorrow the makeup and costume departments want to do a test run of the act break. "It'll be first thing in the morning," she tells us. "As you know—"

Uh . . . not me.

"—that means being seen in all the glory God gave you."

Wait, what?!

"So if you need any maintenance work"—Nikki raises her hand in a "stop" motion—"don't tell me about it. Just do it. Or don't. I don't care. But do not think that we will waste time tomorrow morning while you pluck or shave or wax. Be here on time, wear your crummiest underwear, and be ready to get naked."

"*Onstage?*" The word comes out of my mouth before I think about stopping it. There's a round of muffled giggles, and Ella throws an elbow into my ribs.

"No." Even Nikki smiles. "Not onstage. In the dressing room, you'll all put on body paint together and shower it off. It needs to be fast, which is why costumes and makeup want to do a dry run. So, tomorrow: don't be late. Everyone got it?"

There's a chorus of yeses and one panicked stare (mine). Once again, this is *not* what I signed up for. I didn't know I'd be forced into group bath time. I'm not an *animal.*

Later, as Del has the principal actors run through the golden-apple-of-discord scene (Zeus, a handful of goddesses, and a tug-of-war over a piece of chipped plaster fruit), the costume designer—a pale woman in a white smock—takes our measurements. She scribbles them on a clipboard before assigning us costumes for the scene. We're all going to be woodland creatures. The designer says the costumes are largely responsible for letting the audience know where we are supposed to be—a forest glen—since we don't have movable set pieces. She looks very proud when she says it, and more so when she assigns my part. "Rainie . . . rabbit."

I blink at her. "You want me to be a rabbit."

"You're tall—think of it as a hare." She points to her assistant, who is standing nearby with a pile of costumes and props. "Ears over there. Next!"

I receive my ears—which are long and brown and attached to a wide headband—and an additional item: a giant, ratty stuffed carrot. I tuck the carrot between my knees while I wiggle the headband into place, and suddenly realize Milo is right there, watching me. And smiling.

"Don't say anything," I tell him, which only makes his smile widen. "I'm serious. Zero words about my ears or my carrot or—"

"Your hopping ability?"

"Especially about my hopping ability." I get my headband situated and reach down to grab the carrot. "What am I supposed to do with this?"

"It's a prop. You act with it."

"I've been to London," I inform him. "I've been to New York. I've witnessed many critically acclaimed theatrical performances. No one has ever needed an oversized root vegetable in order to do their job." I look him over. All I see are two wide straps over his shoulders, like he's wearing a backpack. "Hey, what are you supposed to be?" In answer, Milo pulls a cord attached to one of the straps and plastic black wings fan out behind him. "A bat?" I ask.

He feigns a hurt look. "Obviously, I'm a crow."

"Crows have beaks. You have no beak."

"Use your imagination," he tells me. "Caw. Caw-caw."

Since he's basically asked for it, I feel justified in giving him a once-over, running my eyes down his angular, T-shirted body to his jeans and Chucks. I have to conclude that the costume designer isn't far off. With that shiny black hair and dark gaze, a crow probably *is* the best choice for Milo. I raise my eyes, and when they meet his, my face goes warm and my heart speeds up . . . just a little. But all I say is "Sure, you make a decent bird."

Before he can answer, Ella stomps over with a scowl. She's holding something behind her back. "Last year I was a squirrel," she tells us. "The tail was itchy and the belt slipped, so I asked if I could be a different animal this summer. Guess what, my wish was granted."

I run through offensive woodland creatures in my mind. Porcupine? Snake? Beaver?

Ella pulls the thing from behind her back and jams it onto her head. It's a wig, probably the worst wig I've ever seen. It's frizzy and spiky and huge. It's black, except for the white stripe running down the middle—

"A skunk!" I burst out.

"Yes, a *skunk.*" Ella glares at me. "All summer long, I'm going to be a freaking skunk."

"Only for Scene Three." Milo says it helpfully, except Ella clearly doesn't think it's helpful at all. Her glare whips to him and intensifies.

"Shut up, birdbrain."

Milo and I watch her storm away before we turn to each other. My smile feels the way his looks: wide and *this* close to turning into laughter. "My carrot doesn't seem that bad anymore," I tell him.

He flaps his wings. "Caw-caw."

After everyone's gotten their assignments, the woodland creatures are each given two places on the stage: a starting point and an ending point. While the scene is happening—a waltz and an argument over the golden apple—we creatures are supposed to slowly meander from the first point to the second, stopping to sniff around or to make fake conversation with other animal friends on our way. Ella and I start in separate corners of stage right, but Milo is on the opposite side and—as I realize during the scene—he and I are on trajectories to meet in the middle. As the three goddesses dance and bicker, as Eris-the-goddess-of-discord throws fruit around, as other scruffily dressed woodland creatures mill about, Milo and I find each other at the center of the stage.

He glances above my head. "Nice ears."

"Nice wings."

We stand there for a moment, grinning at each other, but then Nikki claps her hands loudly and we both jump. "Creatures! Keep moving!"

So we do.

• • •

From a Greek-chorus standpoint, the rest of the apple scene is easy. The goddesses squabble about who's the prettiest, until Zeus arrives to break it up. In one of his few lines of the show, he asks, "Who can judge among these three?"

The chorus—from our scattered places around the set—answers dutifully. "How about you, Zeus?"

Zeus is clearly a wuss, because he can't bring himself to choose one of them, so instead he finds an appropriate judge. It's a mortal man who is so handsome and spectacular that Zeus bestows on him the great honor of picking the winner.

End scene, and enter Tuck Brady.

As we woodland creatures duck out to deposit our costumes and props in wooden crates just offstage, Tuck strolls on, all tall and blond and perfect. He's gazing at himself in a handheld mirror and self-talking about his good looks. The chorus—now back to being proper citizens of Greece—returns to the stage as the three goddesses arrive, still squabbling. They ask the question via song: Which one is the prettiest?

Nikki stations the rest of us in a half arc against the back of the stage, where we are to watch the action and participate in the chorus of the song. "Who doesn't have a line yet? Raise your hands."

A half-dozen hands—including my own—shoot into the air. It's not that I *want* to speak out loud from the stage, but if I am forced to do it, at least it would be nice if it's in a scene with Tuck. Like we are acting *together*.

"Keep them up," Nikki tells us. While we stand with our arms in the air, she and Del have a whispered confab. After a moment, she writes something on the script in her binder. "Okay, hands down. Bianca, you have the first chorus line on page twenty-two. Let's hear it."

A girl with long pink hair steps forward from our half arc. "However will you choose, Paris? They're all so pretty."

Del Shelby gives her a thumbs-up and, satisfied, Bianca returns to her spot.

"Great." Nikki checks her script. "Rainie, same page at the bottom. The last chorus line."

I scan the page and find my line. Horror rises inside me. I would rather run around the stage butt-naked than say this thing to Tuck in front of everyone. I jerk my gaze back to Nikki, who is waiting expectantly. "Go ahead."

I look at Tuck. He gives me an encouraging smile. I step

forward—because there's no way to wriggle out of this grace-fully while all these people are here—and I say my awful, awful line. "Hey, Paris, how about picking a mortal instead? Like me? Please? Please?"

Except apparently I say it too quietly and too fast, because Nikki waves her hand at me—*speak up*—and I try again. This time, Del Shelby ambles over. "Hey, honey. New this year, right?" I nod, and he points to my script page. "You're doing great. Just give me a pause between the two 'pleases' and add some des-peration, okay? You *want* this guy. Sell me on that." Del gestures to Tuck. "Paris, give her the reaction line." He points to the two girls flanking me, Ella and a girl named Lori. "Then you guys pull her back, like you're saving her from more embarrassment. Everyone got it?"

This is literally the worst thing that has ever happened to me: basically begging Tuck to love me before getting dragged away from him because I'm just too pathetic.

But since I can't say that, instead I spit out my line: "Hey, Paris, how about picking a mortal instead? Like me? Please?" I wait until Del points at me before I say the last word. "Please?"

From center stage, Tuck-as-Paris throws me an incredulous look, as if to say, *Why would you be so stupid as to even think I might be interested in you?* But aloud he says only, "Uh . . . no thank you."

"Great!" Del Shelby claps his hands. "We'll hold a second for laughter—"

It just keeps getting better.

"—and then you'll be pulled back by your friends. Let's run that again."

So we do. Thrice more. By the last time, I've perfected my despondent slump when Tuck—I mean, Paris—rejects me. I definitely wouldn't call it acting, though, because I'm not acting at all.

I would trade my line for Ella's stupid skunk costume any day of the week.

Chapter 7

I stayed up late last night, reading the whole play from beginning to end and typing up a cheat sheet for myself. I finally understand what's going on, but exhaustion meant I was pretty out of it this morning . . . and I forgot all about Nikki's instructions. Everyone else in the dressing room is wearing ratty black or beige underwear that never should have seen the light of day. I look down at my pale yellow lace panties and matching bra.

They're about to get wrecked.

The rest of my clothes are in my assigned locker while I stand with Ella and a half-dozen other girls in the communal shower of the women's dressing room. The ceiling is low over my head, and the tile floor is cool and damp under my bare feet. The makeup assistant—a young woman dubbed "Makeup Mandy" by the rest of the cast—hands out damp sponges and plastic spray bottles filled with green latex paint. I don't want to be on display for these people I don't know, but there's no way out of it. Besides, no one else seems to be bothered in the least. Not the pink-haired girl, who, now that she's nearly naked, I can see is covered in tattoos; not my scene buddy Lori, who is built like an

Amazon and apparently isn't interested in wearing a bra; and not Ella, who is shorter than me, curvier than me, and clearly much more confident than me.

"Bianca, you're first." Mandy beckons Bianca forward and, without any additional warning, squirts her with the spray bottle. A splotch of green blossoms across Bianca's stomach.

She squeals in response. "It's cold!"

"Rub it in." Mandy demonstrates by swiping Bianca with a sponge, spreading the green over her sides. "Everyone else, start squirting. And help each other out. If you see someone missing a patch, let them know."

There's a pause while we all stand around, uncertain. Then Ella grabs a bottle and unceremoniously blasts me in the thigh. I squeal like Bianca. She wasn't just being a dramatic theater girl—the paint is freezing.

"Three minutes." Mandy is holding a stopwatch. "On a performance night, that means you only have two left until you're supposed to be onstage. So unless you want to be out there in your underwear, I suggest you speed it up."

We start squirting and sponging like mad, and very quickly we're all green from our hairlines to our toes. Once we're done, we rush to our lockers; in each hangs a dress the same color as our newly painted skin. I yank mine over my head and tug it down. It barely skims the tops of my knees.

"Go!" Mandy yells at us. I follow Ella and the rest of the girls in a mad dash from the dressing room.

On the wooden deck, an assistant stage manager is also yelling "Go!" and gesturing toward the amphitheater. We charge out of the wings as a stream of equally green boys are pouring from the other side. Nikki directs us into our standard semi-circle at the back edge of the stage, where we're told to situate ourselves in boy-girl order and to link arms with the people next to us. I find myself on the end of the arc, and as I slide my right arm between a hard biceps muscle and a naked rib cage, I realize they belong to Milo.

I also notice (again) that he's tall. And angular. And (for the first time that I've seen) wearing very, very little.

Which suits him.

It is not a thought I can have, so I try to shake it off. I pretend that I don't notice it's him.

More specifically, I pretend that I don't notice his body.

But Milo has no such compunctions about me. "You look like an elf," he tells me.

I compose myself enough to answer him. "Well, you look like an alien." It's less weird than saying what I truly think, which is that he looks like he belongs in a museum. One with a gallery featuring a display of sculpted Greek gods.

Yeah, there's no way to deny it. Ella's ex-boyfriend is *hot.*

But maybe I'm only noticing it because (A) he's half-naked, and (B) Tuck is not in this scene.

Del Shelby and the choreographer saunter onto the stage, and we walk through the basic steps of the final moments before intermission. We will continue to hang out upstage in our semi-circle while four dancers—also completely in green—come out carrying flaming arrows. The dancers will flail around for a little bit before flinging their arrows into four fire pits.

Then King Menelaus shows up. He's yet another green dude, but he's bigger than everyone else and wears a super-crazy giant headdress. Also, he's seriously pissed because in the last scene—while I was slathering myself in paint—Paris crashed his castle and snagged his wife, Helen of Troy. Paris had goddess-permission to do it, because Aphrodite, desperate to get that stupid golden apple, promised Paris the most beautiful woman on earth if he would only proclaim her—Aphrodite—the most beautiful goddess.

I lean toward Milo. "These goddesses have major self-esteem issues."

"It doesn't make any sense," he agrees in a whisper as King Menelaus rages across the stage. "They're grown-ass goddesses. Why do they give a crap how some stupid boys think they look?"

"It's a terrible message."

"The worst."

"Also, what makes Paris so qualified to judge female beauty?"

"Good point." Milo shrugs. "But whatever. I didn't write it."

Nearby, King Menelaus waves two huge arrows over his head while he tantrums around. Finally, he stops on his mark at the center of the stage, where Del Shelby directs him to give a "war whoop." Menelaus lets out something that sounds more like a baby donkey braying, which makes me feel a little relieved. At least I'm not the only one who underplays their lines. . . .

Del makes Menelaus whoop again, and the third time he gets it right. Those of us in the chorus somberly intone, *"This is war."* Nikki explains that during a real performance, this is when all the lights will go off, the arrows will be extinguished, and the stage will be plunged into darkness. We're supposed to run off-stage under cover of night.

I practice running as instructed, and nearly bowl over Ella. She gives me a dirty look even though I say, "Sorry!"

"Where were you in the line?" she asks me.

"Stage left." I say it with more authority than I feel, as I'm still making sense of the directions around here.

"Next to Milo." Ella's voice is level. Calm. I can't tell what she's thinking.

"Yeah." I push past her into the locker room. "Next to Milo."

• • •

The next day is a tiny respite. Del Shelby is going to work with the principals on their deep, meaningful moments, and the choreographer will be onstage with the featured dancers. We peasants—I mean actor-technicians—don't have to be there until midafternoon, so Ella and I get to sleep in.

When we awaken—conveniently at the same time—we find Annette just leaving for work. She looks like a waitress in a movie: crisp white button-up over black pants, little red apron, high ponytail. She pauses in the apartment doorway to invite us to the restaurant for lunch. "We have great sandwiches, and I can give you the family discount. It's a good deal."

Ella and I look at each other. She gives a tentative nod, I do the same, and three hours later I'm pulling into Bel Giardino's gravel parking lot. We get out and head toward the faux-brick building graced by an awning of red, green, and white stripes.

The windows are painted with cartoon renderings that someone must think of as authentically Italian: a heaping bowl of spaghetti with meatballs, a pizza, and a chubby chef in a white suit with a red neck scarf.

"It's supposed to be the best restaurant in town," Ella says as she holds open a door for me.

Just inside, we find ourselves in a lobby that is small and dark and lined with red benches. It smells like garlic and freshly baked bread. Suddenly, I remember that all I had for breakfast was one of Ella's strawberry yogurts.

A college-aged—or maybe slightly older—dude in a red vest looks up from his position behind a host stand. His nametag says *Vic* and, under that, *Assistant Manager*.

"Two for lunch." He sounds bored. "Table or booth?"

"Booth," Ella and I say together.

"Let me see if we have one open." He scours his clipboard, which of course doesn't make sense, since *he's* the one who just asked *us* what we wanted.

Ella steps forward. "Can we be in Annette's section?"

Vic the Assistant Manager perks up. "Are you her guests?" When we both nod, he beams. "Why didn't you say so? Which one of you is her sister?" Ella raises her hand, and the wattage of Vic's smile increases. He grabs a couple burgundy-leather-bound menus. "Right this way."

We follow Vic down a narrow hall and into a larger room with a black-and-white-checkered floor and red-and-white-checkered tablecloths. Low copper lamps hang above all the seating areas, about half of which are filled with customers. The walls are decorated with oil paintings of Italian streets. As Vic waves us into a corner booth, Annette comes out of an arched doorway that probably leads to the kitchen. She gives a little squeal and trots over for hugs. "See, I said you'd get the royal treatment."

Vic smiles at us. "Enjoy your meals." He heads back toward the lobby.

Ella and I slide into opposite sides of the booth as a busboy in a red bow tie arrives with a plastic pitcher of ice water. If nothing else, Bel Giardino is consistent with its employees' accessories. The busboy pours, edging around Annette as she opens our menus and starts pointing at entrées. "We're kinda known for our pizza wrap, but the meatball sandwich is to die for. The chicken pesto is awesome too. Cory here"—she gestures to the bow tie guy—"can start you off with drinks. What do you want?"

Cory—who by the way is very cute and blond—gives Annette a slow smile before regaling us with a list of nonalcoholic fountain and bottled beverages. I order a Coke. Ella asks for a water with lime and is told they only have lemon.

As Cory heads off, Annette leans close to our table. "The guys who work here are the *best*."

After Annette takes our orders and Cute Cory brings our drinks, Ella and I are left sitting across from each other. It's awkward, to say the least. Sure, we've agreed to a meal together. That doesn't change the facts: she's blackmailing me to stay in town, and I'm pissing her off by being friendly to her ex.

However, we do share a history, an apartment, and—I'm assuming—a desire for a peaceful lunch. I decide to wave the white flag. A temporary one. I motion to her water with lemon. "Sorry about your subpar citrus."

"I did assume there would be multiple garnish options." Ella stirs her water with her straw. "Bel Giardino has a bar, after all."

"You should have asked for cherries."

"So I can show off my newly acquired tongue-tying skills?"

"Yup." I take a sip of my Coke. "How was the acquiring of those skills, anyway?"

"You mean, how was Gretchen?" Ella eyes me. "You can just ask. I'll tell you whatever you want to know."

"Is she . . ." I'm not sure what I want to know. *Is she funnier than me? Is she smarter and cooler and better than me? Is she going to marry Tuck and bear his children?* "Is she nice?"

"She's not *not* nice." Ella looks at me like she's considering what to say next. "So what are you going to do about Tuck?"

"I don't know what I *can* do." Other than admit that everything I thought when I came here was completely wrong.

"Well, are you getting to know him? Like we talked about?"

"I guess so." I don't mention that the person I seem to be getting to know best is Ella's ex-boyfriend. "I just don't . . ." I trail off, because saying what's in my brain is too hard. It makes me feel naked, and I've already been more naked than I care to be in front of a bunch of people I don't know. And I still don't even know Ella. At least, not anymore. Not really.

But Ella finishes my sentence for me. "You don't know if it's worth it."

"Yeah." Again, I omit part of my thought: *Or if I screwed up again. Wanted the wrong thing again. Can't figure myself out. Again.*

"Well, I think it is." Ella eyes me across the table. "What he said—about how he was glad you came—I think he meant it. It's just that—" She stops, cocking her head to the side. Like she's weighing something.

"What?"

"I think he meant it. That's all." She takes a sip of water, and the conversation is over.

We sit in silence until Cute Cory returns with the fried mozzarella sticks I ordered as an appetizer. "I brought extra marinara sauce." He sets the basket between us on the table. "Since you're Annette's friends."

"I'm her *sister,*" Ella specifies.

"Even better." Cory grins at her before glancing back at me. "No offense."

"None taken."

Ella and I manage to make small talk through the cheese sticks and most of the entrée (shrimp scampi for me, a meatball sandwich for Ella). Even if we wanted to have deep conversation, we couldn't, because we're constantly interrupted by the stream of waitstaff coming over to say hello. Clearly, Annette is the beloved belle of the Bel Giardino ball.

As we're finishing our lunches, Annette shows up again to ask if we want anything else. Ella sticks to her lemon water, but I ask for an espresso. While we wait for it to arrive, Ella glances around the restaurant. She leans across the table toward me. "Hey, Rainie, who wouldja?"

I blink at her. "Huh?"

"Remember how we used to play that?" Ella grins, and I'm taken back to sixth grade—our first year in middle school—when we were suddenly thrown into the deep end of a much larger social pool. To cope, we started playing this game in every classroom we were in. At the time, the implied word at the end of the sentence was "kiss," but now that we're older, I think it might be a different verb. . . .

"Okay, one sec." I scan the room. Two tables over, there's a dude in a beret who's scribbling in a notebook. The seat across from him is occupied by a guitar, so maybe he's writing lyrics.

"That's a reasonable option." Ella is looking at the same dude. "Maybe he'd play a song after the deed is done."

"Wait, you think that's a *plus*?"

Cute Cory appears at our table with my espresso. "Can I get you anything else?"

We tell him no and watch him walk away. When he's out of earshot, I turn to Ella, but she says it first—"Dibs!"

"Damn." That busboy is definitely the best option in this place.

"How old do you think he is?"

"Twenty, maybe?" Ella grins. "God, if that's how boys grow up, I can't wait for college."

"Why do you have to wait?" I return her grin. "We're here. Give him your number."

"Gross, no."

I'm lost. Weren't we just admiring his hotness?

Ella sees my look of confusion and leans over the table, lowering her voice. "I think Annette's dating a restaurant guy, which means it could be him."

"Or not." I shrug. "If you don't know, he's fair game."

"Nope." Ella shakes her head violently. "If there's even a chance Annette did or does have a thing with him, he's not an option. The sister code is even stronger than the friend code, and you don't share boys with your friends."

Okay, that makes no sense because—

"You theater kids all date each other," I remind her.

"We hook up with each other," Ella clarifies. "It's just sharing tongue space. You don't *really* get together with someone your friend was *really* with. That's bad form."

Huh. I can't tell if Ella is warning me away from Milo, or saying we're friends despite her blackmailing ways, or just making conversation.

"However, Cory is mine for the sake of Who Wouldja." Ella gives me a huge smile. "Guess you're stuck with Beret Guy."

I decide to play along. It's more fun that way.

"Ugh." I slump overdramatically. "You know his songs will all be super emo."

"I bet he smokes skinny cigarettes."

"He'll call me by his mother's name."

"He wears socks to bed. And leg warmers."

"He sits down to pee."

Ella bursts out laughing—"Lazy!"—which makes me laugh along with her.

"Deal breakers." I compose myself and lean across the table, making my face serious. "Also, Beret Guy weeps after sex."

That remark sends Ella into another gale of laughter. I look around the restaurant to make sure we're not disturbing other diners. A new customer is walking in. He's tall and lanky with shaggy black hair and a concert T-shirt from an old British punk band. I reach over to flick Ella on the arm. "Dibs," I tell her.

Ella follows my gaze and, just like that, her smile drops away. "Interesting."

"What?" I take a second look at the guy, which is when I realize he undeniably reminds me of someone.

Milo.

I don't know what that means, but it can't be right. It can't be *good.*

"Nothing." Ella averts her eyes. "I thought you liked blonds, that's all."

All the good humor washes away from our table, leaving us in an awkward silence that goes on far too long. I'm thankful when Annette returns to drop our check on the table. "See, what'd I tell you? Thirty percent off."

I pull out a credit card and toss it onto the paper as Ella digs through her purse for bills.

"Split it?" Annette asks, and we both nod. She takes it and trots back toward the front of the restaurant.

Cory arrives at our table again. He takes our cups and

napkins, and after he disappears into the kitchen, I look back at Ella. "He's really cute. I think you won the game."

Even though I'm confused about the nature of the war currently being waged, my words are an offering of peace. But Ella doesn't seem to realize that.

"Yep." She doesn't even look at me. "I'm a winner."

Chapter 8

We're into the second week of rehearsals. I now know *Zeus!* from start to finish, beginning with Leda's dance and ending with the Greek-Trojan battle in which Achilles is killed by Paris and Paris is killed by Zeus. This theater thing must be growing on me, because I find my heartstrings tugging when Milo falls and then again when the lightning bolt hits Tuck. When Tuck crumples, Pollux runs out and catches him as he "dies," lowering his body to the ground before standing to deliver a stirring monologue about the travesties of war. Then the entire cast emerges from the right wing and trudges across the stage while singing a mournful dirge.

It's a very dramatic ending.

On principle, I'm still irritated by Ella's blackmailing me to stay. In practice, however . . . I'm getting used to being around her.

The Tuesday before our first tech rehearsal, we all end up at McKay's again. I was hoping Tuck would be there (preferably without Gretchen), but when Ella and I take a reconnaissance lap around the place, he's nowhere to be seen. We grab a booth and order the McKay's special to split: a toasted croissant, cut in half and filled with two scoops of vanilla ice cream, then drizzled with hot fudge and topped with a cherry. Our waiter places it between us, giving Ella the chance to yet again practice her new skill. I time her, and she spits the tied stem into her hand at exactly fifty seconds. "I should get a prize," she tells me.

"You're going to get a boyfriend." I motion to the booth across the aisle from us, where a guy we don't know is watching her performance. He shoots Ella a thumbs-up, and I burst out laughing.

A second later, Milo plops down beside Ella. "What's so funny?"

My insides light up with no warning, but Milo obviously doesn't have the same effect on Ella. She abruptly stops laughing, dropping her spoon with a clatter. "Gotta pee."

Milo immediately slides out of the booth, springing to his feet. "Hey, if this is girls-only time, I don't need to stick around—"

"Nope." Ella cuts him off as she also slides out. "I think I might play some darts, after all. Feel free to stay, have some chocolate. My roommate and my ex hanging out—it's just what every girl wants." She says it like a joke, but I don't think she finds it funny. "Stop. Stay. Seriously."

Milo looks startled, and after Ella stalks away, he hesitates before sitting back down. "Do you want to go after her, or . . . ?"

"No." I say it automatically, and then, after a second, I realize it's the truth. I don't need to chase after Ella just because she's having an inscrutable hissy fit. I'd rather hang out with Milo.

However, I really—like, *really*—need to find out what happened between them. In general Ella's overdramatic, so I'm sure it was something that normal humans wouldn't even consider a bad thing. But I want to know, just in case.

In case of what . . . I don't know.

Milo sits across from me. He picks up Ella's discarded spoon and looks at it for a moment before setting it down. "That would be gross, right?"

"Give it." I hold out my hand so that Milo can place the handle of the spoon into it, and then I wipe off the ladle part with my napkin. "There you go."

We both ignore the fact that he used to put his tongue in Ella's mouth, so using her spoon shouldn't be *that* big a deal.

"You are a dream." Milo accepts it and takes a bite of ice cream, apparently not noticing the way my cheeks go hot at his off-handed compliment. "So what do you think of *Zeus!* these days?"

The job is insane, my life is a mess, and I make no sense whatsoever. But, sure, let's talk about the ancient Greek musical drama.

"When I was a kid, I had this book of Greek myths. I remember the one about the guy who flew too close to the sun and the story about Pandora's box." I scrunch up my nose, thinking through what bugs me about our play. "But *Zeus!* . . . I guess I'm confused about our Zeus. About how he's written."

"You mean, because he's supposed to be this big god hero, but then he smites Paris?" Milo gives me a sympathetic smile. "You're not the first person to say that."

"Yeah. It's like he turns out to be a villain, but only accidentally. And the way Hugh struts around onstage, it's like Zeus doesn't even *know* he's the villain of the story."

"To be fair, that's the *deal* with villains." Milo leans across the table. "The best ones—like those who are written in the most complex, interesting ways—they never *know* they are villains. They have their own reasons for their behavior."

I find myself nodding along. "They justify their choices."

"Right. Because otherwise they're just happenstances of plot."

I fold my arms and sit back in my seat, thinking about it. "The best villains are like real people. When they make a bad choice, they don't always *know* they're making a bad choice."

Like me choosing to come to Olympus, chasing Tuck.

"Exactly." Milo points at me with his (Ella's) spoon. "The very best villains have some redeeming quality about them. Something that makes them three-dimensional."

"Something that makes them human."

"Right." Milo grins at me. His grin—and there's really no other way to put this—it's breathtaking. "No one is ever all good or all bad."

I stare at him across the table, and then I shake my head and take another bite. Having fleeting lustful thoughts about Ella's ex-boyfriend is all bad.

It's all kinds of bad.

• • •

When Ella and I step into our dark apartment, we're both startled to find Annette in the living room. She's on the couch, talking in a soft voice into her phone. When we walk in, she jerks to her feet before heading into her room. Ella turns to look at me. "Twenty bucks says it's the busboy."

"Cute Cory?" I smile at Ella. "Well, *one* of the Reynolds sisters should get him, that's for sure."

Several minutes later, Ella and I are in our beds. Moonlight glows between the bent mini-blinds, striping across my comforter. I squirm, trying to get comfortable, before I ask the question that's been weighing on me for days. "So what's the deal with you and Milo?"

There's a silence, during which I wonder if I shouldn't have asked the question. Then I hear Ella shift in her bed. "Why do you care?"

"I don't have any friends here." I didn't realize how pathetic that would sound until the words hit the air.

"Hul-*lo*." It sounds like she's saying it with a smile, but I can't be sure. "I'm in the room."

"Um . . . and blackmailing me." But I say it lightly so she won't take the words too seriously. "Really, Milo is so nice. What gives?"

"Sure, Milo can be nice. He can also be . . . not nice."

"Like how?"

A long moment passes, and then I have to strain to hear Ella's voice. "He cheated on me."

"What?" I bolt upright in my bed. That can't be true. It doesn't sound like the Milo I know.

Except . . . I don't really know him, do I?

"I know, right?" I hear shuffling from Ella's side of the room and see her silhouette rise in front of the window. She's sitting up too. "He doesn't seem like the type."

Suddenly, Ella's attitude makes a little more sense.

"We started dating near the end of last summer," Ella continues. "It was still pretty new when Mandy went to a party and saw him hooking up with one of the dancers. I wasn't allowed to go to parties last year, and I thought maybe Mandy got it wrong, but then I started asking around. It turned out he was hooking up with *two* dancers. Not at the same time. Two different dancers, two different parties."

My heart drops. What Milo said was true: the best villains don't know they're villains. It's too much to explain to Ella, so all I say is "That sucks."

"Yeah. If he had just broken up with me like a normal person, it would have been bad enough, but instead I have to hear about it from Mandy while she's giving me a bottle of green body paint. Milo and I never even had The Talk. We just kind of . . . fizzled."

"You didn't get a real ending."

"It was . . ."

I finish the sentence so she doesn't have to. "Embarrassing."

"Yeah. People started avoiding my eyes. Milo was the asshole, but it was like I got punished for it." She settles back into her bed. "It's fine for you to be friends with him. I just thought . . . you should know."

I'm glad she told me, but I hate having heard it. I don't want Milo to be a villain. I want him to be one of the good guys.

As I slide back onto my pillow, a thought flashes through my brain. One I shouldn't ask.

"I didn't have sex with him." It's like Ella read my mind. "I haven't . . . ever."

"Me neither."

"Are you kidding?" Across the room, Ella props herself up on one elbow, facing my bed. "You're a virgin?"

"Uh, yeah." Should I take her surprise as a compliment or an insult?

"Oh, it's just . . ." She trails off. The moment goes on so long that I have to prod her.

"Just what?"

"You and your little gang of three. You have, like, this all-access pass to every social event somehow. You go to all the parties."

It rubs me the wrong way. "Just because I go to parties doesn't mean I'm having sex at them."

"That's not what I meant. I just thought . . . you and Marin and Sarah seem older or something. Like you've got more going on. I assumed you'd have more experience."

Marin and Sarah have more going on: plans, ambition, a future. Me, though—I'm like a human skipping stone, splashing across life's surface, going after one thing and then another. Sure, I might make a lot of ripples, but they always disappear.

"Who do you think I would have slept with? I never hang out with the same guy for very long."

I never do the same *anything* for very long.

"That doesn't always matter."

"I know, but it does for me." I try to untangle the reasons why. "I don't want to do it just to *do* it, you know? If it's not right."

This time the pause is long enough that I wonder if Ella's fallen asleep. "But how are we supposed to know when something's right?"

"Are we still talking about sex?"

"I don't know."

"Well, I'm clearly the wrong person to ask." It's late enough and I'm tired enough that the truth is coming out. "Just about every decision I make is the wrong one."

Ella shifts in her bed. "Maybe you're not as wrong as you think you are."

Maybe you don't know me well enough to say that.

I pull my comforter up to my chin and nestle into it, beginning to drift off. As I do, the last thing that occurs to me is that this conversation has made things clearer. I need to stop letting myself get distracted by Milo. I didn't come here for him.

I came for Tuck.

Chapter 9

Ella tells me that cue-to-cue rehearsal is the worst, and she's not wrong. For endless hours, we start and stop the show so that the light people and the sound people and the set people and the fire people can all get their crap together.

The most annoying scene is the one I hate the most anyway: when Paris sails across the Aegean Sea so Helen can fall in love with him. The "sea" is made of giant strips of multihued blue canvas. Those of us who are lowly cogs in the vast machine of *Zeus!*—we hold the ends of the canvas strips and wave them up and down to make "waves." Paris and his army traipse between them as we pull the cloth across and off the stage, so it looks like the army has arrived on dry land, simulating their landing in Greece. The first million times we attempt this scene, the lights have to be adjusted because Del doesn't like their colors or focus or something. Finally, the lighting people get that part down—by then my arms are killing me because that stupid canvas is heavy—and I run backstage to green up for the war-prep scene. Except that when we return to the stage, looking like many, many human-sized Statues of Liberty, Del isn't ready for us. So I have the supreme pleasure of sitting beside Ella in the front row of the amphitheater while, over and over and over again, Paris strides into a garden to see Helen for the first time.

Helen is sitting on a rock, chilling with her friends, when Paris arrives to be wowed by her beauty. He lets us know this by pressing his hand to his heart and saying a bunch of extremely poetic things. Helen starts to ask, "Who are—"

But then Eros shoots her with an arrow of love. "—youuuuu?" She finishes the question in a trill because, thanks to the arrow, she's now hopelessly and eternally smitten with Paris.

It doesn't seem so difficult, but Gretchen cannot get her timing right. The love arrow is not a real arrow at all but a stage effect. There's a *twang-zing* sound, and a light beam hits Helen in the boob, which means that she needs to be in *exactly* the right spot at *exactly* the right time, and it's just not happening. The few times she *does* get it right, either the sound tech or the light tech misses the cue. Rehearsal of this scene goes on forever, and the whole time I'm aware of Milo sitting in the row behind us.

I've managed to avoid him all day. He waved at me this morning, but I pretended not to see him. Later, as Ella and I were walking out of the dressing room, he came up to us. "I think I owe you a McKay's special," he said to Ella. "I ended up eating most of your half last night."

"It's fine." She shrugged and walked off.

He looked at me. "I tried, right?"

"Whatever." The word came out of my mouth exactly as chilly as I intended it to be, and I immediately followed Ella as she strode away.

But not before I saw the flash of hurt on Milo's face.

Now, sitting in the first row of the amphitheater, I'm way too aware that he's there, probably wondering what happened between last night and this morning to make me treat him like this.

Or—what do I know?—maybe he hasn't given me a second thought. He wouldn't be the first boy here to barely notice me.

I'm considering turning around, maybe just to make eye contact, when everyone stands and I register that finally—*finally*—stupid Gretchen has gotten her stupid cue right three times in a row and we can move on to the next scene. So maybe later.

Except later never comes.

• • •

The used-book store on Nine Muses Street is small but well stocked—at least the mythology section is. I find a tattered copy of the book I had as a child, plus a newer, slim one that seems to be a family tree of Greek gods and goddesses.

Finding a section of the shop devoted to theater is more difficult, and it takes me a while to locate the most appropriate book: *Theatre for Dumdums.* I wonder if the author is a dumdum or if it's supposed to be a joke, since that's not even how you spell "theater." But since beggars can't be choosers, I buy all three books. If I can learn the language here, maybe I'll understand the people who speak it. Maybe I'll find a way to connect with Tuck.

I'm on the way out when I nearly run into our stage manager, Nikki, heading for the counter. She's carrying a small paperback with a cover that shows lots of flames and skin and palm trees. Nikki and I make eye contact, and she instinctively moves to shield the book, but it's too late. I've seen it and she knows it. She stops in front of me, blocking my path. "I'm not going to ask about your books. You don't tell about mine."

"Of course! I would never—" I pause, looking at her. "I just assumed you read, like, military strategy or something."

Her eyebrows rise. "You think I'm in the army?"

"Maybe. You're so badass and all. . . ." That might actually be the stupidest thing I've ever said. Is there a *Conversation for Dumdums*?

Nikki laughs . . . thank goodness. "Dude, I spend every day and night making sure a bunch of hormonal people stand in the right places and say the right words. When I get back to my apartment at one in the morning, all I want is to be away from it all for five minutes." I look more closely at the book she's holding. The background is a tropical island at night, awash in flames. In the foreground, a bare-chested man with flowing hair holds a buxom beauty who is either fainting or sleeping or *really* enjoying herself. I'm sure that, at the very least, it's entertaining. "I know." Nikki brandishes the book. "It's awful and it's not feminist. But it's escapism, and damn if I'm not allowed to escape a little bit."

"Damn, indeed." If I can't figure out what the hell I'm doing about Tuck, escaping doesn't exactly sound like the worst thing in the world. "Can I borrow it when you're done?"

"No way." Nikki winks at me. "Buy your own book."

• • •

I swing by the apartment to pick up Ella so she doesn't have to walk to the theater. When we arrive at the wooden deck behind the stage, there's a big poster sheet tacked onto the corkboard next to the sign-in spot. Milo's name is written across the top in red marker and decorated with gold glitter. Below his name are messages and cartoon figures and signatures. The board's narrow shelf holds several markers.

It was Paul's birthday last week, so I know what we're supposed to do.

Ella turns to me. "I'll look like a poor sport if I don't." I remain silent as she writes the bare minimum on Milo's birthday poster: *HBD, Ella.*

Ella slaps her marker down on the shelf and waits for me to sign. I scribble a simple *happy birthday,* followed by my name. Part of me wishes I could write something else. Something more. Something to acknowledge that even though Milo cheated on Ella last summer, he also spent the first part of this summer being nice to me.

But I don't.

And Ella approves.

• • •

I'm still feeling guilty about the generic birthday greeting when Milo accosts me in line at the food counter. "Hey, what's going on?" He nudges me with an elbow, and I squelch the urge to nudge him back. Instead, I yank away, putting distance between our bodies. It's necessary because the Appalachian air is sticky hot and I'm wearing a short tank dress and he's in a sleeveless tee. The last thing I need is for my arm to be pressed against his, with everyone's warm skin and hard muscles all over each other.

Not that I'm the one with the hard muscles.

I am not.

When I don't answer him, Milo steps in front of me, peering down into my face. "Rainie?"

I jerk my gaze away—it would be too easy to get lost in those brown eyes—and mumble an answer. "I'm just trying to get a sandwich."

In my peripheral vision, I see Milo's arms folding across his chest and then unfolding. His hands—warm, dry—land on my shoulders and gently spin me around. I allow it, and a minute later I'm in the relatively cool shade of a sugar maple on the deserted path to the parking lot, looking up at him.

"Are you mad at me?" Milo asks.

"Yes," I tell him, even though it's a lie. Even though the person I'm really mad at is me. "I don't like cheaters."

"Cheaters? What are you—" He stops, and his forehead creases in a frown. "Is this about Ella?"

"Yes. Unless you cheat on *everyone,* in which case it's about them too." My hands fly to my hips as I channel theater-girl drama. "It's crappy to cheat on anyone, anytime, for any reason."

Milo shakes his head. "You have no idea what you're—"

"I thought you were different." There's no reason for me to let him speak. "Obviously you are not. You're a villain." Milo's mouth drops open, but by now I'm too far gone to stop. "I'm sure you have a justification all thought out, but it doesn't matter. I don't care. At the end of any story, the villain is still a bad guy."

With that, I whirl and storm toward the backstage. There. I've done my duty as Ella's friend, I've done my duty to all of womanhood . . . and I've successfully removed temptation from my life.

Because—let's be honest—if Tuck wasn't in the picture, Milo would be very, very tempting.

Chapter 10

Final dress rehearsal. We practice in the morning and early afternoon—I avoid Milo's eyes the whole time—and then we're sent home with instructions to rest and "come back at your normal call time." For Ella and me and the rest of the actor-techs, that means arriving at six-thirty for an eight o'clock show. Now that rehearsals are about to be over, we are going to have every single day free for the rest of the summer. And Monday nights too.

It's not a terrible schedule.

Ella and I arrive together, but we split off in separate directions when we reach the theater. She made ramen noodles at home, but I'm starving and want something from the backstage kitchen counter. I find myself next to Hugh Hadley, who flashes me a yellowed grin. "You ready for tomorrow night?"

"I have to be, right?"

It's an offhanded remark, but it makes Hugh roar with laughter. "That's the spirit!" he tells me before taking his burger and wandering away.

I pay the white-aproned boy behind the counter. He gives me a paper plate that holds a sandwich, two dill-pickle spears, and a handful of greasy potato chips. I start to head to the benches at the other end of the deck—they overlook the shaded woodsy paths leading down to the forest behind the theater—when I realize Ella and Milo are standing there. They're deep in a conversation that seems . . .

Intimate.

As I watch, Milo takes a step closer to Ella. He leans over so he can whisper something in her ear. My eyebrows slant down in a frown as Ella smiles up at him. He pulls her into a hug, and as my insides inscrutably tighten, I whirl and head for the locker room, dropping my plate into a trash can as I go.

I've lost my appetite.

• • •

By the time we're into the nest scene, my jaws have been clenched for so long that my teeth ache. Forget cheating, forget villains . . . what's going on between Ella and Milo?

I mean, sure, it's her right to hug whoever she wants. To do *whatever* she wants with whoever she wants. But why is she doing it with *him*?

More importantly, why do I give a flying crap?

As the chorus members mill about, pretending to have conversations while Helen and Pollux hatch from their eggs, Ella meanders over. "Hey, do you want a smoothie after work? I bought frozen fruit today, and supposedly Annette has a blender somewhere."

"No." The word comes out hard and sharp, like a stick breaking. Ella opens her mouth to speak, but I cut her off. "I mean, unless you're going to force me to, in which case, sure. I'll have a smoothie. I guess you can let me know what flavor I like."

"What the hell are you talking about?"

Why the hell were you and your hated ex-boyfriend all over each other?

But what I say is this: "You know, your friendly little blackmail? I'm over it."

Behind us, Helen's egg rocks back and forth. It bonks into Pollux's egg, which also starts rocking.

"Okay . . ." Ella stares at me. "So what are you going to do about it?"

"Tell Tuck the truth." The option didn't occur to me until the moment I said the sentence, but now that I have, it seems like a good idea. My voice scales up. "You won't have any more power over me." Nearby, Paul turns to look at us. I bring it down a notch. "Then I can leave whenever I want."

"Good," says Ella. "You do that. Is there anything else?"

I want her to tell me the truth about what the hell she was doing backstage with Milo, but before I can decide whether to ask her, both of those two damn eggs crack open so the most beautiful woman in the world can be born alongside her ugly brother. Ella and I walk off in different directions.

Stupid, stupid mythology.

• • •

The rest of final dress rehearsal goes really well, which apparently is a problem because there's some dumb theater adage about "bad final dress, good opening night." At least, that's what

Paul tells me when I ask why he doesn't look happy. "I'm telling you, tomorrow's going to be awful. Tonight's the good night. Live on that."

It is, of course, utterly ridiculous . . . and yet when I'm walking to my car and see Tuck across the dark parking lot, those words cross my mind. Without giving myself time to chicken out, I start in his direction. But before I take more than ten steps, Milo is in front of me.

"Rainie, can we talk?" His head is cocked, and his dark brown eyes are looking into mine. Suddenly I'm aware of the muggy North Carolina air. The sound of cicadas at the perimeter of the parking lot. The still-present heat of the sun-warmed pavement rising up through my feet and ankles.

Milo makes me too aware. Of everything.

So I take a step back. I force my gaze to slide off Milo's angular face, to focus behind him, where Tuck is just getting into his pickup truck. "I have to go."

Milo turns to see what I'm looking at. His expression changes. It hardens. Becomes unreadable.

"Oh," he says, but his voice comes from behind me because I've already stepped past him. I'm walking—no, *running*—toward Tuck's truck. The headlights are on, and as I get closer, the engine rumbles to life. I screech to a halt at the passenger side and rap on the window. Tuck turns to look at me, surprised. It's only then that I hazard a glance backward into the darkness.

Milo is nowhere to be seen.

But I can't think about him now.

Chapter 11

The inside of Tuck's truck smells like stale cigarettes. It surprises me enough to say something. "I didn't know you smoked."

"I don't usually." Tuck looks ashamed. "Except when I'm in a show, then sometimes I do. Do you want one?"

"No." I stare at him, at his beauty. So perfect, so blatant. Tuck looks like a thousand male models on a thousand fashion websites. Anyone would want him.

"So what's up?" He cocks his head, and it bumps me back in time to three minutes ago, when Milo did the same thing but my physical reaction was completely different.

Because I *had* a physical reaction.

I shake away the thought. This boy—the one right in front of me—is *why I came here.* I have to be right about one stupid thing in my whole stupid life, and that thing is sitting behind the steering wheel, looking across the bench seat at me. So I say it— "I came here because of you"—and get the satisfaction of watching his blue eyes widen in surprise.

"To . . . the parking lot?"

"No." I take a deep breath and let it out. "To Olympus. To this show. To the summer."

I see it in his eyes—*WTF?*—but the only thing that comes out of his mouth is my name. "Rainie."

I go for it before making the conscious decision to go for it. "It was your monologue," I blurt out. "I understood it. I am so scared of the future. Of *my* future. That what's supposed to happen won't happen because I can't figure out what *should* happen."

Tuck is completely still except for the rise and fall of his chest. I'm glad *someone* in the car is capable of breathing right now.

And then he leans toward me, stopping just over the midpoint of the seat. "What's supposed to happen?"

"I don't know." My heart speeds up. "But everything you said, it changed me. It made me feel like maybe there's something in front of me. Maybe I have a future even if I don't know what it is. Maybe I'm not just treading water after all." Now my words speed up too, matching the desperate thudding of my heart. "What you said made me come here. . . ." I stop because this time I hear the sound of my own voice cracking. I swallow, trying to choke back the terror of what lies ahead. Of my uncertain, cloudy future. "Tell me I wasn't crazy. Please."

Because otherwise I'm just a dumb girl who's looking at the wrong boy.

"Tell me I'm not *still* crazy."

We look at each other, and I have no idea what he's thinking, this blue-eyed boy I don't know. He goes blurry, and I feel something against my forehead. It's Tuck's hair brushing against mine. We've leaned far enough toward each other that we're touching.

Barely.

Tuck slides his hands up my arms to my neck. He cups my face in a way that feels like a scene in a movie. "You're so brave," he whispers.

"I'm really not," I start to tell him, except then he's kissing me. His mouth—softer than I would have guessed—is against my own. The kiss is so light that it tickles, and I have to tilt forward to stop the sensation. Tuck apparently takes this as encouragement, because he parts his lips, sliding a hand to my waist. I close my eyes and try to match his movements because this is everything I wanted. This is why I came to this strange country, where even the directions are backward. . . .

But the soft and the wet and the motions are gone.

He's gone.

I open my eyes. Tuck has pulled back and is gazing at me from his side of the seat. "Here's the truth," he says. "This thing with Gretchen, it's not real. It's temporary."

I stare at him. "You don't like her?"

"No, I do." Tuck's smile is sad. "But not in a strong way. Not in a deep way. Not like I could like . . . someone else."

He means me, right? After all, his tongue was just in my mouth. . . .

"Then why?" I ask him. "Why even bother being with Gretchen? What's the point?"

"This summer." Tuck reaches out and grabs my right hand. He squeezes it between his own hands, looking at me earnestly. "This summer is the point. It's my first professional lead role, and when we're together offstage, I'm better with her onstage. I'm . . ." He swallows and his grip around my hand tightens. "I'm scared, Rainie. I need her."

My heart lurches. Beautiful, confident, rock-solid Tuck Brady is scared? More than the kiss, more than the way he's looking at me now—that makes me feel good. "So now what?"

"Now we're here for the summer," he says. "But you have to know this: you're the real deal. You're . . ." His blue eyes darken, and the corners of his full lips pull upward. "Let's just say I won't be sad when we go back to Dobbs." He pauses and lets go of my hand so he can slide his own back to my face. "But I can't be with you here."

"I know," I tell him, even though I'm not sure I do.

"And, Rainie." He tugs me closer, until my face is inches from his own. "Thank you." He kisses me. "For being so brave." He kisses me again. "But we can't do this anymore." He pulls back and looks at me. "This is wrong."

No. I'm wrong.

He turns toward the front of the car, his movements deliberate. Shutting me out, sending me away. His fingers grip the wheel. "You should go."

So I go.

It's humiliating, but I go.

• • •

Ella's waiting on the hood of my car when I return. Maybe she planned to start a fight, or maybe she was going to apologize. I'll never know, because she takes one look at my tear-streaked face and holds out her hand. "Keys."

She is silent as she drives us home and as I slam the car door and stomp up the apartment stairs. However, now that I've spent a solid twenty minutes lying facedown on the sofa, she's apparently over it. There's a thumping sound as she drops to the floor beside me. When I lift my wet face, there's a strip of tape stretching from Ella's forehead to the tip of her nose, pulling it upward like that of a pig. Ella makes a snorting sound and—even though it's the stupidest thing in the world—I laugh. Because who *does* that?

She holds up a pint of strawberry ice cream and two spoons. "There's no chocolate."

I sit up, wipe my face, and accept one of the spoons. "I didn't know we had any ice cream."

"We don't." Ella peels off the lid and takes a scoop before handing the container to me. "But Annette does, so I'm pulling the sister card."

I also didn't know that such a thing as a sister card existed, but it sounds amazing. I dip a tiny spoonful and let the sweetness melt on my tongue. I'm taking a second scoop when Ella speaks again.

"I never would have told Tuck you followed him here. I just said that to get you to stay."

I lower my spoon and look at her. "What?"

"I didn't even think you'd take it seriously, and then when

- 116 -

you did . . ." Ella sighs. "I was kind of offended that you believed me."

"Why *wouldn't* I believe you?"

"Because we were friends." She looks at me. "We *were* friends," she clarifies, accenting the word. "But I thought if you were here for the summer, maybe we would be again."

I nod, only because I don't know what else to do. Blackmailing me—or even pretending to—was not cool. But getting me here was.

And so is the strawberry ice cream.

"What happened with Tuck?" Ella asks me, and I tell her. She nods and boils the ten-minute pickup truck exchange down to its essence: "He likes you, but not enough."

"Pretty much." I take a second—and larger—spoonful. "What we did, do you count that as cheating?"

"Absolutely." Ella sees my slump. "You wouldn't want *your* boyfriend kissing other girls in his truck, would you?"

Again—as has happened much too often recently—Milo springs to mind. I picture him kissing another girl, and a hot flush of jealousy surges through me. I fight it back, taking a third bite of the ice cream to cool myself down. Milo has kissed other girls. He does kiss other girls. In fact, he's kissed the girl sitting *right in front of me.* More importantly, he's not my boyfriend.

Nor should he be.

I have other dreams.

But because I'm sick of talking about Tuck, I change the subject. If nothing else, Milo makes for an excellent topic shift.

"What was going on with you and Milo before rehearsal?"

Ella's expression darkens. "Nothing."

"It wasn't nothing." My face suddenly feels the way Ella's looks. "You were all huggy with him."

"I was not." Ella snatches the pint away and shoves her spoon into it. "*He* was huggy with *me*."

There's that hot flush again. What is *wrong* with me?

Ella shovels in a couple bites before plunking the pint onto the coffee table. "He wanted to apologize, okay?" She licks her spoon and drops it with a clatter. "He said he was sorry about how things happened last summer, and then he wanted to hug it out like some sort of big, stupid Band-Aid. Like that would make everything okay."

"Did it?" I realize I'm leaning toward her, and I belatedly jolt back on the sofa. "Are you guys . . ."

Getting back together?

"Are we okay?" Ella shrugs, her dark eyebrows winging down toward each other. "Sure. He's forgiven, whatever." She looks at me. "Let's all forgive each other, okay?"

"Okay," I mumble, snatching up the ice cream and taking a big bite. If Milo felt some crazy need to apologize, why'd he wait until now to do it? Why not do it last summer, when he actually made the mistake?

Maybe he just wants more of Ella's dessert at McKay's.

Maybe he wants more of *Ella*.

Maybe I should figure out why it bothers me so much . . .

Or maybe I should just get over it.

Chapter 12

We were told that we should rest. That we should go over our lines. That we should reflect on what the show means, on its deeper place within us, so that tonight we'll be prepared to perform *Zeus!* before hundreds of pairs of eyes. Thus, the *obvious* thing to do is get up at the butt-crack of dawn and drive a dozen foggy miles on the two-lane highway heading out of town, then turn onto a winding dirt road so we can follow a caravan of cars to an unmarked clearing. From there, the best choice is to hike into the woods in search of something called Blue Ridge Rock Colony.

In good news, this morning Ella left the house extra early and came back with coffee, so at least I was caffeinated for the drive. Of course, it also means that before we've arrived at our hiking destination, I already have to pee. I look around from where Ella and I are in the midst of our crowd. Roughly half the cast and crew came—because apparently it's one of the Olympus traditions—and we're all moving along in little clumps: groups of people overtaking each other, then merging, then re-forming. The whole time, although I'm trudging along beside Ella, I'm horribly aware of only two people: Milo and Tuck. Mostly because they're practically stapled together. They spend the entire hike in a weird twosome huddle as we all walk beneath the yellow birches and mountain maples. I try very hard to squelch the part of me that's trying to stare at them. The part of me that's wondering if they're talking about the show, or if they're talking about Ella, or—and this is the absolute worst *if* of all—if Tuck is telling Milo about what happened last night.

Because that would really, really suck.

We're thirty minutes into the hike when I register that not only have I been hearing a sound, but I've been hearing it for a while, and now it's louder and closer. Right as I make that realization, someone far ahead—Paul, maybe—yells that "we're here." The trees break to either side, and Ella and I are suddenly in a beachy area (if you can say "beachy" when not near the ocean) by a mountain stream filled with boulders. Some of the big rocks are rounded and some are flat, making a giant path from one side of the narrow water to the other.

As we step closer, someone lets out a loud "Woo-hoo!" and it's a second before I realize the someone was Ella. More surprising, she's yanking her T-shirt up over her head. She turns to grin at me—in her bikini top and cutoff jean shorts. "Come *on!*"

I'm wearing my swimsuit under my clothes too, but I didn't really think I'd be seen in it. I thought it was one of those things you do as an extra layer of protection. Like, just in case you're suddenly forced into a swimming situation, you won't have to skinny-dip.

I shake my head at Ella. "No way."

"Why? You have an awesome body."

Number one, that's a lie. Number two, it's only one of my issues with the situation. "It's freaking freezing out here!"

Okay, I'm exaggerating a little, but it's definitely not swimming temperature. At least, not yet.

Tuck and Milo clearly disagree with me, because they're stripping down, both of them. Whipping off their shirts, dropping them on the ground. Being all tan and muscled and uncaring. As I watch, Tuck turns to Milo and says something. They might as well be on another planet for all the chance I have of hearing what they say, but their body language is obvious. Milo holds up a fist for Tuck to bump, but Tuck pulls him into that one-armed-dude-hug thing he likes to do. He says something else that makes Milo duck his head and shrug. Milo glances back into the crowd—toward where Ella and I are standing—and then he gives Tuck a small shove before taking off in a sprint toward the boulders. A second later, both of them are jumping from rock to rock, their two heads light and dark flashes over the stream. They bolster the courage of the rest of our group, because now everyone is stripping off clothes, running toward the water. Ella grins at me. "Come on, it'll warm up soon."

I have a hard time believing her when there are still dewdrops clinging to the maples, but I don't feel like I have a choice. And although I don't love the idea of flaunting my body in front of everyone's face, I reason with myself that all the girls here have already seen me full-ass naked in that little communal shower, so it's not a *huge* jump to the boys seeing me half-naked in my swimsuit. This really shouldn't be a big deal.

Except that it's not *all* the boys I'm worried about.

It's only one of them.

Okay, *two* of them.

As my scoop-neck yellow shirt drops to the dirt and I wriggle out of my shorts, I keep my eyes trained on what's happening on the rocks. Milo and Tuck stop leaping around like mountain goats and part as Gretchen makes her way out there. As I watch, she points out a tall boulder to Tuck. He bounds up and then reaches back to help her scramble aboard. Gretchen shakes out a big towel and drapes it over the rock, stretching like a cat . . . or a professional swimsuit model . . . before she lies down on it. Tuck hunkers beside her and, as he does, his head swivels in my direction. His eyes find mine before I can look away.

All I can think is, *I'm so embarrassed.* I whirl in the other direction, which of course means that now I'm staring straight at Milo. God, more eye contact. This time it's a different kind of embarrassed. One I don't know how to identify.

One that makes no sense whatsoever.

• • •

People fell asleep on their rocks. I was one of them—and so was Ella—but that was a while ago. It was after we ran and splashed and played (and also after we returned from a trek into the woods so I could pee; no way was I doing that alone). Now we're both awake and I'm peeling a tangerine, letting the orange scraps dance away in the gurgling water. Normally I wouldn't litter, but Ella reminds me that tangerines are from nature. They're organic and pure.

The only thing I know that is pure is my embarrassment about Tuck.

I finish a final juicy slice and look over at him. He's still at the top of that boulder, but now he's face-suctioned to Gretchen.

Worst.

"I'm going back to sleep," I tell Ella.

• • •

This time when I wake up, I'm baked into our big, flat rock, which is now warm. Very warm. Usually, I wouldn't begin to know how to tell time by the sun, but it's directly overhead and I'm pretty sure that means it's noon. Ella is still asleep beside me with one arm slung over her heart-shaped face when I sit up and push sticky bangs away from my forehead. I'm thankful I slathered myself in sunscreen before we took off this morning. I'm also thankful there's no mirror around. I can just pretend I look like a pretty mermaid instead of a dirty forest person.

I shade my eyes with my hand and scan around for a clump of yellow. I'm fairly certain I left my shorts and shirt by the path, but I don't see them right away, so maybe I'm wrong. Ella is still sleeping and I think about doing the same (again), but I'm getting bored. And cramped. And stiff. So instead I shimmy down from our rock and splash across the shin-deep water.

Holy *God,* mountain streams are cold.

I pull my clothes on over my swimsuit and then find my backpack, which is beside a rhododendron bush. I root through it for a snack and realize—too late—that Tuck is several yards away, doing the same thing. We see each other at the same time, and he stands, waving a granola bar in my direction. "Want one?"

I hold up my bag of chips. "I'm good, thanks."

I think that's going to be it because his girlfriend is here and life is awkward, but then he drops his backpack and walks over. "Hey."

"Hey." What else would I say?

Tuck glances around. Most people are prostrate on the rocks, with a handful of outliers playing Frisbee a little ways off. I have no idea where Milo is. "You look great," Tuck says.

Pretty mermaid, pretty mermaid, pretty mermaid.

"Thanks." I try to smooth my hair in a way that doesn't make me look crazy or paranoid. "You too?"

It accidentally comes out as a question, and Tuck smiles. He takes a step closer, and I automatically glance at Gretchen. She's still asleep on her boulder . . . thank goodness.

"You surprised me last night," he says. "And I think maybe I surprised you too."

With the kiss? Uh . . . yeah.

"You're nice," he continues. "And cute and smart."

He's forgetting some of the other applicable adjectives, like "weird" and "confused" and "unfocused."

Tuck squints down at me. "I like smart girls."

Really? Is that what Gretchen is?

I make an attempt to wrangle back my less charitable thoughts. After all, he did just call me "nice." I should probably make an attempt to actually *be* nice.

"Let's be friends." Tuck takes a step closer and gives me a

smile that is way flirtier than the smiles friends are supposed to give each other. "We can wait and see what happens."

"Okay." Because—yet again—what else am I supposed to say?

"Gretchen, Paris, my monologue, you . . ." His smile goes crooked as he looks down at me. "It all seems like fate."

Even though I'm super *over* this conversation with Tuck, his last sentence strikes a nerve. I think I believe in fate. At least, I *want* to, because otherwise I'm just a dumbass in the mountains. But if fate is real, if every choice I've made is part of some bigger, cosmic plan, then I have to hold on to the part where I came here for a reason. And that Tuck was that reason. And that everything will work out okay in the end.

And that this part—the part where he's saying inscrutable things and isn't even really *doing* it for me right now—is just a bump in the road.

So I nod.

"I shouldn't have kissed you." His gaze wanders to my lips. "I'm sorry. So can we just . . ."

Tuck pauses so long that I *have* to say something. "Be friends."

"Yeah." He breathes out a sigh of relief. "Even though it will kill me."

"Sure." I say it all casual-like—because I'm out of other options—but the moment the syllable comes out of my mouth, it hits me. Something about this *does* feel like fate. I mean, if fate has a feeling.

Which is when Milo shows up.

He addresses Tuck. "Ready for tonight?"

Tuck nods with great confidence, even though just last night he admitted to needing Gretchen out of fear. "You?"

"I'm a punch line who gets killed by a lightning bolt." Milo shrugs. "I'm fine."

There's a pause, during which I flash back to Ella and the strawberry ice cream. *Let's all forgive each other, okay?* I look up at Milo. "Is that a real thing? Achilles being killed by Paris?"

Milo's face broadcasts surprise at my question and—maybe—tentative relief that I'm talking to him. "Are you referring to history?" His own question is careful, deliberate. "The answer is no, but it's beside the point anyway. Pollux isn't supposed to be on the same side as Paris, and he's also not Helen's twin. But none of that matters. *Zeus!* is mythology. What *actually* happened and the dramatic stories made up to *interpret* what happened . . . those are two different things."

He gives me a pointed look and I nod. No, the double meaning is not lost on me.

"I get that." God, he's cute. "And I also get that two different people could come up with two different interpretations of the same event."

"Exactly." A faint smile grazes Milo's lips, and I answer it with my own.

Tuck looks back and forth between us, bemused. "But Zeus and all the Greek gods were only stories to begin with."

"To be fair," Milo says, "the stories were made up by people who were desperate for something to believe in."

I know how they felt.

"They wanted an explanation for how the world worked," Milo continues. "So I guess in that way, the stories are kind of true."

"I don't know if I buy your definition of truth," I tell him. "Just because someone *wants* a thing to be true doesn't mean it *is* true."

"Agreed." Milo crosses his arms, considering. "But sometimes the *actual* truth is different from what *looks like* the truth."

I'm lost again.

"I mean, sometimes there's meaning behind the meaning," Milo clarifies. "Like the wooden horse. It was sent into the city as a fake gift filled with warriors."

"Which didn't really happen," I say.

"Right." Milo looks down at me. "But there's a kernel of truth deep inside it. What's *true* about the story is that sometimes a gift can be harmful to the receiver. That you shouldn't hold grudges that last a decade because they never end well." Milo pauses, turning his dark eyes up toward the treetops. "And . . . I'm struggling for additional meanings here. . . ."

"And sometimes characters are misread, so people are confused about who's the actual villain?"

"Yes." Milo gazes into the distance, stroking his chin in a dramatically thoughtful way. "Also, sometimes when people fight, they look like a big horse's ass."

My eyes narrow until his gaze drops back to me and I realize he's joking. "Nice," I tell him.

He leans closer. "And that sometimes men have trouble thinking straight when a certain chick's around." He throws me a grin that in one of Nikki's romance books would probably be described as "rakish."

Wait.

Am I the "certain chick" in this scenario? Surely not. I *can't* be, because . . .

Because of Ella.

Because of Tuck.

Because of fate.

But all I say is "There you go. Lessons from *Zeus!*"

Milo rocks back on his heels, grinning. "So the next time we're at McKay's, we can have a croissant sundae without it being weird, right? Like actual friends?"

My heart takes a nose dive at the word "friends." Seriously, nothing about this boy makes an ounce of sense. Or rather, about my feelings for him.

"Sure." I fold my arms over my chest, mimicking him. "McKay's dessert, no problem."

Suddenly I make another realization: Tuck isn't here anymore. He hasn't been here for . . . I have no idea how long. I turn to scan the water and . . . yep, there he is. Laid out across a boulder, tongue to tongue with Gretchen.

Gross.

As I drag my gaze back to shore, my eyes land on Ella. She's perched on our rock, awake and staring straight at me. And at Milo, because he's standing right next to me. I can't read the expression on her face, but I still feel guilty.

Chapter 13

Ella and I make it back to the apartment with a full two hours to spare before our call. It gives us both time to take showers at home, even though we'll be showering again midshow with our standard dressing-room audience.

We're in my car, heading up the narrow road toward the theater, when Ella asks the question. "What were you talking to Milo about?" Her voice is overly casual, which I know means the subject is not at all casual.

I answer her truthfully. "The show."

"Really?" Ella doesn't look convinced. "What is there to talk about?"

"You know, the message behind it." I swing into the *Zeus!* parking lot, hazarding a fast glance at Ella. "Like, what it really means."

"The show is produced by a tourist foundation." She makes a snorting sound. "What it really means is 'please buy tickets.'"

I don't realize I'm nervous until after I've slammed my car door. The air suddenly seems quivering and expectant. A minefield stretches from where I stand to the end of the night, peppered with explosions of every way I could screw this up.

I'm terrified.

But because I'm me and Ella is Ella, I don't mention my terror. Instead, the minute we hit the wooden deck filled with cast members and anticipation, I ditch her with an excuse about needing to make a phone call. She goes toward the locker room, and I go to the kitchen counter for comfort in the form of a grilled cheese sandwich. When, two bites in, it still hasn't helped, I throw it away and take the wooden steps down from the deck, heading behind the rhododendrons that screen the backstage from the forest.

Here, the air still feels warm and impatient and jittery, but at least I'm alone. At least, no one can *see* the way I shake my hands in front of my body, trying to catch my breath. It's ridiculous—I know it's ridiculous—and yet I can't seem to get my pulse rate under control. Even though I'm aware of the smallness of my role on that stage, of the fact that no one is going to be looking specifically at me . . .

An entire auditorium is going to be looking *toward* me. If I mess up in a spectacular fashion—the way I messed up this summer—they'll know. Someone will know.

And it's not like I *have* to stay. There's no more blackmail. No more Tuck—at least, not really. Waiting for the school year to figure things out with him is the most realistic plan, anyway. I could bail right now, just flee into the woods and circle back to the parking lot without anyone seeing me. I could pack up my stuff and be back in Dobbs by midnight. . . .

I tighten my fists into hard balls and squinch my eyes closed. I slow-count to ten, then relax my fingers and let all my breath out in a long *whoosh*. When I open my eyes, Milo is there. "Rainie, are you okay?"

"Totally." See, sometimes I speak the truth, and sometimes lies spew out of my mouth like vomit. "It turns out this is how I get ready for opening nights. Walking out into the forest. It's gonna be my thing."

"Right." Milo cocks his head, sizing me up. Seeing straight through me. "But what's up? Really?"

I try again. "I'm getting some exercise before the show."

"You don't look like you're exercising."

I open my mouth to produce another lie, but a version of the truth pops out instead. "I'm kind of freaking out." Milo doesn't answer immediately, so I hasten to lighten it with a wide smile. "I know, it's stupid."

If Milo had been pretty much any other boy, he would say the thing—*No, it's not*—but he's not every other boy, so instead he pauses. He thinks about it. When he finally speaks, he does so slowly. In a measured way. "It's not stupid. But I don't get nervous here because of the way I grew up. It was different from almost everyone else." He stares down at me, and without meaning to, I notice how the early-evening sunlight dapples through the trees, casting speckles across his light brown skin. "When something's normal for you, like going to Thanksgiving dinner with your grandparents, you don't get nervous. It's just what you do. It's a thing that happens once a year."

"But this year is different for you too," I remind him. "You've never played Achilles before."

"True. I guess I could worry about screwing up my death scene. I've never died onstage before . . . so now that you mention it, maybe I *am* worried. Thanks for that." Milo flashes me a grin, but I don't speak. His grin slips away. "Hey, what's wrong? Really?"

"I'm scared." Suddenly I'm even more naked than before, because what I'm admitting is so absurd and dumb. "I don't want to go out there. Why doesn't it make you feel like that at all?"

"Because I don't care—" He stops, like he said too much, and runs a hand through his choppy black hair. "Look, all this . . . it isn't really me." I stare at him and, after a moment, he tries to explain. "I get this place. I've been coming here my whole life. It's like . . ."

He pauses and I fill in the blank for him. "Home."

"Yeah. My parents love it, and it's part of our family life, but it's not . . ." He pauses again, and this time I don't know what to say, so I just wait. "It's not the thing I'm aching to do."

I don't know how it happened, but somehow we're closer together. We're maybe a foot apart, standing in a swirl of acorns and curled rhododendron leaves and scattered rocks. I stare up into Milo's angled face. "What are you aching to do?"

"To create." The minute the words come out of his mouth, he looks embarrassed. "I mean, it's not enough for me to say lines in a script that someone else wrote. You know?"

I don't know specifically—and it suddenly seems very personal to be hearing about it—but there's a part of me that understands a *little*. A part of me that gets it—how it might feel to need something that comes from you, that what already exists just isn't enough. "What do you want to create?" I ask him.

He looks me dead in the eyes. "I want to have babies."

I stare back at him. He wants—*what?!* What high school boy says that? Does he mean *now?* Is he propositioning me? That's an insane thing to let loose with. Is he—

Wait.

Hold on.

The corners of Milo's mouth are twitching, just a little.

He's screwing with me.

"Not cool!" I whap him on the arm, and he mock-flinches away. "I thought for a second—"

"I know." He grins down at me. "I saw it on your face. Like, 'What weirdo teenage dude says he wants babies?'"

"Okay, seriously." I give him my best imitation of Nikki when she's all stern and reading us the riot act about getting here late or standing in the right place. "What do you want to create? Tell me one thing."

Milo looks uncomfortable. He shifts his weight from foot to foot, dropping his gaze to the forest floor beneath us. "I've been taking photographs."

I almost laugh. "I know that. Everyone knows that."

"No, not for the show. Other stuff. Old things, mostly." I swear his angular cheekbones darken. "Abandoned houses. Train stations. Stuff like that."

It sounds cool. No, it sounds *interesting.* I don't know anyone else who does that.

"I'd like to see them sometime." I don't really think about the words—they just come out of my mouth.

"Maybe." He still doesn't look at me. "I haven't really . . . I mean, it's not like I'm submitting to galleries or anything."

"But could you? Submit to galleries?"

He nods, and then we're both silent for a while before he drags his gaze back to my face. "So here's how you do it. Get through the show tonight, I mean."

"If you say I should imagine the audience in their underwear, I might actually punch you."

"To be fair, you already did hit me." Milo rubs the spot on his arm where I whapped him. "But if that does it for you, then, sure, imagine whoever you want in their underwear."

And just like that—right there in my brain—Milo's in his underwear. They're boxer briefs.

They fit perfectly.

Stop it.

"Ready for my wisdom?" Milo asks. I gesture for him to give it to me, and he leans over, bringing his mouth close to my ear. When he speaks, it's in a whisper. "It's. Not. About. You."

I pull back, offended, to find him grinning again. "No, really," he says. "Think about it. It's *freeing*. Everyone out there, they've got their own story. They're on a first date or a last one. They're in a fight with their boyfriend. They're mad at their mom. They failed biology. They're trying to find a job. Everyone's in the middle of their own shit, and they've either been here a zillion times and will recite the lines and sing along, or this is their first time. Or somewhere in between. Or none of the above."

I think back to my most important recent theatrical experience: the high school monologues. When Tuck was standing on a stage, seemingly speaking right at me . . . except he really wasn't. He was in his own head, doing his own thing, thinking about his own girlfriend. I was projecting my own crap onto him. It wasn't about me then. . . .

It's not about me now.

I don't say any of that. I only reach out a finger and poke Milo in that same spot on his arm. "Thank you."

"You're welcome."

"Oh, and happy birthday." I give him a sheepish grin. "Belatedly."

"Thank you."

Chapter 14

The theater is packed. That's what the assistant stage manager loud-whispers as he runs down the wooden deck an hour before curtain. Of course, in the case of *Zeus!*, "curtain" is a metaphorical term, as there are no actual curtains hiding the stage from the audience. It's just a giant expanse of packed (and raked) dirt leading to row upon row of aluminum benches marching up toward the top of the amphitheater.

By the time I'm in my "whites" (costume-speak for the togas we wear as the Greek chorus), everyone is whispering about how *Zeus!* hasn't had an opening night like this in twenty years. Our company manager—also known as Ella's uncle Rob—comes down from the offices to give a little speech about how we're upholding a tradition that has been passed along through generations. When he's done, Del Shelby gives a speech that is all about Art and Truth. After his, Nikki gives her own speech that, when boiled down to its essence, is "Don't screw it up and make me look bad, dumbasses."

Ella and I line up with everyone else on our side of the stage, waiting for our grand entrance. We hear the applause as Eros and Eris walk out into view. It's loud and it's a little unbelievable that all those people are so hopped up about two actors in golden diapers. . . .

But it's really, really cool. The energy is cool.

As Eros and Eris start their monologues, I'm strongly aware that what Milo said is true. This is not about me. I'm nothing but a cog in the immense and lengthy machine of this play, but nonetheless . . .

I think I'm excited about the machine.

Yes, this might be actual excitement.

Beside me, Ella grabs my elbow. "Break a leg," she whispers. There's a smudge of tangerine lipstick across her front teeth. I point it out, and Ella runs her finger over the smudge. She bares her teeth at me in the cheesiest of wide, cheesy grins so I can give her the A-OK. Her goofiness makes me smile in return.

I guess there's just something about opening night.

"Can you believe you're here?" she asks. Since the honest answer would be "Oh, hell no," I shrug and smile again. "Tonight, it's even all right that I'm a skunk."

"Really?" Because there's nothing nice I—or anyone else—could say about that wig.

"Yeah. I mean, when else in life am I going to dress up like a skunk?"

The assistant stage manager beckons us to our places, and we crowd closer to the stage. We're hidden from the audience by a thick row of trees and hedges and carefully placed boulders, but I have a clear vantage of the wings on the other side, where the rest of the Greek chorus waits to go on. I find Milo in the middle of the crowd. He's already looking at me, and when we make eye contact, he jerks his thumb in the direction of the audience. Then he makes a *no* gesture with his hands before quickly miming glasses over his eyes and pointing at me.

They're not looking at you.

I grin back and shoot him a thumbs-up . . .

. . . right as Ella's fingers encircle my upper arm. Eros and Eris have almost finished talking and—

It's go time.

Just like that, I walk out onto the giant stage with Ella and Paul and a bunch of people whose names I still don't know.

And it's fine.

The entire show is utterly fine.

Everything goes just like we practiced.

Zeus falls in love with Leda and then shows up as a swan. The eggs crack on time. Pollux squawks like he's supposed to. Everything is perfect. Even Gretchen's boob is where it should be for the ray of arrow-love to hit it at the exact right moment. In fact, the only surprise—at least, for me—is Zeus himself. I'm in my bunny outfit, getting ready to wander out onto the stage, when I see him up on Mount Olympus, waiting for his cue. He turns his back to the audience, pulls a small flask from inside his Zeusian tunic, and tips it up to his mouth.

Onstage.

Mid-performance.

I almost laugh out loud. If the star barely has any lines *and* he gets tanked during the show, theater is really not what I thought it would be.

When I meet Crow Milo in our Grecian forest, we smile at each other before we start our fake-whispered-conversation-that-is-really-an-actual-whispered-conversation. "You're not dead of stage fright," he tells me.

"Hugh Hadley is drinking," I inform him.

"Oh yeah, that happens. He's been here a billion years and he knows his lines, so . . . I guess everyone puts up with it." Milo glances across the stage, where the three goddesses are fighting over the golden apple of discord. "Almost time to go." He flaps his wings at me.

I twitch my tail in return and immediately regret it. I make a solemn vow to myself that next time I'll wiggle my nose instead. Noses are way less flirtatious than tails.

"Logan's party tonight?" Milo asks. "You and Ella?"

"Yep," I tell him. "Me and Ella."

• • •

Here's both the best and the worst thing about being in *Zeus!*: at the end of the show, the entire cast walks out onto the stage and stands in a great big semicircle. We hold hands, and we bow.

And the audience claps.

A lot.

Chapter 15

Logan lives in an apartment complex called the Oaks. Ella and I walk there because—as Ella says—it's less than half a mile away and maybe I'll want a drink or something.

I *think* the "or something" is a figure of speech, but I'm not completely certain. . . .

As we enter the complex—a series of narrow streets running between brown buildings—Ella slows down. She looks uncertain. "Number twelve, right?"

Her concern is short-lived because fifteen minutes later we're in the middle of the party and she's lost any trace of apprehension. Apartment number twelve is packed wall-to-wall with *Zeus!* people. Some are dancing, most are drinking, and all are engaged in shouted conversations. The shouting is essential because of the blaring music: a mix of pop songs and Broadway show tunes.

Ella leads me to the keg, which is in the middle of the kitchen. On the melamine table beside it is a red plastic cup, overflowing with money. A handwritten sign next to it reads *Suggested donation: whatever you got.*

"Shit." Ella looks at me. "Do you have any cash?"

From an early age, my mother instilled the lesson in me—yes, you might have a credit card, but *always carry cash, just in case.* I'm pretty sure she wasn't talking about this sort of circumstance.

I fish out a twenty and hand it to Ella so she can shove it into the cup. She looks around. "I guess we just help ourselves, right?" She pumps the keg's handle and pours me a beer. I accept it, wait as she gets one for herself, and then touch the rim of my cup to hers. "Opening night!" she says.

We both take sips. The beer is already going warm, and I make a sour face without meaning to. That's when we hear the voice of Logan, portrayer of Pollux and host of the party. "Hey, can I see some IDs?"

Ella rolls her eyes. "Very funny."

"No, really." Logan points first to her plastic cup, then to mine. "Aren't you guys still in high school?"

"Yes." Ella folds her arms in front of her chest. "Kinda like you were last year. When you were drunk all summer long."

Logan smirks. "You weren't at those parties, were you? No. Because your uncle was always lurking around."

"I can switch this out for something else." I hold out my cup, trying to be conciliatory. "I really don't care."

Logan turns his attention to me. "I'm just saying, this is the opening-night party for a professional theatrical performance. You guys are still . . . kids."

Ella's cheeks flush pink, and I take a step forward because I can't stand to see how embarrassed she looks. "Quit it, Logan."

His gaze cuts to me, surprised. "Ah, the quiet mouse speaks."

"Actually, I'm a rabbit." I tilt my head to the side, popping my hand onto my hip in a way that feels vaguely like a power stance. "And you're pretty much a glorified chicken, so maybe lay off."

"It's fine." Ella looks at me in a way that seems beseeching . . . and feels embarrassing. "He's just kidding."

I don't think he is, but before Logan can confirm or deny, Milo is between us. "Hey, you gonna throw me out?" He waves his own plastic cup at Logan. "I'm in high school. Drinking a beer."

Logan looks at him, some sort of war I can't identify waging in his brain. Then he turns back to us. "Don't spill beer on my carpet."

"We'll try," I tell him. He walks away and I turn to Ella. "What's his deal?"

"He's a jackass." She looks at Milo, who's still standing by us. "Thank you." She actually sounds sincere.

"You're welcome." There's a pause during which I think we're all trying to figure out how to make conversation from here, and then Milo waves toward the living room, where most people are gathered. "Here it is. Just like all the parties everywhere."

We look at the crowd on the carpet. The music has changed to an old Britney Spears song that must be Gretchen's anthem, because she's standing on the back of a big upholstered chair, one hand pressed against the ceiling for balance. She sings along while others cheer her from below. Nearby, the assistant stage manager blows soap bubbles, and Paul swing dances with one of the pyrotechnics guys. I don't see Tuck anywhere.

Ella plops her cup onto the table. "I'm going in," she announces. "You wanna come?"

"In a minute." I brandish my own cup at her. "We worked hard for this beer."

Ella's gaze goes from me to Milo and back again. She nods. "Okay." For once, she doesn't say it in a snippy way. Maybe we've gotten somewhere after all.

Several new people come in through the front door and make a beeline for the keg, so Milo and I retreat to a corner of the kitchen. I motion to his cup—"I thought you stayed on the right side of the law"—and he tilts it so I can see inside. "Water?" I ask.

"Vodka."

"Really?" I say the word before I realize he's joking. "That would be a *lot* of vodka."

Milo nods. "Sorry Logan's such a dick."

"Eh." I shrug. "I've met dicks before." I immediately flush at my own choice of words, but Milo doesn't seem to notice.

"He had the same routine last summer. And he actually *was* joking, although he might have let you get all the way outside before saying you could stay. It's not a great joke."

"Yeah, he could stand to work on his material." I almost wore heels tonight—cute ones with peep toes to match my short green sundress—but then Ella wanted to walk, and I didn't want to spend the night in pain. Therefore, I'm in black Vans, so I have to look up to see Milo. "Whatever, it's fine."

"It's not." Milo shakes his head. "But he doesn't get it. The best villains and all . . ."

"They never know they're villains." I consider that for a moment. "But you said the best villains have at least one redeeming quality. What's Logan's?"

We turn to look toward the living room, where Logan has rejoined the party and is taking off his shirt in some sort of bad striptease while the crowd cheers him on. Milo leans against the counter, watching. "He has nice . . . I don't know . . . taste in socks? Good diction?"

I settle against the counter next to Milo, our arms touching. "Maybe he's amazing at crochet."

"Or miming. He could be an excellent mime artist."

I shake my head violently. "I have a hard time imagining Logan's gift being a silent one."

"Good point." Milo assesses for another moment. "Mini golf. I bet Logan is killer at mini golf."

"Or maybe Frisbee golf."

Milo and I say it at the same time—"Mini Frisbee golf!"— and then we both burst out laughing.

"He's basically throwing drink coasters at trees," Milo says after we've settled down.

"That sounds about right."

"There you go." Milo gestures at Logan, now naked from the waist up and dancing with Gretchen. "His redeeming quality is mini Frisbee golf."

The rest of the party is more of the same. I talk to Milo while Ella dances a little and drinks a little. Then she pulls me out onto the floor so I'll dance with her, which I do (a little). At some point, Tuck arrives. Gretchen's atop yet another chair when he walks into the living room. She nearly knocks him over by launching herself at him. Ella and I move out of the way just in time to avoid being clobbered by one of her arms.

As Tuck swings Gretchen around, he makes eye contact with me and winks. I'm so startled that I wink back . . . kind of. It might look more like an eye twitch, because Tuck frowns, confused.

Ella witnesses the exchange and shakes her head at me. "Smooth."

"Shut up," I tell her.

Later, after I've finished roughly a third of my beer and poured the rest down the sink, after I've laughed at many jokes—a few are even funny—and danced with Ella some more, after I've eaten a slice of lukewarm pizza and exchanged more looks with Tuck, I make two realizations in quick succession:

1. There's a lot to like about these people. They're fun and engaging and entertaining. However—
2. I could use a break from them. For weeks now, we have been up each other's butts 24/7. Frankly, I could stand to crawl the hell out.

Which is why, on our walk home when Ella asks if I want to go shopping or hiking on Monday, I tell her "neither. I'm going to take a 'me day.' Cool?"

Ella doesn't answer.

Chapter 16

Sunday's performance goes well. Not spectacularly, but well. There's a technical flub in the final scene that earns us all—even though most of us have nothing to do with it—an extra half hour of squawking from Nikki at the end of the show. What's *supposed* to happen is that after the clashing of wooden swords and the booming of unseen cannons and the death of Achilles, Paris stands alone at center stage. He's all exhausted and triumphant, surrounded by the spoils of war: dead bodies and dropped props. Across from him, Pollux makes a final kill and then casually strolls toward Paris, presumably to hug it out, bro-style. However, before he can get there, Zeus appears on the upstage boulders—otherwise known as Olympus—and shouts, "For Achilles!" before letting a lightning bolt fly at Paris. After that, Paris falls, Pollux delivers a stirring monologue about the travesties of war, and then the entire cast does our trudging and mournful dirge bit.

Tonight, however, someone's off their mark. Everything goes fine through the battle sequence until that final revenge lightning . . . which unfortunately happens just *before* Zeus yells his line. Tuck wavers and crumples to the ground somewhere between the flash-boom and the "For Achilles!" but surely the audience is confused about what actually caused the death of Paris: a bolt of lightning or Hugh Hadley's gravelly voice.

• • •

In every other era of my life, Monday morning has been my least favorite day of the week. The end of the weekend, the start of school . . . nothing about it is good. However, now that I'm part of a theater group, it means something entirely different. It's "dark day," which is theater speak for "no show today." It's my first true free day since arriving in the mountains. No performance, no rehearsals, no company meetings.

Glorious.

I wake up early because I'm excited to savor the freedom. Ella is still asleep, so I grab the clothes I laid out last night and stealth my way out of our room. I keep it simple—jeans, plain V-neck tee, Adidas. After a quick brush of hair and teeth, I head out. Since I already told Ella I didn't want to shop or hike, I feel okay leaving the apartment without a farewell. After all, I have a key and she has a life. We'll both be fine.

Also, it's not just the *other* company members I could use a break from. I wouldn't mind a day without Ella too. Yes, she can be fun, and we've gotten past the blackmail thing, but sometimes she's a little . . . passive-aggressive. Or cranky. Or bossy. Or *something*. I don't want to second-guess my entire day based on what mood she's living through at any given moment. I don't want to plan my day around her, to make decisions with her. In fact, I don't want to plan my day at all. I just want to go with the flow.

My own flow.

However, just as the little bell is *ching-ching*ing over my head as I walk into the coffee shop, I get a text. It's from Milo. I'm not surprised that he has my phone number, since a contact list was emailed to everyone at the beginning of rehearsals, but I am surprised—shocked, in fact—at what he says.

> Milo here. Hitting send before can change mind.
> Am off to create, wanna come?

As I'm reading his text, a second one pops up:

> Look, I hit send.

And a third:

> Shit, if I'm waking you up, sorry.

I stand there in the entrance to the coffee shop, half in and half out—story of my life—staring at my phone. Because I specifically did not want to plan my day, I now have no real plans. Left to my own devices, I'll probably dork around downtown before ending up back at the apartment, probably with a new hemp outfit or some beaded jewelry, and then I'll have to endure Ella being all mad at me because I shopped without her.

But . . .

But I'm attracted to Milo.

There, I've said it. At least to myself.

He's cute and he's nice and he's really funny and . . . I absolutely *cannot* like him. I can't like him for about a million reasons, but the top two are Tuck and Ella. Except maybe I should reverse the order. Ella first, then Tuck.

Milo and I have to be friends.

Just friends.

Of course, one morning of hanging out with Milo doesn't have to mean anything. It can be a morning with a friend, the way these theater kids are with each other all the freaking time. I'm starting to fit in now, that's it.

That's what this is.

That's all it can be.

Which is why I type back to him:

@coffee shop. Pick me up here.

Milo writes back immediately:

You're in charge of coffee.
Except get me hot choc instead.
You allergic to anything? I'll get lunch.

A half hour later, I'm in the passenger seat of Milo's car. It's a navy-blue Impala that has to be at least twenty years old, but, as Milo tells me, the gas and brakes work, so it's fine.

What's less fine is our conversation. It starts off stilted, makes a pit stop at awkward (the high note is a discussion of Olympus's weather conditions), and then heads swiftly to non-existent. Which, metaphorically speaking, is where we are as we wind southwest through the Appalachian Mountains.

It's not that I don't want to talk to Milo—I do. It's just that I'm not sure what we should talk about. In the Venn diagram of our new supposed friendship, I don't know where we over-lap . . . beyond Ella. And that topic of conversation is already weird, so I'd rather not enhance the weirdness by expounding upon it.

With both our windows down, a warm wind blows into the car. It's not too loud for conversation, but I can pretend it is. I kick off my sneakers and pull my knees up to my chin, folding my arms around my denim-clad legs and watching the spruce pines blur by.

"You ever been down there?" Milo points at the sign for Linville Gorge, just ahead of us.

"No." We drive past the turnoff, and I cast desperately through my brain for something else to say, but I'm tapped out. Apparently, I'm not even remotely interesting when I'm with Milo.

"A bunch of us camped down there last year." Milo runs a hand through his shiny black hair, pushing it out of his eyes. "Best night of the summer." He glances at me. "From the look on your face, I'm guessing it's not your thing."

"I like walls and ceilings," I tell him. "Besides, your parents let you do it? You weren't even a junior."

"Your parents are letting you overnight in Olympus for a whole summer."

"Yeah, but that's different. I'm staying with Ella's older sister." Never mind that Annette isn't even remotely paying attention to either one of us.

"We had a whole bunch of people. It was safe. And my parents trust me here. It's kind of like having a family reunion for an entire summer." He pauses for a moment. "I mean, not *exactly* like a family reunion."

Suddenly it's weird again. I think because the implication was that it's not *exactly* like a family reunion because you don't hook up with people at family reunions. So, basically, we're talking about Ella again, and since I don't want to do that, I don't say anything. I just watch the spruce pines for another ten minutes until I remember something.

"Milo!" He jumps, and I lower my voice. "Sorry, eyes on the road . . . but guess what I saw at Barney's?"

"A dude in overalls hawking organic produce?"

"No—"

"A girl carving goblins out of handmade soap?"

"No, although I'm open to buying some of those."

"Interesting," says Milo.

"Actually, it was a notice about a show in the back gallery. They're looking for local artists."

Milo nods. "Cool."

But he doesn't sound like he thinks it's cool. He sounds somewhere between irritated and embarrassed. I'm about to question him about it when I'm interrupted by a buzz from my phone. It's a text from Ella.

Where are you?

In all truth, I have no idea. "Milo, where are we?"

"About an hour outside of Tennessee."

I start to thumb-type that to Ella, but my signal is fading in and out. I slide my phone back into my pocket. "It's not important."

Milo nods and we slip back into silence.

It's killing me.

"Want to play a game?" I watch his dark eyebrows rise at my question. "To pass the time. Like a trivia game or the license-plate game or . . ." I trail off, feeling like an idiot.

"That song game?" Milo doesn't sound like he's mocking me, but still—

"Just a guess here, but does the song game involve singing?"

"Yes." Now he sounds amused.

"I don't sing."

"I don't either, but I will if you want."

Of course. Because the theater people don't have a filter the way I do. Wait—did I say "filter"? Mine is more like a suit of armor. A protective bubble. The Great Wall of China.

"How about truth or truth?" Milo asks. This time, the glance he slides toward me is more tentative.

"Like truth or dare?"

"Yeah. Except we're in a car. And we're not twelve. So we won't be running outside in our underwear or anything."

Second time I'm picturing Milo in his underwear. This is not good.

"I'll start," he says. "Truth or truth?"

"Do I really have to answer that?"

"It's part of the game."

"Really." I shift so my back is in the corner where my seat meets the passenger door. "How often have you played this game?"

"Never." He slides the Impala into a passing lane so a muscle car can roar by us on the left. "Come on, say the word."

"Truth." This is absurd, but I'm intrigued by what Milo might want to know about me. And by what I might find out about him.

"Do you have any siblings?"

"Nope. Do you?" I wait. Milo also waits. "You want me to say the thing, don't you?" I'm rewarded with a wide grin, even though Milo keeps his eyes on the curvy road ahead of us. "Fine. Truth or truth?"

"Truth." He sounds smug. "And yes. One sister, three years older than me. Her name is Cat. Goes to Chapel Hill. This is the first summer she's not here."

There's something in his voice that makes me ask the question. "Do you miss her?"

Milo nods. "Although she'd call me a liar if she heard that. We don't have a lot in common. We're pretty much the opposite of each other."

"Wait, let me guess." I think about what would be *opposite* of Milo. I decide not to say the first things that come to mind—that his sister must be ugly and boring and dumb—and instead go with something safer. "She knows sports?"

Milo looks offended. "I know sports."

"Really? I mean . . . sorry. You don't seem like a sports guy."

"I used to play soccer. Now I mostly just watch it on TV. And I go to the school football games." He raises his chin. "Also, you might recall that I'm amazing at darts."

"I recall you being mediocre at darts." I gaze at his profile, still trying to figure out what his sister is like. Mostly because I'm trying to figure out what *he* is like. Here I am, driving through the mountains of North Carolina with a guy I don't know. "Does your sister love math or something?"

"No." Milo smiles. "What I meant is—she's always in trouble. Not like drugs and parties, but she's constantly in an argument with someone. She's all about civil rebellion and fighting the establishment and righting the injustices of the world. Whatever her thing is at the moment, she's a million percent in."

"And you're not?" I thought it was a rule that you had to be filled with passion if you're in the theater world.

"Not like that. Not like Cat. She's . . . she's a bomb waiting to go off. She and my mom—" Milo shakes his head. "One time Cat slammed her bedroom door so hard that a hallway picture fell down and smashed on the floor. Later, when she was gone, Mom took her door off the hinges and put it behind the garage."

"That's kind of brilliant."

"I know, right? Cat was so pissed." Milo shakes his head.

"But it makes me crazy. She got suspended from high school, like, five times. When I was a freshman, people were always asking me why my sister was in the principal's office."

I can see how that would be annoying. "So you're the good one?"

"Yeah, I guess so. It makes life easier because they let me do whatever I want. I think they figure no matter what I do, I'm not going to get in trouble the way Cat does." He reaches over and taps me on the knee. "How does that work when there's only one of you? Do you have to be the good one *and* the bad one?"

"Yeah. I guess so." I pause for a moment before saying more. "Actually, I'm the neither one. I'm never really in big trouble, but I'm also not—"

The focused one.

The passionate one.

The interesting one.

"—the good one," I finish lamely.

Milo doesn't say anything. He just drives.

We pass a sprawling Christmas tree farm, a gas station advertising *CASH ONLY* on a hand-painted piece of cardboard in the window, and a wooden fruit-and-vegetable stand. Finally, as we're passing a sign that tells us we're thirty-two miles from the Tennessee border, he speaks again. His voice is mild. "It seems like you're a good friend."

Images of Marin and Sarah flash through my brain: stealing fries from each other, smiling at me over cups of coffee, pulling me into a bathroom at school to whisper gossip.

But Milo's never seen any of that. The only thing he knows is me trying to fit in, me living with Ella, me mooning over Tuck.

All I say is "Maybe."

"Truth or truth?" he asks.

This time I answer definitively. "Truth. Absolutely truth."

We play the game for the rest of the drive. I find out Milo's favorite food (Italian, especially manicotti), which countries he's visited (Canada, Mexico), and when and where he had his first kiss (youth group lock-in, thirteen years old). He discovers that my favorite animal is the platypus, that I wanted to be an astronaut when I was little, and that if I could take a vacation anywhere in the world, I'd pick New Zealand. Once he and I are through the awkward part, it's fun. And *easy*. I'm not trying to impress him. I'm just being . . . me. We're in the middle of a spirited debate about barbecue—wet ribs versus dry—when Milo hits his turn signal and pulls off the two-lane highway. We curve around to the right, onto a smaller road, and then into a parking lot. "Pit stop," he tells me.

I step out, looking at the two-story building before us. Narrow white wooden slats cover the front, broken by windows with bright green frames. The double doors are painted the same color, and so is the sign that hangs above them: *Round Wheel General.*

"Great, right?" I look over the hood of the car and see Milo watching me size up the store. "Wait until you see the inside. Come on."

I follow Milo across the gravel, past a very old German shepherd that lifts its head at our arrival, and through the green doors. We step onto roughhewn oak floors and stop to breathe in the scents of wood and leather and something sweet and yeasty. Dust motes dance through the sunlight filtering in the front windows, and soft fiddle music plays from hidden speakers. Shelves line the walls, some metal and some made from a dark wood. A row of rusty file cabinets and old crates runs down the center of the room. From where we're standing, I can see a sampling of the store's wares: thick woolen socks, small barrels of old-fashioned stick candy, plaid flannel shirts, metal canteens, yo-yos, books about hiking trails. There's no rhyme or reason to the place, so it *should* feel cluttered and crazy, but instead it's a little magical. Like we've stepped into the past.

I turn to Milo and find he's watching me again. "It's one of my favorite places," he says.

Milo's words make me extra happy. This isn't just a cool old store; it's something special to Milo. And he wanted me to see it. Like maybe I'm special to him too.

Of course, I don't say any of that. I only smile.

We wander around for a while, looking at postcards and old Coca-Cola signs and handmade candles before splitting up to use the restrooms. We meet up by the cash register, where Milo buys sodas for both of us and I buy a bag of assorted candies to share.

Back in the Impala, Milo pulls a tattered map from the glove compartment. He spreads it over the steering wheel and places a finger on what I presume is our current location. "Don't be nervous," he tells me. "I'm sixty percent sure I know where we're going."

"Then I'm only forty percent nervous."

Milo flashes me a grin, then goes back to the map. He leans closer to the paper, his narrow shoulders hunching toward his ears as he traces his finger along a line. A flop of black hair swings in front of his forehead, and I fight an urge to reach out and tuck it behind his ear. I cannot have these feelings about Milo. I *cannot*.

And yet the reason I'm out here with him is—clearly—because I was already having them.

Shit.

With a flourish, Milo folds the map in half and hands it to me. He turns the key, and the Impala's engine groans to life. "I'm up to seventy percent."

"I think I'm still at forty."

This time, he laughs out loud.

It's a nice laugh.

Shit shit.

We go another ten minutes down the road before Milo pulls off again, this time into the dirt area beside a tiny white church. "Are we here to pray?" I ask.

"Nope, just to park."

Poked into the ground is a bent metal sign telling us that the church is called Round Wheel Baptist. "Wait a minute." I look at Milo. "Is this town . . . or whatever . . . called Round Wheel?"

"Yep." His eyes dance as he nods. "Cute, right?"

"Yes. And redundant."

"And repetitive."

"It also repeats itself."

"Exactly."

This time when we exit the car, Milo opens the back door. He grabs something and looks over the roof at me. "Here."

I manage to catch the plastic bottle he tosses. "Bug spray?"

"Unless you wish to be eaten."

"Does it keep away bears too?"

"No. But that's what *I'm* here for." Milo makes what I think is supposed to be a fierce face, and I burst out laughing.

"Very scary," I assure him. "No bears would dare come near us."

"Thank you."

After we're both sprayed, Milo pulls on his backpack and slings a duffel bag over one shoulder. I offer to carry his tripod, and we strike out on a narrow path heading into the forest. The dogwoods at the edge quickly give way to tall maples, shading us from the hottest of the sun. The path is narrow, so I follow behind Milo. He's wearing a black T-shirt over long gray cargo shorts and his standard Chucks. As I watch, he pulls his purple bandanna over his hair. I watch him tie a knot at the nape of his neck, and again, I squelch the desire to touch him. There's something about the brown skin of his knuckles. And the long lines of his calves, moving rhythmically beneath the edges of his cargoes. He's just . . . touchable.

We walk for another twenty minutes or so. It's quiet except for the sounds of our feet on the path, the occasional scurry of wind in the trees, and the songs of thrushes and warblers. Then the trees fall away and we're out in the sun again, in a giant meadow with scattered patches of grass. It's warmer now, and a trickle of sweat runs down the middle of my back. The tripod, which felt so light when I took it out of the car, has become hot and heavy. I keep switching it from arm to arm.

Ahead of me, Milo stops walking. He's looking at a dribble of water running across the way we're going. It's not really even enough to call it a stream, but Milo shakes his head in frustration. I touch his arm. "If you're worried about me, you should know that I'm capable of jumping over two feet of water."

"We came the wrong way." He looks at me. "Are you good to keep walking?"

Even though I'm hot, I nod. Milo must read my mind, because he takes off his backpack and unzips it, pulling out a metal water bottle. He unscrews the lid and hands it to me. I take a sip and nearly gasp at how cold it is. It still has tiny chips of ice from the cubes Milo must have put in this morning. I take three more long gulps before handing it back so he can do the same. We pass the water back and forth until it's gone. "Good?"

This time when I nod, I mean it.

We double back on our path. We've almost returned to the edge of the forest when I hit my foot against something and trip, catching myself before I fall. Milo turns around. "Are you okay?"

"I'm fine." Other than feeling a little stupid, that is.

Except Milo's not looking at my face anymore. His eyes have dropped to my shoes. "Hold on." He sets his hands on my shoulders and gently pushes me back a step so that he can look at the ground beneath my feet. I stay where I am, staring up at him because . . . well, because I can. What Milo sees makes him suck in his breath quickly and then jerk his gaze back to my face. "You found it!" In one motion, he pulls me in, wrapping his long arms around me. The hug lasts only a second, but that's enough time for me to clearly feel the hardness of his rib cage against my own, and his chest muscles beneath his thin T-shirt. When we part and step away from each other, I duck my head to see what he was looking at.

And also to hide the flush staining my cheeks.

There, barely visible beneath the grass, are metal rails and a broken wooden slat. It's an old train track, cutting across the middle of the meadow. "You're a genius." Milo sounds excited. "Come on, this way."

We walk, side by side now, following the tracks. They lead us back to the edge of the forest. There are no huge mature trees here, only saplings and shrubs. The track—and we with it—cut along the periphery until Milo points ahead. "There it is."

I shade my eyes with my hands, and after a moment I see what he's looking at. It's a building, crouched in the shade of the large trees that stand beyond it. As we get closer, I can see that it's actually only part of a building. The rest has fallen down and fallen away, gotten lost in time.

"It was a train station," Milo tells me.

"Does that mean there's a town here too?"

"There used to be. We'll see what's still around."

The station is tiny, smaller than Annette's apartment. It was once yellow, but now most of the paint has peeled away, exposing gray slats. It sits on a slab of concrete atop a crumbling brick foundation. A wooden roof still sags over the tiny porch area. There are spaces for two doors. Only one still exists, tilting forward from its hinges.

"Do you think it's safe?" Milo turns toward me, and I say it automatically. "Don't make the face again." But he does, and because it's oh-so-fierce, I laugh and he laughs with me. Then I give him a stern look. "But, really, I don't think we should go inside."

"You're probably right. If there's even a floor left in there, it can't be stable." He heads around the corner of the building. "Besides, that's not what I'm interested in, anyway."

"Then what?" I call after him. He doesn't answer, so I lift the tripod from where I rested it on the ground and go after him.

I catch up with him behind the building, finding him staring in awe. "Look." He points to something on the rear wall of the station: a crude marking made long ago with black paint. It's a square: missing its top line, faded from the sun and the years.

Milo nudges me. "You know what that is?"

"A . . . 'U'?"

He shakes his head. "A vagabond mark. Probably a hundred years old. They're also called hobo codes, but 'hobo' is pejorative. You know."

Actually, I didn't know, but I accept it.

"Quick history lesson." Milo drops to his knees, setting his backpack and duffel bag before him so he can pull out equipment. "Vagabonds didn't have homes. They stowed away on trains, going all over the country looking for work."

It sounds romantic. Romantic and dangerous, that is.

"They had a code of honor," Milo continues. "They would help each other out because they were all in the same boat, so they'd leave messages for the travelers who came after them. Except that most of them were illiterate, or they came from somewhere else and didn't speak English. So they had these symbols instead. Like 'be careful of guard dogs' or 'someone here might feed you.'"

I tilt my head, sizing up the unfinished square. "What does that one mean?"

"I think that it's 'safe to camp,' but I'll have to check online once we're back in cell range."

I watch Milo select a lens and carefully attach it to his camera. I'm intrigued. Messages left in plain sight for each other. Information you only get to know if you're accepted into the brotherhood. And everyone else—those outside the secret circle—could look right at a sign and not even know they were missing something. "How did you find out about vagabonds?" I ask Milo.

He's squatting before the symbol now, taking pictures. "My great-grandfather was one."

"Wow." I try to imagine it. Leaving your family for the dream of a better life far away, unable to communicate with anyone. And then finding a community of fellow wanderers. Amazing.

We spend several hours at the train station and nearby, stopping only once to eat the lunches Milo packed for us. Deeper in the forest, we find a little group of other abandoned buildings and a bunch of other marks. Most are in discreet areas on the buildings—the corner of a porch railing, the support beam on a collapsed fence, a brick of an old well—but there's also one barely visible on a big oak tree, and another painted on a boulder. That one looks fresh, and I wonder if it's a true vagabond mark or if it was put there more recently. "Do people still do this?"

"I don't know, maybe." Milo runs his finger along the arrow symbol on the boulder. "But there aren't as many train stowaways these days. The hobo lifestyle is kind of a faded institution."

I'm listening, but my gaze is drawn to a pile of fist-sized rocks near the base of the boulder. I plop down and lift one, then hold it up for Milo to see.

"Oh wow." He looks awed again. "You found a nest of them."

"They're vagabond eggs," I tell him before continuing to look through the rocks. There's one with a triangle and another with an 'X.' One looks like a top hat and another has a stick-figure cat. "Do you think this one means they'll feed pets too?" I start to ask Milo, but when I look up, he has the camera lens pointed at me. I instinctively duck my head away, holding my hand up to block his sight of me.

"No, don't do that." Milo pulls the camera away from his face. "You're this modern girl looking through messages from another time. It's awesome."

I hope the camera can't pick up my sudden blush.

I look back at the pile and try to ignore the clicking sounds coming from Milo's direction. I consider taking the cat rock when we leave, but I decide it should stay where it is. It's a little piece of history. I don't have any right to it.

We're going past the train station on our way back to the car when Milo stops. "Hold on, come here." I follow him to the porch area, where he drops his bags on the lowest step. "We should leave our own mark," he tells me. "Nothing permanent. Like with a stick in the dirt."

I like the idea. An impermanent telling of our incomplete story.

"Of what?"

Milo turns to me, and suddenly I'm all too aware of how close we are to each other, standing there beside the old train station. He reaches out and takes my left hand.

I let him do it.

He turns my hand over and runs his finger in a circle over my palm. My heart speeds up, and I absolutely cannot lift my eyes to meet his. I keep them fixed on my hand as Milo traces a line through the center of the invisible circle. "What does it mean?" I hope my voice sounds normal, because I suddenly feel very *not* normal. I feel hot and excited and terrified.

"The road is safe," he says. I manage to raise my chin to look at him. Even though his eyes are a dark, dark brown, out here in the sun they have flecks of lighter brown. Those eyes are crinkled up at the corners. He's smiling. "Either a safe road, or get out fast because it's dangerous."

"Maybe we should pick something else, then." Impossibly, my voice is steady.

"Hmm." He looks back down at my hand. "Okay, I remember this one." He brings his finger to my wrist, drawing what looks and feels like a little snowman next to three triangles. My skin tickles when his finger moves across it, and even when he lifts his hand, I can still feel his touch.

"Shovel snow for food?" I guess.

"No. It means there's a nice lady here."

"Are you saying I'm a nice lady?"

"Not at all." But he smiles in return.

"Why the triangles? I don't understand that one."

"That's because you're not the intended audience. You're not supposed to know what it's saying. Like this." He slides his left hand farther up—like he's erasing the snowman and triangles—to just inside my elbow. My entire arm tingles in response. He touches the tip of his right index finger there and scribbles something—it might be words—down the length of my arm. It burns under his touch, and I have to swallow to collect myself before I can ask the question: "What was that?"

But Milo only positions my arm a little higher in the air. "Hold still." I keep my arm extended as he pulls his camera back out and *click-click-click*s at the blank space on my skin. When he's done, he flashes me a grin that is brighter than the sun overhead. "Hidden messages."

• • •

I think we're both tired from the walk and the heat because we mostly listen to music on the way back through the mountains. The few stations we can pick up come in and out intermittently, so we're subjected to easy listening, nineties pop, and, for one tragic stretch of time, country. As we cross the border into Olympus, Milo stops paying attention to the music. I can tell because he's not drumming on the steering wheel with his thumbs anymore, and as we cruise down Nine Muses Street— bright and bustling in the afternoon sunlight—the radio goes to static, and Milo doesn't change the station. I reach over and click it off as we turn past the Blue Ridge University sign. Milo doesn't say anything and neither do I, because somehow the silence has suddenly become its own entity, filling the space between us. We head onto Crestline Drive, and as the gray apartment building comes into view, Milo clears his throat. "I have to tell you something."

A million thoughts spin through my head, many of them having to do with what Milo invisi-scribbled on my arm and what he does or doesn't know about my feelings for Tuck.

Never mind that I don't even understand my feelings for Tuck anymore.

"What?"

"I didn't know Ella was upset about last summer. It didn't even occur to me that she would be."

Oh, so we're talking about Ella, then.

"No offense, but that sounds ridiculous." I frown at him. "You cheated on her. Who *wouldn't* be upset about that?"

"No, I get that." Milo pulls off his bandanna and wads it in his right hand, steering with his left. "Except that I didn't think I *was* cheating on her. We weren't a thing. We definitely weren't a boyfriend-girlfriend thing. At least, I didn't think so."

Well, that's surprising.

"Really?"

"Yeah." He shoves the crumpled bandanna under his thigh

so he can use both hands to turn the car into the parking lot. "We didn't—" He stops, choosing his words very carefully. "We didn't do much. Like . . ." He stops again, and I decide to help him out.

"Physically, you mean?"

"Yes." He slides a grateful glance at me. "Like, not really anything. And it was only two times, kind of."

"What does 'two times, kind of' mean?"

"I don't want to—" He swings wide and pulls into a spot facing the building. "We're in a gray zone here, you know? It's her privacy, and I'm not an asshole."

"You're the one who brought it up." I fold my arms in front of my body. "And you're the one saying it's not a big deal, but apparently she thinks it is. So explain."

Milo puts the car in park and kills the engine, staring in the direction of the apartment. After a moment, he turns to me, crooking one knee up onto the console between us. "Fine." His dark eyes are fixed somewhere over my shoulder. "Once was backstage, on that bench near the bulletin board. It was near the end of the summer, after the show. Almost everyone was gone for the night. My dad was in tech, writing his end-of-season list. Ella's uncle got held up in the company office, so we were both stuck there. We were just waiting, and then we were . . . kissing."

The jolt of jealousy is sharp and hot and surprising. I already know something happened between Milo and Ella, so why the hell is it affecting me now? Probably because now that Milo has described it, I can *see* it. The bench. The empty wooden deck in the evening heat. The postshow exhaustion.

I shake my head in an attempt to get rid of the image.

I came here for Tuck, I came here for Tuck, I came here for Tuck.

"What about the second time?" I ask in a level voice.

"We were at McKay's. A bunch of people were there in the afternoon before the show. Ella asked if I wanted to see the coolest graffiti in Olympus. I was just starting to get into photography, so I said 'sure.'" Milo plucks the bandanna out from under his leg and twists it between his slender fingers. "Someone else was going to come too—I think it was Paul—so it didn't feel like a *thing*. It wasn't a big deal. But then suddenly I'm on the sidewalk with Ella and she tells me Paul's not coming. Which is still fine, except then she takes my hand, like to pull me in the right direction. But when we start walking, she doesn't let go. And I feel like I'm a jerk if I *do*, so I just keep walking with her, holding her hand."

The heat of my jealousy turns into shame. Shame on behalf of Ella, unable to read Milo's cues. And on behalf of Milo . . . a little blind, a little spineless. "Then what happened?"

"We went down this alley, saw this graffiti, and she kissed me. I should have stopped it, but I didn't get what she was doing. I thought it was a hookup, like everyone hooks up all the time. Stupid, right? I mean, stupid of me." He shakes his head, irritated. "It's not like we were at a party. It was a deliberate decision to peel off alone together, and I just . . . didn't get it. I didn't think we had anything important between us, so nothing about it felt important." Finally, his gaze floats back to mine. "Does that make sense?"

"I don't know." I try to unspool the moments that made Ella think that she and Milo meant something more. "Some couples have lasted here, right? Some people stay together?"

"Maybe, I don't know." Milo frowns, considering. "I mean . . . look, I've been coming here my entire life. Once I was old enough to know what I was actually seeing backstage, I started realizing it was the same thing every year. It's a summer thing. It's what you *do* when you're here. Like a hobby."

"But that's so . . ." I pause, trying to home in on what I don't like about it. "It's *hopeless* or something. Pointless."

"Or fun." Milo shrugs. "Summer flings have been happening since the beginning of time, right? You kiss the person next to you, and you move on. They weren't invented at Olympus."

I think back to what Tuck said about Gretchen. He was basically saying it wouldn't last, right?

"I should have had the conversation with Ella—I get that now." Milo grazes my leg with one knuckle. "But I didn't think it was important enough. Talking about how we kissed a couple times and I didn't want to do it anymore? That seemed *worse*. For her, I mean."

All I can think is that if Ella could hear this conversation, it would be the most embarrassing thing that ever happened to her.

"I didn't cheat on her," Milo continues. "At least, I didn't think I did. She wasn't my girlfriend. You can't *cheat* on someone you're not dating."

He's not wrong.

But he's not totally right either. I'm not so horrified by either his behavior or Ella's as much I am by the awareness of how appalled Ella would be if she heard any of this conversation. She'd be mortified to find out that Milo never considered her a girlfriend. Or, really, anything at all . . .

But it does put everything into context.

"When Ella said that thing at McKay's, about me being her ex, it was a wake-up call." Milo's eyes rove over my face. "That's why I wanted to talk to her about it."

I remember when I saw Milo hugging Ella backstage. So that's what was going on. It was exactly what she told me: that he apologized to her about last summer.

"You know what would make life easier?" I ask Milo. "If people were just freaking honest about things." Like, if I had talked to Tuck about his stupid monologue in Dobbs, I would have known it didn't have anything to do with me and I wouldn't be in stupid Olympus having this stupid conversation right now. "Just say what you're thinking when you think it. Then people's feelings don't get hurt." Then it would never have gotten all muddy between Milo and Ella, which means it wouldn't be all muddy between Milo and me right now.

"Maybe." He tilts his head a little to the side, like he's sizing me up. "But there's a case to be made for keeping some things on hold until the right time, don't you think?"

"Until the right time," I repeat slowly.

"Hidden symbols." That grin again. "They're only understood by the people who are supposed to find them."

I look at him—the angles of his cheekbones and the darkness of his eyes—and the air in the car goes still around us. It's charged. Electric. Almost without my directing it to, my hand slides up my own leg, moving toward Milo's hand where it's still perched on his knee. I'm almost touching him when I realize his gaze has shifted past me again. I turn my head to see . . .

Ella.

She's crouched on the wooden stairs, scrambling to grab what look like cans or bottles or boxes or . . .

Groceries.

Ella went to the store, and one of the bags ripped as she was almost back at our apartment. Now she's trying to gather all the groceries before they fall between the slats in the stairs.

In one motion, I undo my seat belt and open the door. Milo and I make eye contact for a brief second.

"Do you want me to—" he says just as I answer him.

"Go." I jump out of the car and then poke my head back in. "Thanks. For . . ." I pause, not a hundred percent sure exactly what I'm thanking him for. "Just thanks."

"Thanks to you too."

I slam the door and go to help Ella pick up our fallen groceries.

Chapter 17

It's Del Shelby's last night at the theater. I guess he's tweaked and changed and moved us around enough for his satisfaction, and now he will go away. I'm astounded that his job exists. It seems so . . . easy.

I voice my thoughts to Milo as we stand around in the Greek forest. "That's why Nikki's here," he tells me. "She gets to execute Del's vision. She's really the one with all the power."

"She could wait until he's gone and then completely change the show."

"Yeah, it could become a . . ." He pauses. "Actually, I can't think of anything weirder than a Greek musical tragicomedy."

I wave my carrot at him. "It could become an improv show."

"It already practically is." Milo flaps his wings. "Were you paying attention last night during the battle? Paul dropped his sword and one of the cannons never went off. Tuck tripped when he was trying to kill me, and for a second I thought I was going to live."

A smile is trying to take over my face. "I did notice you nearly living."

"The Trojans almost lost. We were almost mythologically accurate."

Suddenly I notice we're practically alone. The other woodland creatures are heading toward the wings as the stage goes dim. Upstage, Zeus is climbing onto Mount Olympus. We've missed our cue. Milo and I exchange startled wide-eyed looks and immediately bolt in opposite directions, me hopping and him flapping.

As I charge offstage, I catch sight of Tuck waiting to go on for the next scene. He's seen the way Milo and I were more focused on each other than the show, and . . .

And he's frowning.

• • •

It's Olympus Summer Festival, which I'm told is to commemorate the forty-third anniversary of the night a group of local drunken businessmen decided that a stock theater focusing on Greek mythology and set in the Appalachian Mountains seemed like a totally reasonable idea.

A two-block stretch of Nine Muses is cordoned off with orange cones so that street vendors can sell Olympus-themed food while adults wrangle their kids into participating in a contest to fashion togas out of toilet paper. It's been a sticky heat all day, so when a late-afternoon rain shower starts up, everyone seems glad except the vendors, who rush to stash their Minotaur burgers and Gorgon fries and paper torches filled with popcorn. The kids don't even seem to notice the rain. They keep frolicking as their togas clump and stick to their bodies. Ella and I watch from the hood of my car, where we've managed to find a parking spot on a side street adjacent to the craziness. We've both been sweating for hours, so when the rain starts, we're bothered about as much as the kids are. After hurrying to toss our phones onto the car seats, we go back to the hood and stretch out on our backs. My car is warm beneath us as our clothes mold to our bodies under the steady onslaught of water. I'm still wearing sunglasses, but Ella has taken hers off. Her eyes are squeezed tightly shut.

It's stupid, but I'm happy. Tuck doesn't matter. Milo doesn't even matter. I've got nowhere I'm supposed to be, nothing I'm missing, no decisions I'm not currently making. "This is the life," I tell Ella.

She doesn't say anything, so I'm not sure if she heard me through the rain and the kids' squeals, but that's okay. I was almost talking to myself, anyway. I raise my hands over my head, laying them back against the windshield. My right arm brushes against Ella's left, and I feel her fingers enclose my hand and squeeze.

It takes me a second, but then I squeeze back.

• • •

That evening after the show, there are fireworks. Ella and I—and most of the other younger company members—trudged up a nearly vertical residential street near Nine Muses, finally huffing our way to a cul-de-sac where, in groups of three or four, we took turns cutting through a private yard and across a rocky outcropping to the grassy plateau beyond it. Now we're all scattered across the area on blankets and pillows, waiting for the show to begin. Down below, Olympus is a fishbowl of twinkling lights amid the dark mountains. Up here, we're lit by the moon and stars and the handful of assorted lanterns that someone set up.

Many people have cans of beer or mystery flasks, but Ella and I take turns sipping from a thermos of hot chocolate. Annette had offered to make an adult purchase for us, but Ella made the very good point that we were already going to be trespassing, and it was probably better not to add underage drinking to our list of violations. Besides, now that the sun has been down for several hours, it's chilly. I'm glad I brought the Olympus hoodie I bought last week at the office.

Nearby, there's a muffled giggle. I turn toward it, but Ella grabs my wrist. "Don't," she says.

Of course I look anyway, and of course the sound came from Tuck and Gretchen, most of their bodies covered up by a quilt. Tuck has no business frowning about me talking to Milo if this is going on.

"They're not *actually* doing it right now, are they?" Ella asks.

I peer through the murkiness at the wobbling lump that is my supposed crush and his girlfriend. "That would be so gross."

"What would be gross?" It's Paul, plopping down between us. He holds up a plastic bag. "Want some Poseidon's licorice?"

"That name makes no sense," I tell him as I accept one of the twisted ropes.

"Yeah, you'd think they'd at least pair the sea god with something appropriate." Ella shakes her head. "Like calamari."

Paul pulls out a lighter and flicks it to life. He holds it close to the bag so we can see the licorice inside. It's blue.

"Huh." Ella shrugs. "I guess ocean-colored is a step in the right direction."

"Still tastes like cherries," I inform her.

From far away, we hear a hiss and a pop. A flare of orange light shoots up from a darkened spot that is apparently the theater's parking lot. "No trees close enough to explode," Milo had explained earlier in the day.

Speaking of which . . .

Milo lands on the other side of me, so now I'm flanked by him and Paul. "Hey."

"Emilio." Paul holds the bag over my lap, but Milo waves it away, pointing to his mouth.

"Gum." He catches me staring at him. "What?"

"Emilio?"

"It's a family name." He grins and then reaches over both of us to poke Ella. "Hey there."

"Hi." She gives him a fast smile but turns back to watch a cluster of fiery white blooms fading away.

I shrug at Milo—*she's just being Ella*—but he doesn't seem to notice. He's still looking at her, thoughtful. Then he leans over my lap, planting an arm between Paul and me to support his weight, and reaches for Ella's hand. She looks surprised but allows him to take it. He bats his eyes at her—super goofy—then kisses the back of her hand. "When I kiss you, I see fireworks." He says it in a terrible accent that's somewhere adjacent to British.

Ella blinks at him. She pulls away. "Dumbass." But she doesn't look mad, and there's a faint smile gracing her lips.

Meanwhile, I'm having a hard time paying attention to anything about Ella, because I'm so aware of the warm weight of Milo's torso stretched over me. Not to mention the smell of his hair or his laundry detergent or whatever it is that's all fresh and soapy and is making me want to press my face against him.

As Milo pulls back to a sitting position, Paul flutters a hand in his direction and Milo immediately grabs it. "When I kiss you—"

But Paul yanks away. "Dude, I was kidding."

"Tease," Milo tells him. He turns toward me, and I nearly lose my breath. Moonlight doesn't generally make people *less* attractive, and Milo is no exception. His eyes are dark smudges against the glowing bronze of his skin. When he smiles, his teeth flash white. "Hand," he demands, and I hold mine toward him without question. Milo pauses, then gently turns it over so my palm is facing up. He dips his head and presses his mouth against the inside of my wrist. His lips are warm and soft, but there's a faint prickle around the edges, where he must have a touch of five-o'clock shadow. Above the parking lot, a triple crimson explosion lights up the sky. Milo lifts his head, and somehow I manage not to move my hand along with him, just to keep our skin still in contact. He looks into my eyes. "When I kiss you, I see fireworks."

This time he doesn't use an accent. This time his voice is low and serious and makes my insides quiver.

It's too much.

Especially with Ella sitting right there on the other side of Paul. Especially with Tuck and Gretchen mere yards away, making gross teenage love under their quilt. Especially with the way I make every wrong choice, every time.

I yank away from Milo and fold my arms over my chest, tucking my hands beneath the edges of my hoodie. "Look, a blue one," I say, focusing my gaze on the starburst display that is lighting up the town of Olympus.

"Pretty," Milo says, and after a second, I hear a rustling as he shifts his weight away from me. We don't touch again, but it doesn't matter. Poseidon's entire ocean couldn't cool the heat scorching through me.

Chapter 18

That Saturday, there's a party (natch). Since it's not at asshole Logan's apartment, I agree to go with Ella, even though Gretchen is one of the hosts. While I'm onstage that night, helping create the waves of the Aegean Sea so that Paris and his army can sail across it, I hear Paul ask Milo in a whisper if he's going to the party. Milo shakes his head, and I am filled with both disappointment and relief.

When Ella and I arrive at Gretchen's townhouse—I've heard her parents own it and let her live alone with roommates—she and Katrina and Finley are thrilled to see us. It's not like we're the first ones—at least a dozen people are already hanging around, drinking and snacking on pizza—but we're greeted like we haven't seen each other for a thousand years.

"You're here!" Gretchen squeals, throwing her arms around me as Katrina and Finley sandwich Ella in a similar embrace. "What do you guys drink? Beer?" She steps back and looks me over from head to toe. "No, you're classier than that. Wine girls? Come on, I'll make something you'll like."

I exchange glances with Ella as we follow Gretchen up the

stairs from the landing and into the kitchen. I'm sure wine *is* the classy choice, but I've never had any that didn't make my mouth pucker up. "Whatever," I tell Gretchen, looking around for the obligatory cup in which to stuff some cash. "Where do we put donations?"

"Stop it." Gretchen waves off the question. "Our party, our treat." She starts grabbing glasses and bottles from one of the marble counters. "Hand me that lime, will you?" A few minutes of stirring and pouring and slicing later, two goblets of sparkling amber liquid sit on the counter. I know ginger ale and vodka went into it, but I'm not sure what else. "You guys walked, right?"

Since in fact we *did* walk here, and since Gretchen is so interested in making sure we're going to have a good time, and especially since neither Milo nor Tuck is anywhere to be seen, I accept the drink. Ella does the same, and we clink the edges together gently. "God, she doesn't even use plastic cups," Ella whispers before taking a sip.

I follow suit and . . . the drink is delicious. Like, stupid delicious.

"What *is* this?" I ask.

"Do you like it? My mom's best friend made it up. Her name is Carol, so we call it 'The Carol.' "

Ella raises her goblet in response. "Inventive."

"I know, right?" Gretchen beams. Apparently sarcasm doesn't have an effect on her. Kinda like how you can't see vampires in mirrors.

I take tiny sips of my drink because it would be way too easy to slam it back like a fool. Still, not long after the townhouse has filled with partygoers and the dance music is blasting and my head is fuzzy, I find Gretchen putting a second drink into my hand and then Ella's. "You too, Ella-Bella."

The nickname must remind Ella of Gretchen's boyfriend because she asks, "So where's Tuck?" and Gretchen's face freezes.

"He's coming," she says after a moment. "But—and tell me if I'm being a controlling bitch—I kinda thought he'd be here by now."

Ella looks at me and I shrug. I'm not sure how you answer that.

Luckily, Gretchen doesn't seem to really be looking for an answer. "When you're the boyfriend, you come at the beginning of the party, right? To make sure it doesn't suck?"

Again, Ella and I look at each other. There's no way—like, literally no way—that one of Gretchen's parties would ever suck. She's just too pretty and popular and wild and *fun*. "Sure," Ella says. "But I think you're doing okay."

"I wish I could suck like you," I say, and immediately regret it when Gretchen howls with laughter.

"I taught her the cherry-stem trick." Gretchen points at Ella. "I can teach you anything you want. I'm sure we have a banana around here. . . ."

"That's really okay," I tell her.

Happily, Gretchen seems to immediately lose track of the conversation. She sets a hand on her hip. "You know what would make this party better?"

"Strippers?"

Gretchen's head swivels to me. She purses her lips like she's considering it. "Where could we get strippers right now?"

"I'm kidding," I tell her. "You don't need strippers. Your party is awesome."

"It's the best party we've been to all summer," Ella confirms.

"Yeah," I continue. "There's music. People are drinking and dancing. It's *fun.*"

What I don't say is that, BTW, part of what makes it so great is that Gretchen's place is kick-ass. It's not a shitty college apartment like Logan's, but rather a full-out townhouse. It's like something my parents would rent if we were skiing in Colorado. There are ivory candles and framed artwork and Oriental rugs. Not a movie poster or beer pyramid to be seen. Seriously, it's awesome.

"Wait." I look at Gretchen. "What were you going to say? What would make your party better?"

She sets her hands on my shoulders and stares at me. I can't tell if she's trying to glean information from my face or if she's forgotten what she was going to say. When she finally speaks, her black-fringed eyes go really wide. "A *game.* Don't you think we should play a game?"

The memory of my first Gretchen sighting flashes through my brain. It was her screaming "Trust fall!" before flinging herself backward into a sea of her quick-reacting friends. It stands to reason that any game Gretchen wants to play might be . . . dangerous.

But before I can record an opinion, I catch movement in my peripheral vision. It's Ella nodding her head. "I'd play a game."

"Yay!" Gretchen flings her arms around Ella and then, maybe for good measure, hugs me too. "Come on, let's get dirty."

Gretchen strikes off toward the living room—I assume to round up the troops—and I look at Ella. "Dirty?"

"Don't ask me." She takes a swig from her goblet. "But whatever it is, I bet it's more interesting than dancing."

"I'll meet you there," I tell her.

After a trip to the restroom, I head to the kitchen to covertly dump my The Carol into the sink. The last thing I need is to be a wasted jackass at Gretchen's not-sucking party. I fill my goblet with ginger ale and am starting to thread back through the crowd when I'm surprised by the sight of Milo heading toward me. He raises his hand in a halfhearted wave and—despite the lackluster greeting—I go to meet him. "I thought you weren't coming."

"Who told you that?" He cocks his head, and I remember that no one told me, that I'd overheard him telling Paul during the show.

Whoops.

"I mean, I didn't know you were here." The attempt at clarification seems to mollify him, because he nods. Still, he keeps standing there, arms crossed, looking at the party around us. I can't quite put my finger on it, but there's something different about Milo tonight. It's not just that there's a darkness around his mouth and chin, like he's a day behind in shaving. *He* seems darker. Moodier. Maybe even angry. "Are you . . . okay?"

Milo's earth-brown eyes widen and dart down to mine. "Sorry. Just . . ." He shakes his head. "Nothing."

That single drink must be controlling my appendages, because one of my hands reaches out and touches his forearm. It's hard, as if he's tensing the muscle. Or maybe it just always feels like that. Either way, I definitely like it a little too much. "You can tell me."

Milo looks at me, weighing his options. Finally, he nods. "Just this thing with my sister."

"Cat?"

"Yeah." He looks surprised that I remember her name. "She came in for the weekend and . . . it's stupid. She's all judge-y about why I'm here. It turned into a thing."

"Here at the party?" I'm having trouble following the conversation. That first The Carol was chock-full of alcohol.

"No, in Olympus. Cat thinks I shouldn't be doing the same thing I've been doing literally every summer since birth. She thinks I'm wasting time, that it's dumb to be here again when I know it's not going to mean anything later in life. That I don't love it."

To be honest, it sounds like Cat has a point. "What does she think you should be doing?"

"There was—" Milo pauses, running his fingers through his hair. "There was this photography internship. I filled out the application in December and . . . I never sent it. Whatever."

"Why didn't you?" Milo's eyes narrow, and I attempt to clarify, to soften my question. "I mean, if you already filled it out. Why not just send it in?"

"I don't know." We both stand there for a long moment. "Yes, I do. Know, I mean." He sighs. "I didn't want to put myself out there because if I didn't get it, maybe it would mean I'm not good enough."

"But what if you *did* get it?" I'm not being facetious. It's a genuine question. I can't imagine a world in which Milo doesn't get what he wants. He's so competent at everything. Able to stride across a stage as a crow or a tragic Trojan, no problems talking to a girl he doesn't know in a coffee shop. He doesn't seem like someone who worries about making the right decision. He acts like every decision he makes will automatically *become* the right one.

He gazes down at me and seems to be turning it over in his mind. "Remember opening night? How you felt?"

"Like I was going to screw it up." And, worse than that . . . "And everyone would see."

"Yeah." Milo's eyes crinkle up at the corners, just the tiniest bit. "That."

I nod. I get it. . . .

I get *him*.

As we look at each other, the music cranks up a notch. Someone makes a beeline for the fridge, bumping into me. I lurch sideways, and Milo grabs my elbow to steady me. "Hey, watch it," he says to whoever's in such a rush to get more booze. He glances toward my goblet. "What's in that?"

I hold it up so he can take it from my hand. He takes a sip before handing it back. "Ginger ale and . . . ?"

"Just ginger ale."

Milo nods and then, like there was never a break in the conversation, he keeps talking. "I honestly don't know which one freaked me out more, the possibility of getting the internship or not getting it. Which I recognize is a very manly thing to say."

I answer his wry smile with an encouraging one of my own. "It's a very human thing to say."

"Maybe. Either way, I wasn't planning on getting attacked about it. We were supposed to have a nice night—maybe play Scrabble or something dorky like that—and suddenly Cat's giving me the third degree. She doesn't get it, that we missed her, that we want to hang out. She just blows into town and causes drama."

"Is that why you came to the party?"

"Yeah." He leans forward, and suddenly I realize he's still holding my elbow. "And I figured you'd be here."

"Me?" It comes out in a startled whisper.

"Because you're all brave and crap."

"I'm brave and crap?"

"When you had your freak-out, you still went onstage." He grins. "It's probably what they'll write on your tombstone. 'Here lies Rainie Langdon, she's all brave and crap.'"

"But I'm not." The Carol–infused truth spills out of me. "Ask around, ask anyone. I second-guess everything. I can't make a decision to save my life."

"You're here, aren't you?" Milo lets go of my elbow, spreading both hands wide to indicate the party, the theater, the town. "You wanted to try something new, so you did it. You marched in like you owned the place."

I stare up at him. There's no way—like, seriously *no way*—he can view me like that. There was no marching. There was no owning. I practically slithered. I crawled along like a worm after a boy who never wanted me at all.

But of course Milo doesn't know that. How could he? I've been trafficking in half-truths ever since I met him.

Milo moves closer. "My sister was like, 'There was an opportunity you didn't take because you wanted the safe choice. Olympus is easy, and the other thing is dangerous. Stretch your wings and effing fly already.'" He reaches out and touches my collarbone, right at the edge, where skin becomes shirt. He slides his finger down the length of my arm. "And all I could think was that I know someone who doesn't take the safe choice, someone who sees something she wants—"

Or someone *she wants . . .*

"—and just goes for it. So I'm a dumbass for not sending that application, fine. But I don't regret it, because already this summer is better than any of the others." His eyes are warm and serious again, like the night of the fireworks. "I mean, you're here."

Except he's wrong.

Because he thinks the wrong thing about who I am.

Because I am wrong.

But of course I don't say that. Instead, I deflect. I take a step backward. I pull my arm away. "Gretchen wants everyone to go downstairs and play a game."

"Uh-huh, one of Gretchen's games. That means drinking or kissing. Or both." Milo looks at me in a way that I can't quite read. "You're going to play?"

"Sure. I mean . . . yeah." Wait, what is he asking? Is he trying to ascertain if he's going to kiss me?

"All right, then." He opens the refrigerator and scans its contents before grabbing a can of beer. "I guarantee I'll need one of these. Are you good with your ginger ale?"

"I'm good," I tell him. It's a little bit true.

Downstairs, a rousing game of "Never Have I Ever" is in full swing. As Milo and I descend the steps into the low-lit den, there's a burst of uproarious laughter, followed by the sound of Paul defending himself: "It's only because I have Ivy League aspirations!"

I plop down next to Ella, who is cross-legged on the rug, with her back against the sofa. At least a dozen other *Zeus!* cast members are wedged around the floor and furniture in similar positions. Ella gestures toward Paul, who is atop an ottoman across the coffee table from us. "He's never skipped a class."

"Not even once?" I ask.

Hearing us, Paul gives me a despairing look. "Ivy League!"

Milo ambles to a space across the room from me. He leans against the wall, crossing his legs at the ankle. I'm reminded of when I first met him, at Wendell's party. Tonight, Milo looks like one of those James Dean cardboard cutouts sold at kitschy stores in the mall. All he needs is a red leather jacket. Plus shorter hair, lighter skin, whatever . . .

"When did he get here?" Ella asks me.

"I don't know." More important, why does *she* want to know? "I had to pee. He was in the kitchen when I came out." My answer seems to mollify Ella. "What did I miss?"

"Let's see." She takes a swig of her The Carol. "Pretty much everyone here has smoked a cigarette before. Most have tried weed. Katrina and Jon have both stolen lipsticks from a drugstore. Tuck is the only one who's ever been naked on school property."

"That seems about right." Belatedly I realize that—indeed—Tuck is here. He's perched on the arm of the sofa behind me.

When we make eye contact, he winks and raises his glass in a silent cheer. I return the gesture and then can't bring myself to look in Milo's direction.

Luckily, there's a thudding on the stairs, and Gretchen bounces in with a pitcher and a six-pack of beer. "Who's thirsty?" she sings out.

Several people raise their hands, including Paul, who first chugs whatever's in his glass before waving it for a refill. As Gretchen sloshes some of what I presume is The Carol into the glass, Ella nudges me. "That's not going to end well."

"What do you mean?"

"It's, like, his fourth one already."

I look down at my drink—still only ginger ale—then over at Ella's The Carol. They're both still full. "I'm good with this," I tell her.

"Me too." Once again, we clink our rims together, but this time we don't take sips.

Gretchen sets the empty pitcher and three remaining beers on the coffee table, then waves her pointer finger around the crowd before zeroing in on Paul. "You. Mr. Attendance. You're next." She clambers into the empty seat behind me, tucking her legs beneath her. I've turned to look at her, which means that—unfortunately—I get to witness the way she flings her arms around Tuck's neck and her tongue into his mouth. I whip around to face forward, and I see that Paul's grimace is mirroring mine. I assume they're for different reasons. Behind me I hear a slurping sound, which is apparently Gretchen extracting her tongue, because next I hear her speaking to Paul. "Come on, make it a good one."

"Okay, got it." Paul sits up straight. "Never have I ever kissed someone of the opposite sex."

A chorus of groans swells through the room. Someone throws a pillow at him. Gretchen yells, "Lame!" and we all take a drink.

Paul shrugs. "You don't go straight to the deed," he says in a mild voice. "It's foreplay. You have to ramp up to the good stuff."

Ella nudges me. "Do you think Paul knows about ramping up to the deed?" I shrug, and she raises her hand. "I'll go," she tells the room. "Never have I ever kissed Paul."

Paul looks comically shocked as everyone bursts out laughing. I raise an eyebrow at Ella, and she shrugs. "I'm curious, okay?" she whispers. "He's kinda cute."

I give Paul the once-over. He's half lying, half sitting in his chair, and his eyes look a little drunk, but . . .

"Yeah, he's definitely cute," I whisper back.

As everyone looks around at each other, it becomes clear that Paul has kissed no one here. He pulls a look of mock despair, which makes Gretchen rise to her feet and shake her hair back from her face. She arches an eyebrow at Tuck. "You're going to have to forgive me this one."

People start to hoot and clap, but Tuck's expression stays

blank as Gretchen sashays to Paul and leans over his chair. She presses her mouth against his in an exaggerated kiss, being careful not to spill the glass she's still holding. After several seconds, during which I very specifically do not look at Tuck, she straightens and takes a big gulp.

As the room explodes into laughter and applause, Paul shoots Tuck an apprehensive look. "You know I didn't instigate that, right?"

"I know," says Tuck. I can't tell if he's pissed or jealous or doesn't care. Either way, Gretchen immediately bounces back and straddles him, which I imagine must distract him from whatever he's feeling.

"It's just a game." Gretchen coos it into Tuck's ear loudly enough for us all to hear. I avert my eyes from their sudden make-out session. My gaze lands on Paul, who's looking at Ella.

"Thanks for that," he says.

"You're welcome," she tells him.

It's super unclear whether one or both are being sarcastic.

Ella points to Bianca, leaning against the opposite wall. "Bianca hasn't gone yet."

"Okay, hold on." Bianca thinks, twirling a strand of her long pink hair between her fingers. "Ooh, I've got one! Never have I ever hooked up with someone backstage." Victorious, she slams back her beer.

Ella throws me a sideways glance before taking a drink. Paul and Gretchen and Katrina and probably half a dozen others also drink. One of them is Milo, which makes my stomach clench because I know it was with Ella. I look down into my glass of ginger ale. Whereas everyone else is running a race to Drunk Town, I'm now playing a one-person game of Who's Gonna Pee First. I start to regret dumping my The Carol.

Joanna from props raises a hand. "Never have I ever hooked up with someone *on* the stage."

There's another round of laughter and applause. This time, Milo doesn't drink. Gretchen and one other girl on the couch do. When I'm glancing back there, I catch sight of Tuck. He looks annoyed. I whip around, away from him, but I'm close enough that I can hear the question he whispers to Gretchen. "Has anyone asked a question tonight that you *didn't* drink for?"

"Please," she whispers back. "Like you're one to talk."

"What is that supposed to mean?" Tuck asks her.

Although I stay facing forward, I can feel Gretchen rearranging her body on the couch behind me. "Hey, everyone," she calls out. "I got one."

I cringe, although I don't know why.

Gretchen's voice rings out behind me. "Never have I ever kissed Tuck Brady."

Along with a burst of giggles, there's an immediate parade of glasses moving to lips. Every girl in the room—except me but including Ella—takes a sip of her drink. So do Jon and a really cute pyro guy named Roy. Ella doesn't say anything, but I can *feel* her next to me. Lowering her glass. Being hyperaware of me sitting, paralyzed.

And so I do it.

I lift my glass and take a sip. It's fast, but not so fast that Milo doesn't see it. He looks startled.

And upset.

And—maybe—angry.

Because even though I've told half lies the entire summer, apparently this is where I tell the truth. I could choose to ignore the rules of the game, but I don't.

Never Have I Ever is my hill to die on.

Awesome.

Chapter 19

The next day as I go into work, I do all my normal things: parking lot, trail down to the backstage area, food from the kitchen. Milo avoids me everywhere. Last night, he left midway through the game. I don't even know when it happened. One minute I was talking to Ella about whether Gretchen noticed that we'd both kissed her boyfriend (which Ella did sometime last year at a theater party), and the next minute we looked up and Milo was gone. I know his departure had something to do with my admission about Tuck—I'm not an idiot—but I can't figure out why, exactly. Every girl in that room has kissed Tuck before. Even if Milo is desperately soulmate-forever-in-love with me (and I'd bet money that he's not), why would he give a crap that I've kissed Tuck? This is theater, for crying out loud. Everyone here has kissed everyone else. By Milo's own admission, it's a *thing*. If he has feelings for me, he still doesn't get to own my history. He can't be upset about things I did that came before him. That's not fair.

After all, he had his thing with Ella, and I'm not being a jerk about that. And if he *does* have feelings for me, he can't be mad if he hasn't done anything about it.

Which he shouldn't do.

Which he definitely should not do.

I finally meet up with Milo on the walkway. And by "meet up with," I mean "accost." He's hanging around the backstage right entrance—which is, of course, the one farthest from the girls' dressing room—when I march up to him. "Hello." I purposefully say it in a challenging way.

"Hey." His eyes touch on mine before skating away.

"Why did you leave so fast last night?"

"I didn't. I walked at a normal pace," he says. I might have smiled if he sounded like he was trying to be funny instead of sarcastic. "My sister left this morning. I didn't want to sleep in and miss her."

"Better to go home and get your beauty rest?"

"Something like that." He folds his arms in front of his body and gives me a long, level look. "You don't get it, do you?"

"I don't," I tell him. "I really don't." Because if he's jealous about Tuck—if he *wants* me—I'm sure as hell not going to be the first one to mention it. That's his job.

"You called me a cheater."

Wait, what?

"Your whole shit fit about how cheating is awful." Milo's gaze darkens. "When all along, you've hooked up with Tuck."

"I didn't 'hook up' with him. It was a kiss, all right? One kiss." I fold my arms, mimicking his stance. "And why do you even care?"

Yeah, why? Tell me.

Please.

But he doesn't.

"Hook up, make out, whatever it was." Milo leans closer to me, lowering his voice. "You did it while he was with Gretchen."

"Milo, it wasn't anything—"

"You were mean." He glares at me. "You called me a villain for cheating on Ella when I didn't even do it, and meanwhile you're sitting around, playing Tuck's mistress!"

It takes my breath away, the accusation. That he is this mad at me. I stare up into the angry angles of his face, my face flushed and my heart pounding. "It's none of your business what I do with anyone," I retort. Milo can't *claim* me. He doesn't *own* me. "Don't slut-shame me!"

"Ha!" Milo's laugh is loud and scornful. It rings out against the rock retaining wall between the path and the amphitheater. "Kiss whoever you want. Hook up with whoever you want. I'm not *slut*-shaming you, I'm *liar*-shaming you. I'm *hypocrite*-shaming you. And guess what—you deserve it."

"Wait." Something is bumping me, edging against the back of my brain. "Tuck and I go to the same school. Maybe I kissed him in ninth grade. Maybe I kissed him in *kindergarten.* Why do you just *assume* I never kissed him before this summer?" It's not that he's wrong; it's that I want to know why he's right. How he knows. Because if Milo knows my history with (or without) Tuck, it means he must have gotten it from somewhere. He must have gotten it from—

"Tuck told me." Milo looks almost victorious. "At Wendell's party."

My hands fly to my hips. "Why was Tuck telling you anything about me?"

"Because I asked him, okay?" Milo's eyes are dark and furious. "You were pretty and I didn't know you, so I asked if you were interesting."

I stare at him. Finally, we're getting somewhere. Finally, he's admitting he has feelings for me. Finally—

"But, as it turns out, you're not." He shakes his head, and the weight of his disapproval lands on me like a wet, heavy blanket. "You're just another girl chasing after the guy at the center of the stage. Giving lip service to what's right and wrong unless it's not what you want. You're a piece of work, Rainie."

"You're jealous." It's not a strong comeback, but it's the only one that manages to make it through the painful fog in my brain to escape from my mouth. Plus, I'm pretty sure it's true.

"Yeah, I guess I was for a second." Milo cocks his head to the side, regarding me. Sizing me up. "But there's no reason to be." He shrugs. "Cat was right. I shouldn't have come here again."

His voice is bitter, and this time before he glances away, I see the pain in his eyes, barely visible through a crack in the anger. I'm reminded of the way he looks in the last scene of the show, when he slides off Tuck's sword and curls forward to collapse onto the dirt. I ache to slide my arms around him, to feel the warmth of his skin and the hardness of his rib cage beneath it. I've hurt him, and now, seeing his pain, I'm hurt too.

I'm touching him before I even realize I've stretched my arm out. His eyes dart down to look at my fingers clenched around his wrist, and then his gaze returns to my face. I take a step toward him. "Milo, please. Just listen."

But he shakes his head and pulls away. "I think I'm tired of listening."

And then he's gone.

• • •

We don't have a huge audience, which is why there aren't very many people to notice that in Act I, Scene 3, a certain crow and a certain rabbit don't talk to each other when they meet in the middle of the Grecian forest.

Chapter 20

Marin and Sarah arrive three days later, and we all do a bunch of squealing and hugging and giggling in the apartment parking lot. When we're done, Marin points to the spray-painted dumpster. "Please tell me those are the gang signs."

I follow her finger. "Yeah. Although I've never seen any illegal activity—"

But Marin and Sarah have doubled over in a gale of laughter. Sarah finally pulls herself together enough to explain to me. "Those are fraternity letters, dumbass."

"Ever heard of the Greek alphabet?" Marin asks.

Huh. Well, that's good to know.

"I took Spanish," I inform them both. Once again, there are signs right in front of my eyes that are clearly readable to others, but I've somehow missed the memo.

Sarah gestures to the apartments. "This is amazing. You're living on your own, like a real person."

"Yeah." Marin grins at me. "You're so lucky."

I stare at the building—at the candles and wind chimes, the

giant tie-dyed sheet—and manage a smile. If my heart weren't heavy about Milo, I'd probably agree.

Ella's uncle Rob was so kind as to hold tickets for my friends at the box office, but unfortunately we can't reserve seats on the amphitheater benches. Because of this inconvenience, Sarah and Marin insisted on arriving early. It's preshow, and I'm on the backstage deck, peering out between two wooden slats. I locate my friends in the third row, munching on hot dogs and chips. I wonder—as I've been wondering all day—what their reactions will be. A ton of people have poured their hearts and their time and their energy into this production. I hope Marin and Sarah will be kind.

I'm able to pay attention to the third row for most of the first act. During the woodland scene, as the three goddesses are fighting over their golden apple, I wander closer to the audience than usual. I do a little extra hopping and carrot waggling, earning some squeals of amusement from Marin and Sarah. Out of the corner of my eye, I catch Milo flapping around at the center of the stage.

Once we're past intermission, I can't see the third row, because the sun has gone down. Torch flames and stage lights illuminate the fictional land I'm occupying, which always helps me feel like I'm really in ancient Greece. By the time Milo and Tuck are nothing but corpses and the rest of us are mid-dirge and mid-trudge, I'm again caught up in the drama of it all. When I trot back onstage with the rest of the cast for our group curtain call, I find my friends' faces in the audience and flash them a giant smile before taking my bow with everyone else.

Even though I'm not scheduled for the postshow meet and greet tonight, I go onstage, still in costume. Marin and Sarah rush across the stage and fling their arms around me.

"You never told us you'd be dressed as a *rabbit*," Sarah says.

"Yeah, and I didn't know you would dance!" Marin pokes me in the toga. "By the way, what are you wearing under that thing?"

"Grecian panties," I tell her.

"Dobbs in the house!" It's Tuck's voice, booming from over my shoulder, and then he's right there with hugs for Marin and Sarah. "You drove up to see me, right?"

He's joking . . . I think.

"Totally," Marin assures him.

"We didn't even know Rainie was here," Sarah says.

"McKay's tonight," Tuck tells me. I don't answer, because I'm distracted by the sight of Milo. He's heading into the wings, removing his armor as he goes. His wiry, tight muscles are clearly visible under his thin linen shirt, which is now damp from exertion and is clinging to his back.

"Rain?" I jerk my gaze back to Tuck, who's staring down at me.

"Right, McKay's." I look at Marin and Sarah. "Sure, if they want to go."

"You have to take them. It's part of the authentic Olympus experience."

I vaguely remember that talk of authenticity was part of what got me into this mess in the first place, but I shrug away the memory of Wendell's party, along with the image of Milo's retreating body.

• • •

"I have a lot of questions," Sarah says as she and Marin and Ella and I walk into the familiar raucousness that is McKay's.

"Yeah, like are we supposed to believe the hot chick fell in love with a *swan*?" Marin is clearly amused by the plot of the show. "And has *sex* with it?"

"She has sex with the ruler of the Olympian gods," I inform them both. "He just happens to be disguised as a swan at the time."

"But, like, how is that even physically possible?" Marin wants to know. "Which one is on top?"

"I've always assumed it was the swan on top," Ella says.

"But what about all those feathers?" Sarah asks. "How would you even find his—"

"Gross!" I elbow her before she can complete the sentence. "Let's remember that I know the actual man who plays Zeus."

"Yeah, and he's roughly a million years old," Ella chimes in. "We don't like to think about where to find *anything* of his."

"Maybe he has a very talented beak," Sarah says, and the rest of us groan.

Ella and I lead everyone through the front of the restaurant— where we know people at most of the tables—to our favorite booth. I sit down, and Ella immediately slides in beside me. Marin and Sarah take the opposite side, grabbing menus. "What's good?" Marin asks.

"The McKay's special," Ella says before I can answer, which bugs me a little. After all, I'm trying to spend time with my two best friends. Ella's only here because I always drive her home after the show, and it seemed rude not to invite her along. "We'll need at least two."

Sarah sets her menu aside. "Okay, walk me through this. Because the chick screws a swan, her children are born from eggs."

"You should stop calling her a chick," Ella says. "It makes for a confusing metaphor."

"I don't understand why her kids are full-grown adults when they hatch," Marin chimes in.

"Technically, they're half gods," I explain, which—judging by the looks on Marin's and Sarah's faces—isn't enough of an explanation.

"Okay, then how come the Trojans don't think twice about hauling that horse into their village?" Sarah asks. "Haven't they ever heard of a Trojan horse?" She stops as Marin and I giggle. "Never mind. That was a stupid question."

After the server has come and gone and our two McKay's specials with four forks have arrived in front of us, Marin brings up the obvious topic of conversation. "So can we ask about the Tuck thing?"

"Yeah, where is he?" says Sarah. "I thought he was going to be here."

I'd seen Tuck in the theater parking lot as we were walking to my car, but I hadn't totally registered him. Now, as I think back, I realize he was having some sort of intense conversation with Gretchen. "I don't know," I tell my friends. "Maybe he changed his mind."

"The Tuck thing is good." Ella leans over the table toward Sarah and Marin. "Not, like, asking-Rainie-to-prom good, but it's definitely getting-to-know-her good."

"He's hot in a toga," Marin says. "And you know I don't usually like boys in togas."

I flick a glance at Ella before I give my *own* answer to my *own* friends. "It's fine. He still has the girlfriend, so . . . whatever. It is what it is."

What it is, is weird. Tuck is the whole reason I packed up my life and came here for the summer, and now I'm not even thinking about him. Instead, I'm thinking about Ella's pissed-off, cheating, hurt ex-boyfriend. Which is something I could talk to Marin and Sarah about if Ella weren't here.

Ugh.

Tuck never shows at McKay's (and neither does Milo), so we eventually head back to the apartment. Annette is nowhere to be found—as usual—when we all troop into the living room. Marin immediately drops to her knees beside her backpack, still in a pile of stuff on the floor where she and Sarah dumped it when they arrived earlier today. "You know Zeva from art class? She's waiting tables at that Italian place downtown." Marin pulls out a bottle of red wine. "The bartender lets her buy from him."

Sarah nudges me. "Yeah, and Marin has a thing for Zeva."

"Shut up," Marin says. "I do not. Anyway, this is supposed to be good. It's Chianti. They drink it in Italy."

It takes me a minute to find a bottle opener in one of the kitchen drawers, and when I return with it plus three glasses, Ella is sitting cross-legged on the living room floor. "Oops." I set the glasses on the coffee table and turn to her. "Do you want one?"

Ella looks from me to Sarah and Marin on the couch, and then back to me again. "Actually, no. I'm tired."

"Okay." I hope my relief doesn't come through in my voice. It doesn't seem like so much to ask that I have a little alone time with my friends. "I'll come get my comforter and pillow now so I don't wake you up."

Ella looks startled. "Are you sleeping out here?"

"Yeah." I see her look of surprise but don't know what to do about it. I haven't seen my two best friends in six weeks. Why *wouldn't* I want to stay out here with them?

Later, when Ella has left us alone and we've all brushed our teeth after managing to grimace our way through a half glass of wine each (the Chianti was really sour), I'm sprawled atop my comforter on the floor beside Sarah. Marin is already asleep on the couch.

"So really." Sarah rolls up onto one elbow to face me. "You and Tuck. Nothing?"

"Not *nothing,*" I tell her. "But it's not *something* either. I guess we're kind of friends, but he's with this other girl who knows how to tie cherry stems with her tongue."

"The cherry stem thing is learnable." It's not so dark that I can't see Sarah's smile. "I could teach you."

"Jesus, does everyone know how to do that but me?"

"It's a survival skill. Like knowing how to swim."

I take my pillow out from under my head so I can whap her with it. Sarah squeals and I quickly shush her. "Dude, people are sleeping." I pause and then decide to tell her a little more of the truth. "Tuck and I might be a thing eventually. Like, later. After the summer."

"Huh?" Sarah looks surprised. "Did he *say* that?"

"Kind of. I mean, we talked about how we have some mutual interest." As the words come out, I realize how absurd they sound. "But there's this other guy and . . . I don't know what I'm doing."

"Who's the other guy?"

"It doesn't matter. He's Ella's ex and—"

"So?"

"So you don't date your friend's exes."

There's a moment of silence before Sarah jostles me. "You and Ella are friends now?"

"Yeah?" It sounds like a question. I try again. "Yeah, I think so. Anyway, that guy is friends with Tuck, too, and I think Tuck might be weird about me hanging out with him, so—"

"Maybe that's a good thing." Sarah jostles again. "Let Tuck see what he's missing. You know how guys are when they get compete-y."

It's easier to get a job when you have a job.

It's easier to get a life when you have a life.

Is it easier to get a boy when you have a boy?

"Maybe," I tell Sarah. "But I still don't want to make it weird with Ella."

Sarah makes a snorting sound. "*Ella's* weird."

Two months ago, I would have agreed with her. Tonight, though, I don't. I just wait a second before rolling over and nestling against my pillow. "Good night," I tell Sarah.

Chapter 21

Homesickness sets in about a week after Marin and Sarah leave. Maybe it's because Tuesday will be my birthday and I've never been away from home on my birthday. Or maybe it's because of what my friends said before they left. We were all out in the parking lot and had just finished a round of hugs. Sarah squeezed my arm and said, "You seem different."

Marin heard her and grinned at me. "You seem *happy*."

Looking back now, I don't know which one of them was right. I miss Milo. I miss being silly with him onstage during the show. This whole week, whenever we met in the Greek forest, we made awkward small talk. We were both . . . formal. I'm not sure how to get back to the way we were, when it was easy and good and fun. Maybe it's because I don't know how we got here in the first place.

Meanwhile, Tuck is going out of his way to talk to me. Several times this week, he's been hanging around the girls' locker room when I arrive for the night. Once he split a grilled cheese with me at the kitchen counter. He hasn't done anything romantic, and as far as I can tell, he and Gretchen are still together—but I'm seeing more of him than I used to.

On Saturday it's drizzling when we get to the theater. Backstage, everyone is on the wooden deck, speculating about whether we'll go on tonight. Some people are perched on the railing separating us from the forest behind the theater. Those lucky enough to get here first have snagged places on the benches. Everyone else either stands or sits on the floor. Tuck—naturally—is on a bench next to Gretchen, which I guess answers any questions I might have about the two of them.

I drop to my knees on the wooden planks and belatedly realize I've picked a spot next to Milo. He nods at me but doesn't speak.

"Hey." I cast through my mind for anything to say, and come up with a safe bet, since it's what everyone's asking everyone else. "Do you think we'll go on tonight?"

"I don't know. There are people in the audience already."

"Ridiculous people."

"The theater doesn't like to cancel the show unless it's raining really hard." Just then, the drumming sounds on the tin roof above us increase in frequency and volume, setting off a chorus of exclamations all around us. Milo flashes me a wry grin, and my heart jolts at the sight of it. I give him a tentative smile in return. He holds my gaze for a second before nudging my knee with a knuckle. "Good news, we'll still get paid."

His look, his touch, his grin . . . it all makes me want to fix things between us. I want us—whatever we are—to be okay again.

I nudge him back. "I'm sorry. You were right to be mad."

Milo doesn't say anything, but he ducks his head toward me, listening. "But just so you know, the thing with Tuck—it really did only happen once. It was . . ." I pause, trying to figure out how to phrase what I mean. "It was a brief moment of villainy."

Milo considers that before giving me the smallest of smiles. "Maybe you're just well written."

"Huh?"

"It is possible that the best heroines have at least one brief moment of villainy."

"To be fair," I tell him, "I have *lots* of those. It's just that only one of them is a tiny slipup with Tuck."

"Cool." He stares at me for a long moment before taking in a breath, like he's getting ready to say something. But before I can find out what it is, we're interrupted by the sound of someone starting to sing the *Dora the Explorer* theme song in a high, sweet voice. After a second, I realize it's Gretchen. Several other people join in, but even if I wanted to, I couldn't, because I don't remember the words. Across from us, I see Ella wiggle onto a sliver of bench beside Paul. She's singing along.

As the song ends amid a lot of giggling, I glance back at Milo. When he sees me looking at him, he puts his hands around his mouth in a makeshift megaphone and calls out, "Who lives in a pineapple under the sea?"

The response is immediate and exuberant, and now just about everyone is singing the *SpongeBob* song. When it's over, someone else starts up the *Scooby-Doo* theme, which is followed closely by the Meow Mix jingle. I clap along, and by the time we're full tilt into the song from the Oscar Mayer commercials,

I'm singing too. In fact, everyone is engaged in some way: singing, humming, clapping, drumming on the deck. We're not even worried about those few ridiculous audience members in the house, or if anyone is seated close enough to the stage to hear what's going on behind it. It's absurd and ridiculous, but it's also raucous and joyful and fun. In fact, it's the most fun I've had in a long time. It's the most fun since . . .

Since the vagabond codes.

I turn to look at Milo, but he's not singing anymore. In fact, the singing is stopping all around us, people shushing each other and trailing off into silence as heads turn in one direction.

Nikki is marching across the walkway toward us. Her face is very stern.

"Whoops," Milo says, scrambling to his feet. He reaches a hand out to me, and I allow him to pull me up before—I think—either of us realizes what we're doing. "They might have been able to hear us from the audience," he tells me. "That's not good."

Nikki's gaze roves across our crowd, waiting until the last murmurs stop. "Announcement from the front of house: we're holding the show for twenty minutes to see if the rain will break." We don't move, and I wonder how much trouble we're in. After all, if we really screwed up by being so loud back here, the theater can dock our pay. But then Nikki's mouth twitches upward, just a tiny bit. "As you were."

Milo and I and everyone around us bursts into laughter. As Nikki strides away, someone starts up the theme song from *Fuller House,* and we all join in with vigor. We're out here on this damp wooden deck with warm rain showering down just past the railing, singing for no other reason than it's fun. For once, I'm not censoring myself. I'm just going along with it. Pretending I'm not apart from it but rather *a part* of it. Because in this silly moment, that's what I want: to be one of these people.

By the time Nikki is back twenty minutes later, we already know what she's going to tell us, because we're practically shrieking the songs over the sound of rain pounding on the roof. "It's official—we're rained out." Nikki waits for our cheers and applause to die down. "Be here at your usual call time tomorrow. You have the night off."

I rise to my feet and am about to trudge back to the dressing room when suddenly Paul and Ella are in front of me, both with wide smiles. "Onstage," Paul says. "Now."

"What? But we're rained out."

"The *show* is rained out," he tells me. "We're not."

I turn my gaze to Ella. She beams, grabbing my hand. "Come *on*." I allow her to pull me toward the stage at a jog as, all around, others are doing the same. I risk a glance back to see Milo trotting after us.

Onstage, the lights are on, so even though the rain is coming down in buckets, everything is lit up. The stage is muddy, and there are deep puddles in some areas, as I cleverly discover when I step into a particularly big hole. Water fills my shoe and sloshes up my shin. I'm thankful I'm wearing my most disposable Chucks, the red ones I'd probably be throwing out by the end of the summer anyway.

I'm soaked within seconds. The warm rain plasters my tank

top and shorts to my skin, and my hair to my face and neck. I let go of Ella's hand so I can pull the ever-present elastic band off my wrist and twist my hair back into a messy, wet knot. When I'm done, Ella's gone. I peer through the raindrops for her. Everyone's here, splashing and jumping and running and screaming, so it takes me a second to locate her. She's over by the rocks with Paul. He has her around the waist and is spinning in circles. I smile and head toward them, when I'm intercepted by Gretchen. "Red rover!" she yells, grabbing my hand. Her other hand is in Tuck's, and *his* other hand is in Mandy's. Gretchen looks past me. "Red rover!" she yells at someone else.

Of course it's Milo, and of course—after a brief pause—his hand is folded around mine.

Moments later, we're standing in a line with half the cast on one side of the stage in the pouring rain, looking at the other half, who are doing the same thing across from us. After some conferring among ourselves, Gretchen starts off the call "Red rover, red rover—" and we all join in for the end part: "SEND ELLA ON OVER!"

Even through the rain, I can see the comical look Ella gives us before letting go of Paul and Bianca and charging across the mud. Right before she reaches our line, she slips. She catches herself, but she's lost too much momentum and can't get through the spot she picked, right between Gretchen and Tuck. After some laughter and screaming, they unclasp their hands and each takes hold of one of Ella's.

Across the stage, the opposite line discusses among them-selves before starting their own chant: "Red rover, red rover—"

I feel a tightness on my right hand, but I can't bring myself to look at Milo. Instead, I squeeze his fingers in return, right as the opposing line finishes their chant. "SEND MILO ON OVER!"

And then he's gone, splashing through the rain and mud to the other side of the stage, leaving me there in the line, where I can still feel the slippery, wet pressure of his fingers against my own.

Chapter 22

I don't see Milo on our dark day, but I do see Ella. Mostly because she spends it up in my business. All I want is some me time, and Ella can't seem to understand that. I try curling up on the sofa under a blanket to watch a show on my computer, but Ella keeps bustling through the room. Sometimes she plays music on her phone, and sometimes she sings a cappella (because *that's* not annoying). When she's not doing either of those things, she's putting away dishes in the kitchen. Or maybe she's putting away xylophones and wind chimes, because whatever it is, it's loud and crash-y and bang-y. I try headphones, but they don't help. I try moving to the bedroom. That doesn't help either, because next thing I know, she's in there, folding laundry and making her bed and putting things away. She asks if I want to go to lunch at Annette's restaurant, and I decline as politely as I can, but she still scowls. She asks if I want to go to the library . . . and the grocery store . . . and on a hike . . . and I say no to everything.

I just need some time to my damn self. Why is that so hard to understand?

By the time Tuesday evening—otherwise known as my

birthday—rolls around, I'm thrilled to go to work. I silently vow that next Monday I'll leave the apartment for the day, even if it means I have to watch movies on my computer at the library. And even though Ella seems to get extra crabby when I'm gone on Mondays.

I drive Ella to the theater as usual, but we're both quiet on the three-minute ride, and we split apart as soon as we reach back-stage. I head off to change into my costume and she heads . . .

Actually, I have no idea where she heads.

A minute later, however, Ella's standing in front of me in the dressing room. "You should go out there," she says.

"Go out where? The stage?"

"No, duh." She rolls her eyes. "The deck."

"Why?"

"Whatever." She shakes her head. "I told you, okay? I've done my friend duty."

Whatever, indeed.

Still, I drop my toga on the yellow bench and shove my flip-flops back onto my feet so I can circle back out to the deck. At first I don't notice anything—just the usual cacophony of cast and crew getting ready for the performance. But as I move along the walkway, I see it: the corkboard hanging on the wall. With a big poster sheet attached to it. My name is written across the top in purple and festooned with tiny foil stars. Below, the paper is covered with notes and signatures.

I stand in front of the corkboard, my smile huge. As people stream around and past me, jostling my body in their rush to get to the locker room or the pyro closet or the kitchen counter, I stay there. Smiling like a big dumbass. Names pop out at me: Paul . . . Bianca . . . Katrina. Gretchen's greeting is—true to form—giant and splashy and right in the middle: "Happy birthday, gorgeous!"

Milo's message is also easy to find. It says "Happy birthday" above a crude drawing of a woman. Below it is the word "From" and then something that might be a tombstone or might be a top hat—it's impossible to tell. I pull out my phone and, after a quick Internet search, discover it's the vagabond symbol for "gentleman."

It makes me smile, both the drawing and the sentiment. It's a tiny, coded act of friendship. Because that's what this is. That's what it has to be.

Ella's signature is small and at the bottom, but it's there. Alongside it are two tiny stick figures that—judging by the long curlyish hair on one and the thick fringe of bangs on the other—are depictions of me and her. The stick figures are holding spoons on either side of a giant croissant—the McKay's special, I'm sure—and are smiling out from the paper. They look way happier than either of us has been with the other in the last few days. A wave of gratitude surges through me. I don't know if Ella's the one who set up the poster, but it doesn't matter. She got me here, to this place where *someone* set it up, and that's pretty awesome.

It's only later in the dressing room—after I've found Ella and hugged her, and after her look of surprise and then her awkward "you're welcome"—that I realize I have no idea whether Tuck signed my birthday poster. I didn't even look.

• • •

During the show, I make a decision to impart a message of my own. After the dirge march, I rush to change my clothes and bolt away from my locker. I trot down the walkway and stop by the entrance to the boys' dressing room, lying in wait for Milo. My heart is thudding low and slow in my chest, which is about the stupidest thing in the world. This shouldn't be a big deal. It's nothing; it doesn't mean a thing. . . .

And yet.

When Milo swings out the door in his black T-shirt and rolled-up cargos, everything in me speeds up a little. It gets worse when he sees me and his eyes brighten. "Hey, thanks for coming by so fast."

"You're . . . welcome." I blink up at him, confused. "Wait, what?"

"Didn't you get my text?"

"No." I scramble for my phone and there it is—a text from Milo.

Got a question for you.

I shove my phone away and look up. Milo seems bemused. "So then why are you here?"

Dammit.

But now I'm in it, so here goes nothing. . . .

"I talked to this guy a few days ago. Downtown, I mean. An old guy. Really old." So this is going well. Babbling, just what I'd planned. "He told me about an abandoned train station just over the Tennessee border. He said you can't find it with GPS, but he gave me written directions."

Milo looks thoughtful. "I wonder if it's part of the Virginia Creeper. It was a line that closed forty or fifty years ago."

"I thought maybe we could go check it out."

Milo hesitates, and my self-doubt deepens. He thinks I'm asking him on a date. Worse, I might actually *be* asking him on a date, and now he's trying to let me down easy or figure out a graceful way to say no—

But then he shrugs. "Sure. I can always use more candids of you in a forest."

"No, I meant for the vagabond symbols!" God, if he thinks I'm looking for a wilderness photo shoot, this is really mortifying.

Except that his eyes are sparkling, and his lips have tilted up at the corners. "I know. We should do that."

"Okay, then."

He doesn't say anything else and neither do I, which might be because I've suddenly gotten lost in the sharp planes of his face and the golden-brown curve of his neck. I try to remember the moment I first saw him, back in Dobbs at Wendell's party. At the time, did I notice how beautiful he was? I take it as a sign that I've matured drastically in the past few months. . . .

"Rainie." Milo interrupts my thoughts. "I was going to ask if you want to do this thing on Monday, but it's self-serving and maybe you'll think it's boring and . . . it's a big ask." I nod at him to continue. "Do you want to go to Greensboro?"

That's not what I expected. At all. "The city?"

"Yeah. More specifically, do you want to drive? My cousin in D.C. has an art show there, but it leaves the gallery next weekend. I've been meaning to go all summer. I thought I'd go Monday, but I usually drive my mom's car, and the air conditioning just broke. She has an appointment to get it fixed. I can't take Dad's car, because they'll need it. I feel like a dick if I don't ever make it to his show and . . ."

"I can drive you." An art gallery? It's so sophisticated.

Milo doesn't seem to realize I've already said yes. "I'll fill up your car with gas—"

"You don't have to do that."

"And pay for dinner—"

"You brought the picnics when we—"

"It'll be a reasonable dinner. None of this grilled cheese nonsense we're always eating here." Milo's eyes are dark and earnest, trained onto my own. "Plus—and this is an added bonus—I promise to entertain you with witty comments on the way to and fro."

"Fro?"

"It's fancy for 'from.'" He grins down at me. "So you're in?"

"You had me at 'do you want to go.'" Getting out of Olympus for a day sounds amazing and, truth be told, doing it with Milo sounds even more amazing. It sounds . . . almost like a date.

Or maybe I'm a bona fide crazy person. At this point, anything's possible.

• • •

The week goes by slowly. *Really* slowly. It drags on and on and on. Except for the moments when I'm onstage and Milo is near me and there's this new electricity between us. Those moments go by like flashes of lightning.

Of course, the last time I felt lightning, it turned out that I'd made it up entirely in my head.

So maybe it's nothing.

Or maybe it's everything.

I have no idea anymore.

● ● ●

Monday finally arrives. I have high hopes of sneaking out of the apartment without having to explain to Ella where I'm going, but I know the chances are slim, since I'm not meeting Milo until after lunch. It does occur to me that I could just get up early and head out to a coffee shop, but I decide that's absurd. I'm *allowed* to have a life that doesn't include Ella.

Thus, I sleep in for most of the morning, which is delicious. When I finally roll out of bed, Ella is still a blanketed lump, so I'm able to tiptoe into the bathroom without encountering any-one. However, both she and Annette wake up while I'm in the shower, and by the time I'm dressed and heading out the door with my backpack, they're sipping coffee on the sofa.

"You look nice," says Ella. "Where are you going?"

"Oh, just out. Maybe downtown or something." Yep, my half-truths have devolved into whole lies. Perfect. Especially since Ella's already clocked the fact that I've spent extra time on things like hair and makeup and wardrobe choices . . .

"If you give me ten minutes, I'll go with you." Ella starts to get up, but I shake my head.

"No." Ella's eyebrows dart together in the middle, and I hasten to explain . . . or rather, to *lie.* "I mean, I don't have any real plans. I think I'm going to read for a while in the coffee shop." I don't *want* to tell her the truth. I don't want to share this day with her, with anyone. I don't want to share Milo with her.

All I've *done* is share Milo with her.

Ella looks hurt, but there's nothing I can do about it. She's not invited on my road trip back to friendship that might actually be some sort of half-assed date.

Annette waves a hand at me. "You'll be back before tonight, right?"

"Yes," I tell her, mostly believing it.

"There's a house party out by Sugar Mountain. You guys should come. This girl from the restaurant is in a band. They're gonna play."

"Sounds fun." Just not as fun as hanging with Milo.

"Everyone will be in college or older," Annette continues. "But you guys are cool. You can handle it."

"Okay." I shrug. "Maybe."

Or maybe not.

I give them both a tiny wave and head out.

Milo asked me to meet him at the theater. He was planning on walking from his family's sublet. I said I could pick him up at home, but he wanted to grab his paycheck. God forbid the good people of the *Zeus!* payroll company make their way into the twenty-first century and the wonderful world of direct deposits.

I cruise into the nearly empty parking lot. My music is cranked, and I'm bopping along by myself when Milo swings out of the low brown building. His purple bandanna is on his head, and—from this distance—he has returned to looking like a pirate. Every inch a tall, thin, angular marauder of the high seas. "All you need is a hoop earring," I tell him when he slides into my car.

"Excuse me?"

"To complete the look." I turn the engine as he buckles himself in. "And maybe a parrot."

"Ah, your pirate thing." He gives me a knowing nod. "I forgot how much you like those."

"Excuse me, I didn't say I *like* them. I'm merely implying that you *resemble* one." I pull out of the parking lot and onto the road, wondering if we're flirting. I used to *know* when I was flirting with a boy, but now—with this boy—I'm all turned around.

"See, and here I was thinking you liked them." Milo reaches into his pocket and whips out another bandanna, this one pink. "I thought you might get a wild hare and want to be a pirate yourself."

I have no desire to be a pirate, but the idea of wearing a pink bandanna to match his purple one is kinda . . . I don't know. *Cute.* Like a weird version of wearing someone's class ring in the fifties. It makes me go warm inside. I hold out my hand, and Milo plops the bandanna into it. "I can't put it on until we're stopped." I place it on my lap. "But your wild hare has been accepted."

I drive us down the hill from the theater, past campus, and

onto the road that leads toward Greensboro. We're both silent until we reach the outskirts of town and the speed limit goes up by ten. Milo reaches over and taps me on the knee. "Wild hare. I never understood that expression."

"It means doing something out of the ordinary, doesn't it?"

"Yes, but what's the symbolism of it? Where does the expression come from?"

I consider. "I think it's like if your pet bunny goes berserk one day and jumps out of its cage and foams at the mouth. Like everything is different. Instead of having your normal life, now you have this wild hare."

"Wait, what?" Milo moves in his seat. I glance over to see that he's turned to face me. "You think it's H-A-R-E, hare?"

"Well . . . yeah." Am I wrong? "What else would it be?"

"It's H-A-I-R. Like on your head."

"That doesn't make any sense."

"But your crazy rabbit analogy does?"

Okay, so maybe that's not right after all. Except . . . "Well then, how would yours work?"

"You know, like if your hairstyle is normal, but then you have one strand that is all crazy and sticking out. A wild hair . . ." He trails off into laughter, the kind that's so infectious that I'm laughing too. It takes a minute before both of us can pull ourselves together. Finally, Milo speaks again. "*Neither* of them makes sense."

I'm so caught up in the amusement of the conversation, which is followed by a much more normal talk about our schools that rolls into a debate about which one has the most ridiculous mascot (mine is an otter; his, a marching apple), that we're passing through Yadkinville before I remember why I wore this particular outfit today. "Hey, Milo, do you like what I'm wearing?"

He looks over at my little slip dress, topped with a thin cardigan and made more casual by a pair of white Vans. "This feels like a trap."

"Just answer the question."

"Sure. I like your outfit."

"Thank you." I flourish a hand over my body, as if I'm showing off a new car to a game-show contestant. "Milo, what color is my dress?"

"Blue." He says it so fast that I know he's two steps ahead of me.

"Gray!" I reach over and flick him on the arm. "You know it's gray!"

"It's definitely blue." I glance away from the road and over at him in time to see the sly look he's throwing at me. "Just like it was the night I met you."

I laugh again—not only because it's ridiculous, but also because my heart is light and hopeful at the reminder that Milo *saw* me that night, that he paid attention. That even now he remembers it. That means something, right?

It takes two full hours to drive to Greensboro, but it feels like much, much less as I pull into a parking lot in front of a large brick building. We go through a set of frosted glass doors to the lobby, where Milo insists on paying our small "requested donations." As we walk over the polished wooden floors into the gallery itself—a large, open space partitioned by white walls—the first exhibit we run into features large painted quilts with hand-embroidered details. I've never seen anything like it. They're haunting depictions of abandoned houses, occasionally stitched across with phrases. "I like those," I tell Milo.

But he only nods. His expression has gone still and dark. "Are you okay?" I ask him.

He looks startled. "Yeah, sorry. I just . . ." He stops, looking around the space. "This place is really cool."

"It is." Truth be told, it's way cooler than *me*. All big and airy, with spotlights hung on ceiling tracks, pointing at the exhibits on walls or displayed on tables. There are collages and jewelry and textured sculptures. Everywhere I look, there are things that I just don't *understand*. I look at Milo. "You could have an exhibit too. Your photography would be perfect here." His eyes go lost and unfocused. I immediately know I've said the wrong thing, and hurry to make it better. "I mean, you could *try*. You're talented and—"

"You don't know that." The words sound harsh, but his voice doesn't. "You've only seen me *take* pictures. You haven't seen the pictures themselves."

"True." I try to make sense of how and why I am completely positive that Milo is amazing and special. "But the way you look at the world—it's not like everyone else. So when you capture pieces of it, you have to do it in a way that's unique and interesting. That *has* to translate to something beautiful. That *has* to—" I pause because he's staring at me. "What?"

"Nothing." He smiles, and it's like the sun coming out from behind a cloud. "Thank you."

A few minutes later, we find Milo's cousin's exhibit. Her statement says that she works in "mixed media." What it means is that she makes oil paintings of landscapes, but also sculptures out of wrought iron and tin and found materials. I'm looking at one of her pieces when something jumps out at me. It's a piece of barbed wire, twisted into the shape of a—

"Doesn't that mean dishonest man?" I ask Milo, pointing to it.

"I think so." He leans forward from where he stands behind me, his chest bumping into my shoulder. His artist cousin must be from the vagabond side of the family. "We're all kind of into our history."

"How long was your great-grandfather a vagabond?"

I turn to look at Milo, but then I'm so freaking close to his tan skin and dark eyes that it's too much and I have to turn back to the art. He isn't just taking photos of something that's weird and cool. He's invested in a piece of history that is deep and intricate and personal. Once again I'm faced with evidence that other people have a depth I haven't figured out.

"About fifteen years. He went back and forth across America. I don't know how many times." I keep my eyes trained on the exhibit as Milo's voice comes from behind me. "He followed jobs because they were a necessity. I don't think he had a plan."

I feel an instant bond with Milo's long-dead ancestor. After all, I know what it's like to move through life because you *have* to, because it's what's expected of you, and yet not to have a concrete idea of where you're going.

"Did he ever stop and settle down?" I ask Milo.

"Yes." Milo glances down at me. "In North Carolina. That's why my family lives here now. They say it's the first place he ever felt like he was home."

I get that part too. The desire to stop and plant your flag in the land you've discovered. If you find the place where you belong, why would you ever, *ever* leave?

We're both standing there, looking at Milo's cousin's artwork, when another customer . . . or audience member . . . or whatever the hell you call someone who looks at art . . . that person walks between us and the exhibit. I take a step backward, and Milo . . . does not.

I bump right up against him, the full length of my body against the full length of his. He should move backward, because that's what you do. Or I should move forward, because that's also what you do. But he doesn't, and neither do I. We both just stand there like statues.

Except *not* like statues, because statues are cold and hard and unfeeling, and right now I am anything but that. With Milo's body leaning against mine so lightly, I feel *everything*—the rise and fall of his chest, the slight exhale of his breath in my hair, the way my knees are trembling and my skin is going warm— and all I want is to feel even more. I tilt back the tiniest bit, almost like an accident, and I think—I *think*—that Milo shifts forward. Maybe. Our movements are so subtle that I can't be certain they're even happening. . . .

Until he's gone. Milo takes a step backward, putting space

between us, and disappointment floods through me. To be fair, it's probably good that I can breathe again, because oxygen is a vital part of existence and all that, but I don't want him to stop touching me—

And then he *is* touching me again. Not with the length of his body this time, but only the tip of one finger. I feel it on my left shoulder blade, tracing a line straight down—maybe three or four inches—on my back. Before I can react, Milo lifts his finger and replaces it a little to the right. This time, he doesn't make a straight line but rather a collection of curves, like he's drawing a picture.

Or writing a word.

It's what he did on my arm at the train station, but now he's moving slower. Taking his time.

Milo's finger loops across the width of my back, tugging against the thin cardigan I'm wearing over my gray (or blue) dress. I stand there, frozen. Feeling his touch like tiny electric charges against my skin. When he reaches the curved edge of my rib cage, he lifts his finger again and drops it lower. I raise my shoulders the tiniest bit, curving my back ever so slightly against his hand. I want to feel him more. I want to feel him everywhere.

But then he stops touching me. He steps even farther back. I ask, because I have to: "What was that?"

"A vagabond symbol."

"Which one?" Again—just like when he wrote on my arm—it's much too long and complicated to be a symbol.

"It's a secret one." I hear the smile in his voice and turn to look at him, but the moment is gone. He's pointing to another of his cousin's pieces. I walk over to look at it, and then we're back to discussing art. What we *don't* discuss is what's really going on here. Maybe because we're both pretending it's not happening.

At least, I am.

Milo doesn't touch me again for the rest of the afternoon, either at the gallery or when we leave and walk around Greensboro's downtown area. We end up grabbing dinner at a little sandwich shop, which Milo says does not count as the reasonable meal he promised me. We don't even get on the road until the sun is setting, so it's dark when we crest the hill into Olympus. Milo gives me directions to his family's apartment, and as I pilot us there, I realize I don't want the day to be over. It's been too easy and too fun and too different. I'm not tiptoeing over the shards of Ella's passive-aggressive glass. I'm not pining over Tuck. I'm just . . . *being.*

I pull into a spot in front of Milo's home and put the car in park. I turn toward him and, in an instant, the air changes. It's alive—like when he was touching me in the gallery, like it's tingling with anticipation. Like me.

Or maybe it doesn't. Maybe there's nothing to the air, nothing to the feel of Milo's fingertip against my back. If there's one thing I'm consistent at, it's at misreading cues. Seeing what I want to see instead of what's really there.

I might never know, because before I can ask if he wants to grab dessert at McKay's . . . or thank him for the fun day . . . or lunge across the seat into his face—

—my cell phone rings.

I check the display. Ella. Of course. I decide not to answer, but before I can decline the call, Milo sees and tells me to go ahead. I'll feel like a jerk if I don't. Thus . . .

"Hello?"

"God, finally." Ella sounds flustered and hollow, like she's calling from an airplane hangar or an amphitheater. "Where are you?"

I don't know if Milo can hear her from the passenger seat, but because it's a possibility, I answer with the truth. "I'm dropping Milo off at his place."

Silence. I pull the phone away from my ear and look at the screen. Yep, still connected. I bring it back. "Ella?"

"Can you come get me? Me and Annette, I mean? I'll text you the address."

"Wait, what?" My voice scales up, and Milo raises his eyebrows. I beckon him closer so he can listen to the conversation. "Where are you?"

"At that party. Annette can't drive her car, and I don't know how. It's a stick shift. Can you come get us?" She pauses. "Please?"

She sounds . . . desperate. Ella, always a bastion of confidence, sounds scared and desperate. "Of course," I tell her. "I'll leave right now."

"Thank you." Her relief comes through the phone. "GPS gets a little wonky near the house. When it tells you to turn left onto Cedar Hills Lane, you have to ignore it and instead take the left two roads later. Try to call if you get lost. The reception sucks up here."

"Okay." I hang up and look at Milo. So much for our moment. "And I guess . . . see you soon too."

Except that he's shaking his head. "I'll come with you."

"You don't have to." I say it because it's what you say, but I really hope he doesn't listen.

And he doesn't. "It's dark, and you don't know the mountains. You're not driving to Banner Elk with crummy directions."

"Thank you." The relief in my voice echoes Ella's.

Chapter 23

The party is half an hour out of Olympus, and by the time we find the house, I'm even more thankful Milo is with me. If I'd been out here alone, I don't know how I would have found this place. As it is, we took several wrong turns, and one time we had to go back to the main road for a cell signal so we could look up the address on the map again.

Loud nineties music pumps from inside as Milo and I navigate our way up the gravel driveway, packed solid with cars. A whole bunch of people are hanging out on the front porch, smoking and drinking. It's a lot like walking up to Wendell's party . . . or to Logan's party . . . or to Gretchen's party. No matter where you are, parties are kind of the same.

I text Ella to let her know we've arrived, but I can't tell if my message goes through, so Milo and I head inside. The music is louder here, and—even though there are a bunch of guitars and a microphone set up in the living room—it's coming from a set of giant speakers. Milo and I make our way through throngs of drunkards to the kitchen, which features two kegs and a water bong, but no sign of Ella. "You're welcome to partake," I yell at Milo. "After all, I drove."

"That's okay," he yells back, scanning the crowd for Ella. "You should have someone sober helping you get home. Maybe over there?"

He's pointing to a wall of floor-to-ceiling beads hanging across an exit off the kitchen. We push through them to a narrow hallway, where—halfway down—we find Ella sitting on the floor in front of a closed door. "You're here," she says to us as a handful of partiers arrive from the other direction. To them, she waves her hand in a shooing motion. "Use the upstairs bathroom." They depart in a wave of good-natured grumbling, and Ella scrambles to her feet. She gives us a wry smile. "There *is* no upstairs in this house."

"Where's Annette?" I ask.

"Are you okay?" Milo wants to know, which I guess I should have thought to say also, except I'm a little annoyed I'm at yet another stupid party instead of alone in my car with Milo.

"I'm fine," Ella tells him. To me, she says, "It's not pretty," and then knocks on the closed door. "Time to come out," she calls. "Our ride is here."

The knob rattles, a lock clicks, and the door opens to reveal Annette. Her outfit is sexy—a short skirt with a pink off-the-shoulder blouse and strappy heels—but her mascara is smeared and her eyes are red. They well up when she sees me. "Hey." She lists to one side in the doorway. "I need to go home."

"That's why I'm here," I tell her.

"I can't be with all these people anymore." Annette's words slur together. "They're all *his* friends."

"It's okay," Ella says. "Let's go."

Annette's wobbly enough that it takes a good fifteen minutes to get her out of the house, down the driveway, and to my car. Milo helps us load her into the backseat before turning to Ella. "I'll drive her car back. You guys can follow me."

Ella looks like she's considering arguing, but apparently she decides against it, instead digging into her pocket and pulling out a key ring. By the time we're following Milo's taillights onto the main road, Annette is passed out in the back. Ella sits in stony silence beside me, her arms folded. I finally ask the question: "Was it the busboy?"

"Assistant manager." Ella shakes her head. "That guy who sat us when we had lunch. Vic."

I do remember Vic, barely. Red vest, pleasant once he knew we were Annette's guests. And also—"How old is he?"

"Twenty-eight. With a fiancée in Ohio." Ella's voice is hard and bitter. "Who showed up tonight."

"Oh crap, are you serious?"

"Yeah. She didn't know anything about Annette." Ella gives a short laugh. "Still doesn't. But Vic's friends do. It was awful. Vic was dancing with her but looking over her shoulder at Annette. Then, one by one, his friends came over to check on Annette. I tried to get her out of there earlier, but one of Vic's friends started giving her shots to cheer her up."

"Recipe for disaster." Public humiliation, heartbreak, and

alcohol? Even I know that's a bad combination. "Why didn't she want to leave?"

"I don't know." Ella sighs. "She kept saying that she'd show him and she was going to be a bigger person, but honestly—I think she was just drunk and wanted to be near him." She pauses. "I mean, *Vic.* He's not even hot. I don't get it."

"I guess you can't choose who you fall for."

"You can choose what you do about it." Ella's voice hardens. "You can choose your actions."

After that we're quiet for the rest of the drive.

When we arrive home, Milo helps us walk Annette up the stairs to our apartment. Her eyes are at half-mast as she mumbles words of gratitude and apology to us all. "Shh," Ella says. "It's okay."

"No, it's not," says Annette before stumbling inside.

Ella takes a step into the apartment, then stops and turns back. She looks at Milo. "I accept your apology."

He stares at her. "What apology?"

"About last summer. I was just making you work for it." She gives him a tiny smile. "Thanks for driving Annette's car."

Then she disappears inside. I blink after her. She's thanking Milo but not me? I can't win with Ella.

"Hey." Milo nudges me. "That sandwich didn't count as a reasonable dinner. I owe you one."

"But after this nonsense"—I gesture toward the apartment— "it seems like maybe I owe you." Even though it wasn't my plan or my sister or my drama.

"Nah." Milo shakes his head. "Totally worth it to get off Ella's shit list. So we'll still do that dinner. Cool?"

"Totally cool," I tell him, which is the understatement of the year.

"It's a date." He grins, and his teeth flash brighter than white in the moonlight. "Okay?"

I swallow. "Okay."

Milo's eyes do that thing where they get all dark and serious. "Good."

I watch him amble away down the deck, and I wonder if he meant it as an *actual* date or just as an expression. Also, I wonder which one I was agreeing to.

Chapter 24

Annette spends the next day going back and forth from her bedroom to the bathroom. She tells us she doesn't want anything, but before we leave for the theater, Ella brings her soup and crackers. "How is she?" I ask as we get into my car.

"She's been better."

Since Ella doesn't seem to want to talk, I don't push it. It's not until we've parked and are walking down the side trail to backstage that she speaks again. "Only three more weeks."

My heart drops. I'm not ready to go yet. Not until I've figured out what I'm doing: with Milo, with Tuck, with my life.

Being this confused doesn't make for good theater, it turns out. In the very first scene, I trip on the edge of my toga and nearly fall. Paul—who enters right behind me—grabs my arm to hold me up, but then he stumbles, which makes Bianca bump into him. Graceful it is not.

I'm flustered, but not as much as I am during the woodland scene when I meet Milo at the center of the stage, where his eyes drift down my body and then back up to my ratty ears. "I just realized something," he whispers. One corner of his mouth tugs up, and his eyes crinkle. "You're not any old rabbit. You're a hare. A wild hare."

I burst out laughing, which earns me several glares, plus a squawk of disapproval from an actor-tech in a bedraggled pheasant costume. Milo winks and heads in the opposite direction. I wish he'd mention our potential date, but there's time. Or at least, there's three weeks.

Except that he also doesn't mention it in Scene 6, when we're slick with green paint and nestled together in our upstage line with our arms linked together. Nor does he say anything when we meet downstage after the first Greek-Trojan throwdown. Or during any of the times we pass by each other near the wooden horse . . . or before the final battle . . . or as everyone's starting the mournful dirge.

Or for the rest of the week.

By the time Friday's performance rolls around, I'm not just confused. I'm irritated. I'm beginning to believe that, once again, I've made something up in my head. I've invented a boy's interest in me. After all, Milo has been pleasant. He's been friendly. He's been nice. But he certainly hasn't been romantic. Not even a little bit.

I don't know if Ella notices, because she's spent the last several days avoiding me completely. She's been going to sleep immediately when we get home at night, and she hasn't been making her usual requests to do things together during the days. Although it's been nice to have a break from feeling like I'm disappointing her all the time, I miss chatting from our beds and grabbing lunch downtown.

Tonight, as I'm driving her home from the theater, she asks, "You're not going to McKay's tonight?"

"Nope."

"A bunch of kids are going. Bianca. Katrina." I feel rather than see the look she slides toward me. "Tuck."

"I didn't get an invitation." It comes out sounding huffier than I feel, which is more bewildered than upset. "Are you going?"

"No."

She doesn't speak again until after I've parked and we're clomping up the splintered wooden stairs to our apartment. Halfway up, Ella stops walking. "Hey, Rainie." I stop also and look at her. She's twisting her hands together, not meeting my eyes. "Annette's not usually like that."

I'm not sure what kind of answer she's looking for, so all I say is "Okay."

"I know how it seemed. Drunk and crying about someone else's guy." Ella shakes her head. "I just don't want you to think that's who she is. Or that I think it's all right to be like that."

"I don't." I'm still not sure what Ella's looking for, but my answer seems to satisfy her, because she nods.

"Cool." She hoists her backpack and continues up the stairs. I wait a moment before following.

• • •

On Saturday, two things happen. The first is that Tuck comes to talk to me before the show. I'm perched on the deck rail when we lock eyes over the swarms of people going every which way to get changed or find props or make plans for the night. He waves, and I tighten my grip on the post beside me as he starts pushing through the crowd. His grin when he reaches me is bright enough to blind an auditorium of lovestruck girls. I almost want to shield my eyes against it. Completely objectively speaking, Tuck Brady is beautiful.

"Hey." Tuck's gaze dips to my legs, braced against the lower rail to keep my balance, then back up to my face. "You look like a little bird in a nest."

"Caw," I tell him, because that's what Milo would say.

Tuck gives me a bemused smile. "I heard that on our last dark day you got the hell out of dodge. Did you have a good time?"

"Yeah." I wonder if Milo's the one who told him about our day trip. "It's nice to be somewhere else for a few hours."

"I hear that." Tuck takes the tiniest step toward me, close enough that he's almost touching my knees. "You want to do it again?"

I stare at him. *What?*

"Camping in Linville Gorge. A bunch of us are going. Logan, Paul, Milo—"

Milo.

"—Richie. Everyone fun. Girls too. You and Ella should come."

"I'll think about it," I tell him, hopping down from my railing.

Tuck doesn't step back, which means that now we're right in

front of each other, our bodies an inch apart. "Good," he says, just like Milo did on my apartment deck.

Do these *Zeus!* boys know how to be clear about anything?

• • •

The second thing that happens is I lose a tooth. At least, I pretend I do. Last week, Ella and Bianca stuffed pillows under their togas and went onstage as fake pregnant during the hatching scene. Nikki was pissed, but as Ella explained later, when you do the same show six times a week, sometimes you have to mix it up so you don't die of boredom.

Since I'm feeling more and more like I want to mix things up, this seems like my chance. After I put on my ears and tail, I steal a dab of oil paint out of Mandy's tray. When I hop up to Milo in our Grecian forest, I beam really big at him. He stifles a bark of laughter.

"Subtle," he says, staring at my mouth, where I've blacked out one of my front teeth.

"Just mixing things up," I tell him.

Milo flaps his wings. "Hey, remember opening night? Would you ever have believed that someday you would mix things up onstage?"

"No." I hop a little and do some intentional tail wiggling.

Milo grins. "Now you're not scared of anything."

I look up into his angled face and lose my breath for a second. Something about him is extra hot tonight. "There are still things that scare me," I tell him when I can speak again.

Milo looks like he wants to say more, but the three goddesses are almost done with their dancing and bickering, so we have to head off in opposite directions.

• • •

The next time I run into Milo onstage, he dips his head close to mine. "You should do one of the things that scare you," he whispers. "I am."

My green-painted arm is between his rib cage and bicep as we stand in our upstage line. I feel his muscles, tense and lean, against my own. "When?" I breathe, hoping against hope—

"Monday. You'll be the first to know."

I smile, even though right now I'm supposed to be a very serious Muse.

The camping trip.

"That's a good plan," I tell him. "I'll do my scary thing then too."

"It's a deal," Milo tells me.

"It's a date," I tell him back.

• • •

Ella is adamant that we need our own set of wheels. It took a lot of convincing to get her to agree to come, and it only happened after I promised that I would leave if she wanted to go. "If it turns into a minus-Ella hookup fest, we're out," she told me.

"Fine," I replied.

Now, as we follow Bianca's car off the road and into a parking lot, I desperately hope it doesn't happen. My legs are shaved, mascara is on, and I'm ready to do the scary thing: to tell Milo how I feel. That I want to be more than friends. That I think we already *are* more than friends. And then, when I've done that, I'll have to do the even scarier thing . . .

I'll have to tell Ella.

Paul hops out of Bianca's passenger seat. He points to the other cars parked nearby. "Tuck's already here, and Logan. There's Gretchen's ride; I think Milo was riding with her. I don't know if Katrina and Finley are coming."

I try not to think of Milo riding with Gretchen or about why she and Tuck drove separately.

I'm here to do the scary thing.

The hike is fairly easy—the trail loops back and forth against the mountain—but it's got to be two miles, if not more. And since it's all downhill, it is not lost on me that coming back tomorrow will be a slow uphill climb.

When we finally arrive down at the gorge, it isn't too different from the rock colony. Trees overhang a dirt floor sweeping up to a stream, except the water is running faster here, and it's not scattered with boulders.

There are three tents set up already, and Logan and a guy I don't know are working on a fourth one that is bigger and—based on the amount of swearing—more difficult to assemble. There's a big pile of wood in the center, but no fire yet, which is fine with me because I'm sticky from the hike down. The last thing I want is a bunch of smoke and heat.

Speaking of heat . . .

I see Tuck straighten from his seat on a stump. His hair blazes bright in the spots where the sun dapples through the leaves to hit it. He looks like a Ken doll, perfect and all-American. He waves an arm in our direction and calls out, "Hey!"

We all wave back. As he starts to trot over, Ella leans close and brings her mouth to my ear. "Someone's happy to see you."

"He's happy to see all of us," I retort, right before Tuck arrives and scoops me into an enthusiastic hug that lifts me off my feet. I make eye contact with Ella over his shoulder, and she gives me a knowing look.

"So glad you came," Tuck tells me as he sets me down. He launches toward Bianca and bestows a hug upon first her, then Ella, then Paul—prompting me to return Ella's look—before grinning at us. "Check out the tents. Richie got a new one. It was a bitch to carry down, but it sleeps six."

"I'm gonna get wet," Paul says, which causes everyone to make grossed-out noises and throw sticks at him. He and Bianca head toward the water and, after a glance at me, Ella does the same.

I watch them go before turning to Tuck. He's gazing down at me with a half smile on his face. "Can you believe we only have two weeks left?"

God, why does everyone keep talking about that?

"Yep. Two weeks, back to Dobbs."

He keeps smiling at me, and I look away because it feels oddly intimate. My gaze falls on Logan and his friend working on the tent. "Who else is coming?" I ask Tuck.

"No one. Everyone's here."

I look around, but there's no sign of Milo. "Where's

Gretchen? I heard she and Milo drove together." I hope that last part sounded more casual than it felt.

"Milo's not coming." The way Tuck says it, it's like he barely notices his own answer. Me, however—it hits me like a bomb. A bomb filled with disappointment.

And humiliation.

And failure.

Once again, I'm wrong. Whatever Milo's scary thing was, one thing is certain: it has nothing to do with me. I came here for nothing. I came here for a lie of my own making.

Just like always.

"Rainie." Tuck's smile has slipped away. He's peering down at me, all intent and serious. No idea of the turmoil he's caused inside me. "I feel like I should tell you something."

"What?" I ask, because it's the polite thing to say.

"Gretchen and I broke up." Tuck reaches out to touch my arm as if he can hear the perfunctory "I'm sorry" rising toward my lips. "It's fine. It's not ugly or anything. We're good. We'll stay friends."

"Congratulations?" My word scales up at the end like a question. If it had happened at the beginning of the summer instead of the end, everything would be different now. Maybe it would be *right*.

Tuck's smile deepens. "Do you want a beer?"

That's the last thing I need. "Maybe a water."

"You have a good-girl thing about you." His lips part in a grin. "You're a breath of fresh air."

It sounds like a veiled insult against Gretchen. I frown

without meaning to. "I don't know if I'd call myself that." I instantly wish I'd said something else, because now that the words are out of my mouth, they sound like I'm flirting.

"Whatever you are, I like it." The wind shifts and the tree above us rustles. Sunlight hits Tuck's eyes, making them even bluer than usual. He's looking at me like I'm the only girl in the world and . . . it warms me. Because at least it's something.

At least it's someone.

"Come on," he says, and I follow him down toward the others. I know I should be doing backflips at the news I've just learned, but it's no longer a victory. I only feel numb.

As we reach the campsite, Logan lets out a war whoop of conquest. The big tent is finally up. Beyond him, the water sparkles under the summer sun. I fade out for a moment, returning to different water, to a different boy, dark-haired and leaping over the rocks.

I fade back in to find Tuck grinning about something he just said about Logan and the tent and getting it up. In a flash second, I decide the only thing I can do is get it up myself. I throw back my head to laugh really long and really loudly.

What is *wrong* with me?

• • •

The next few hours are a blur of the same: chatting with Tuck, keeping track of Ella, wondering what to do . . .

Some of the guys pull out weed and cigarettes—neither is my thing—to go with the beer. Obviously, it's not like I'm never around weed or cigarettes or beer, but right now we're far away from civilization. Everything feels a little less settled. A little more dangerous.

Ella partakes, but I'm pretty sure she has only one beer, which she shares with Paul. They drift in and out of my orbit and appear to be in a heavy discussion about music. Tuck alternates between hanging out with the guys and talking to me. I try to pay attention to what he's saying—which is mostly about our upcoming senior year at Dobbs High—but I keep getting distracted by thoughts of Milo. By wondering what scary thing he's doing today . . .

And yet when the sun is high and the fire is lit, I allow the inevitable to happen.

Tuck strolls up and hands me a hot dog on a bun. It's wrapped in a napkin and drizzled with mustard and ketchup. "I guessed on condiments. You like?"

Actually, I can't stand mustard, but it seems rude to mention, since he's gone to the trouble to make it for me. "Thanks," I tell him, and take a tiny bite.

We sit in silence for a moment, both of us chewing, and then Tuck leans close. "Rainie."

I swallow and meet his gaze. Those blue eyes are very bright. And also very, very close to me. I don't answer, because he hasn't asked a question. He glances around at the dozens of people throwing Frisbees and cooking meat and generally ignoring us. Then, with no further preamble, Tuck tilts his head and kisses me. His mouth is cool from his beer, and slick with lip balm. When he pulls back, I can still taste the coconut residue he left on me.

"I shouldn't have waited so long to do that," he says. "You were right from the very beginning."

Was I?

"But like I said in the monologue," he continues, "you can't see the path until you've walked it."

Except here I am, walking around and still not knowing a damn thing.

Because I'm so frequently wrong, because I seem to possess an uncanny ability to march straight down every wrong path, I decide to change my tactic. I decide to—once again—mix things up. This time, I do the exact opposite of what feels right and good and true.

I lean forward, I grab Tuck by the front of his T-shirt, and I yank him to me. I kiss him: hard, long, and with plenty of tongue. When I finally pull back, he looks dazed.

"Wow." He blinks at me. "You're amazing."

"Thanks," I say, because I just confirmed the undeniable fact that I've been a zillion percent wrong from the moment Tuck spoke on our high school stage.

I don't want him.

I don't want him at all.

"I'm so sorry," I tell Tuck Brady. "But I have to go."

Chapter 25

Ella—stomping along the path in front of me—is furious. "I suppose you think I should thank you."

"For helping you escape from a place you never wanted to go in the first place? Sure, I'll take some gratitude."

"I told you that now I wanted to stay."

"We had a deal," I remind her. "One wants to leave, we both leave."

"That wasn't the deal. We said if *I* wanted to go, we'd go. But of course, who am I talking to here?" She throws her hands up in the air. "Rainie! And we all know who makes the rules. Rainie!"

"Please! What rules have I ever gotten to make?"

"Oh, let's think about that." I don't need to see Ella's face to know how mad she is. Even her back looks squared and angry. "You decide when we go to work, when we come home, when we do or don't hang out . . . which God forbid we ever do, because you hate it so much."

"I don't hate hanging out." That's about the stupidest thing I've ever heard. "Why would I hate hanging out?"

"Oh. Sorry. I wasn't specific." I'm almost surprised Ella's voice can carry back to me, since it's so weighted down with sarcasm. "What I meant was how much you hate hanging out . . . *with me.*"

"Hanging out with you is fine!" It bursts from me like a small explosion. "At least, when it's my *choice* to do it. When you're not blackmailing me into it. Or guilting me somehow. I've spent the entire summer hanging out with you!"

"Seriously? You can't see what you've been doing? God, you can't see anything." A burst of hard laughter echoes back to me. "You just walk around in your fifty pairs of shoes or driving in your fancy car, doing whatever the hell you want—"

"My car isn't fancy!" What is she even saying? My dad got it used from some dude he knew on the arts board. "And talk about doing whatever you want! All you want to do is control me." I allow my voice to go high and whiny in an exaggerated version of Ella's. " 'Rainie, where are you going?' 'Rainie, when will you be back?' 'Rainie, can we glue ourselves together?' "

"Oh, that's nice." Ella pauses to glare back at me before taking another turn on the path. "I help you get a job, I help you get *friends,* and the second you have what you need, you're nowhere to be found. It would be awesome if you would actually behave like a human being and help out now and then."

"Help out?" My voice scales up. "Who drove you out here? Who drives you *everywhere*?"

"I don't have a car!" Ella is yelling now. "And that's not my fault. But you have one, and you don't even care. You take off without it and just *leave* it with no explanation and no keys, so I have to *walk* to pick up our groceries!"

"I never asked you to get our groceries!"

"Because you don't *need* to! Because I always get them while you're off with Milo."

"Oh, there it is." I almost laugh at that one. "Milo. I'm not allowed to be friends with Milo."

"Is that what you call it? Friends?" Ella shakes her head. "Although it is highly amusing, the way you throw yourself at him—"

"What?! I'm not—"

"—since the summer started off with your whole sob story about Tuck. You already have everything, so of course you need the guy everyone wants. Are you going to throw him away, too, the same way you throw everyone away? Or keep trying to get Milo, because one prize is never enough for you?"

"What the actual hell are you talking about?" I stomp faster until I've caught up, and now we're storming along beside each other. "What *prize* do I ever get? I can't help it that I have a car—"

"And your own room. And you don't have to have a job, like, *ever*. You don't need anything." Ella's cheeks are stained dark red. "I thought maybe you finally did need something, like just a little bit. But no. Same old Rainie. You never need anything. You never needed—"

She breaks off in the middle of the sentence, taking another turn so she's once again ahead of me, pacing along the trail. For several minutes, I follow her. The path has inclined and it's gotten hotter, if that's possible. There's a trickle of sweat rolling down my spine. I push my damp bangs out of my eyes, trying to work through what Ella is really mad about. So maybe I wasn't always aware about the car—I get that. But Ella also could have said something. If she had *asked* to borrow my car, I would have let her. No big deal. And as far as Tuck goes . . .

"I screwed up." I direct the words toward Ella's back. "I followed Tuck here without thinking anything through. It was stupid and I was embarrassed and then I basically threw myself at him in his truck and . . ." I'm furious about the tears welling up in my eyes. "You *knew*. You knew what it was like here. You knew what *he* was like. You let me come up here and make an ass out of myself and . . . why? Did you just think it was funny? Was I, like, your big practical joke?"

"No!" Ella pauses, and I almost bump into her before she starts walking again. "I thought it would be cool to have you here. I knew Annette wasn't going to hang out with me. And you—" Now her voice sounds suspiciously thick. "We used to hang out." I don't know what to say to that, so we just walk in silence. After a while, Ella's arms move like she's wiping away tears. "And then you just bailed on me. You were gone."

Okay, now I don't know what to think anymore. She's talking about seventh grade. Or eighth. Or whenever it was that we stopped hanging out. "I didn't bail," I tell her. "We grew apart. People do that, you know."

"I didn't."

"Yes, you did!" It's not fair for her to act like a martyr, years after the fact. "You started auditioning and going to theater club. You were wearing all black and hanging out with Bradley and Traymor and that girl with the nose ring—"

"Sabrina."

"Yeah, her." I remember how I felt at the time, how Ella stopped caring about all the things we used to talk about, like what boys were cute and the Who Wouldja game. How she was doing her own thing, so I started doing mine. How I became friends with Marin and Sarah because they thought I was fun. "You acted like what I said was stupid, like I was stupid."

"I needed a distraction," Ella tells me. "My parents were—" She pauses, and again I see her hand rise to wipe her face. "My mom cheated on my dad. They split up."

"What?" That is shocking indeed. "But they were fine when we drove up here—"

"They *are* fine now. Or at least they act like it." Ella shakes her head. "But they weren't. Not at first. It was bad for a while. There was so much screaming and crying. My sisters and I talked about it a lot—at least Annette and I did, because Olivia was too little—but I wanted someone who wasn't a part of it, who wasn't all mixed up in it and . . ." She pauses. "You were with Marin and Sarah."

"You should have told me." I'm not psychic, after all.

"If you'd been around, I would have." This time, Ella stops walking. It's so abrupt that I almost bump into her before I can stop too. "And then I thought part of why you were coming to

Olympus was to be friends again." She stops and lets out the smallest laugh. "It's stupid."

"No, it's not." I say it automatically, but a half second after it flies out of my mouth, I know it's true. "We *are* friends."

Ella shifts so she's facing me. "Are we?"

I stare into her gray eyes, peering at me from beneath the edge of her thick bangs. We stay that way—looking at each other—for a long time, with the sun beating down on us even as it slides toward the side of the mountain.

Finally, I open my mouth. Finally, I drop some actual truth.

"I'm freaked out," I tell her. "Everyone else seems like they have their crap together. They take pictures of their food and their clothes and their vacations, and they post it online like it's all perfect. Like it's *correct*. And I can't do anything right. Every time I try to do something new, I change my mind. Either I don't like it the way I thought I would, or I suck at it, or it's just wrong. I'm tired of being wrong all the time."

"Why did we leave the gorge?" Ella asks. "Why were you so desperate not to stay down there?"

"Because Tuck and Gretchen broke up." I sigh. "So I kissed him."

"And you didn't like it?"

"No." Impossibly, a giggle creeps up my throat. "I didn't." The giggle comes out between my lips, turning into a full laugh. After a second, Ella joins in.

"Wait, wait," she says, trying to pull it together. "Was it *bad*? Is Tuck Brady a bad kisser?"

"You should know," I remind her. "You kissed him once."

"I know, but . . . I don't remember what it was like."

"Being unmemorable is hardly the hallmark of a *good* kisser," I tell her, and then we're laughing again.

"Hey, guess what I did back there," Ella says between snorts.

"What?"

"I kissed Paul."

"What?!" I stare at her. "How was it?"

"Really good!"

We're still laughing when we reach the parking lot.

Chapter 26

Ella and I were so starving last night that we stopped for dinner on the way home. We were considering Bel Giardino (family discount!) but saw a steak chain on the edge of town and decided we couldn't wait. By the time we trudged up the stairs to our apartment, we were exhausted and pretty much insta-crashed.

We didn't set any alarms, which means we both slept until almost noon. Ella showers first, so I dork around on my phone until she's done. Then I shower and get dressed, once again spending a little extra time on fixing my hair. Presumably, when we get to the theater, Milo will tell me all about the brave thing he did yesterday. Even though my heart is broken that it's not about me, I can't let him know that. I'll listen to his story. I'll be there for him . . . as his friend.

Just as his friend.

• • •

Ella and I are perched on opposite ends of the sofa, sipping coffee, when it happens. First, Annette wanders out from her bedroom, yawning. Then she disappears into the bathroom. We hear water running, and a little later she emerges in a robe, her hair wet. "Morning," she says as she heads back into her bedroom. But only a second passes before she pops her head out again. "Rainie, did you see the thing that guy dropped off?"

What.

Thing.

What.

Guy.

I make eye contact with Ella a split second before we both leap off the couch. "Where?" we ask together.

"I put it in the kitchen," Annette tells us as she goes back into her room.

Ella and I have a mad scramble into the kitchen, where we see exactly nothing. "Where is it?" Ella yells.

We get a muffled response from Annette's room, but it doesn't matter, because I've already spotted the scrap of blue on the floor, sticking out from between the counter and the refrigerator. I swoop down to pull out the . . .

Flyer.

It's a flyer advertising Barney's current gallery opening: a photography exhibit by local artist Milo Cabrera.

I suck in my breath and flip the paper over. On the other side, written in black marker, is my name followed by the vagabond symbol for "safe place." At the bottom of the page are the words "Scared Shitless," and then Milo's signature.

Ella grabs the flyer from me at the same time my phone buzzes. It's a text . . . but it's not from Milo. It's from Tuck.

Back from camping. Okay to come over?

I look at Ella, panicked. She brandishes the flyer at me. "Milo's opening was yesterday."

Dammit.

I fast-type a text to Tuck:

No, about to leave for coffee. C U @ the theater.

Later, I'll deal with the aftermath of kissing him. Right now, I need to go see Milo's exhibit.

• • •

The little bell over the door of Barney's Bagelry makes its familiar *ching-ching* when Ella and I enter. I was hoping that none of our crowd would be there, but of course there's Gretchen, picking up a coffee from the counter. When she sees us, she comes over. "Hey, you guys took off early yesterday."

"We remembered we hate nature," Ella says, which makes Gretchen laugh. I only stand there awkwardly, since—after all— I bolted after kissing her newly exed ex.

"I need coffee," Ella says, and heads for the counter, leaving me alone with Gretchen.

"Hey." Gretchen nudges me. "You know we're cool, right? About the Tuck thing. I don't do gross girl competition." Panic rises in my throat, nearly strangling me. Apparently, Tuck told people about our kiss. Or maybe she saw us. It's hardly like we were hiding at the time. Gretchen grins. "Go with God. Seriously. He's fun."

"Thanks." I manage a weak smile, zeroing in on the rear door, the one with the *Gallery* sign overhead. "I'm going to check out the exhibit," I tell her. My voice sounds high and reedy in my ears.

"See you onstage," Gretchen says with another grin.

I don't wait for Ella to get her coffee. I just make my escape.

The rear gallery is small, but there's enough room for white partitions, just like the one in Greensboro. I walk through the display of pottery by the entrance, past a row of silver jewelry, and to the back wall. There they are, Milo's photographs marching in a row down the center. I start on the left side, where there's a scattershot of small black-and-white images laid out in a star pattern on the wall, each of them a close-up of a single rock bearing a crude chalk drawing. I don't recognize any of the symbols. Milo must have made them up himself and sketched them onto the stones. Telling a story in a language only he can read.

Farther along, he's done something different. There are several photos of clouds, except he's used a computer program or maybe some kind of photography paint to swirl forms into the formations. There's one with the figure of a ballerina, and another with a faceless bride holding a bouquet of flowers. In another, what looks like a young boy rides a horse. The card stock beneath them proclaims the group to be *Daydreams,* which makes sense to me. They're all images of things someone might fantasize about while looking up at the sky. Never in a zillion years would it have occurred to me to explain that phenomenon in such a visual way, but as I've learned during this summer, Milo's mind works differently from mine.

More interesting.

Better.

I walk slowly past his other photographs, drinking in each: a bridge; a crumbling church; an empty road . . .

Until I reach the very last one.

The one that means the most.

This photograph is also a black-and-white, but it's larger than the others. It's framed in gray wood and set off from everything else, so you have to work just a little harder to get to it. I center myself in front and breathe slowly, taking it in.

Milo took the picture in front of the abandoned train station we visited. I can tell because the crumbling brick foundation is visible in the background of the photo, and because a loop of Milo's canvas backpack is curved in the corner. But mostly I can tell because I'm the star of the picture. That's my arm, stretched across the foreground. My fingers, curved against my palm, the polish on two of them chipped. My leather bracelet tied around my wrist.

But it's Milo's handwriting that is scrawled down the length of my arm.

I remember the moment Milo asked me to hold still so he could take the photo. I remember how he traced his fingertip across me, how I felt the light burn it trailed across my skin. Now that he's captured that moment and put it here for everyone to see, I can read the message he hid away in plain sight. There it is, superimposed over the photograph in glowing blue letters:

I want to kiss you.

Right out here in front of everyone, except I'm the only one who knows it's a message for me and me alone. A message that Milo's been trying to tell me all summer and that I've been doing everything in my power to pretend doesn't exist. To pretend that I am not also hiding. My gaze drops to the title card below the photograph.

Hidden Message.

Of course.

I'm standing there, shattered by the knowledge of how he feels and the courage it took to put it out there like this, when suddenly familiar hands slip onto my waist from behind. A familiar voice speaks into my ear. "Hey."

I turn, finding myself—as I knew I would—standing in the protective circle of Tuck's arms. He's gazing down at me, all handsome face and white-teeth smile. "I wanted to see you before the show."

I swallow, unable to move. I'm not sure where I would go, anyway.

I hear Ella's voice. It's loud and strained, coming from somewhere nearby. "I think she might have gone to her car. Maybe we should go check—"

And Tuck's mouth lands on my own. His lips are warm and his breath smells like coffee. It happens so fast that I don't have a chance to respond before it's over, before he's pulling back, smiling down at me, turning us both to greet Ella, who is standing at the other end of the wall . . .

Next to Milo.

Tuck keeps one arm slung casually across my shoulders, which—even though I'm horrified—makes me mildly grateful because it stabilizes me. With Tuck holding me, there's less of a chance I'll fall over.

Although now that I think of it, if the wooden floor wanted to open beneath me and swallow me in a single gulp, maybe that wouldn't be so terrible. Because then Milo wouldn't be staring at me the way he is.

Surprised.

Confused.

Devastated.

Chapter 27

Extricating myself from Tuck and Milo and everything awkward is a blur, but I'm pretty sure Ella is the one who makes it happen. All I know is that somehow I end up in the passenger seat of my car, with Ella driving us up the road to Olympus. "I can't go on," I tell her as she pulls into the parking lot. "I don't want to do the show tonight."

"You have to. It's your job."

"I feel sick."

"No, you don't." Ella cuts the engine and turns to look at me. "You're not sick. You're just messed up about boys."

"I'm *too* messed up," I tell her. "People as messed up as me shouldn't be in front of other people."

"Please." Ella rolls her eyes. "Have you ever read a trashy magazine? People way more messed up than you are on display all the time, so pull it together. You have two boys who like you. I'm having a difficult time feeling sympathetic."

"I hate you," I tell her.

"I hate you too." She opens her door. "Come on. Let's go. It'll be fine."

• • •

It's not fine. It's a disaster. When we all come out in our white chorus robes, Milo refuses to meet my eyes. During the woodland-
creature scene, he doesn't meet me in the middle of the stage.
When I start toward him in the way I've been doing all summer,
he changes course and flaps in another direction. I follow, but
again he moves away, and because I can't exactly play this game
of tag in front of an audience, I eventually stop and stand around
by myself. The saddest rabbit in the world.

Tuck has the exact opposite reaction, which I guess I should
have expected. He does nothing but pay attention to me. When
Aphrodite offers him the most beautiful woman on earth, he first
looks at me before giving his dramatic agreement. Later, when
he's sailing to Greece, he gazes directly into my eyes the entire
time that I'm helping the other cast members pull the Aegean
Sea across the stage. I guess this is what I had hoped for when
I originally imagined the summer, but now that we're here, it's
terrible.

It's also a little bit ridiculous.

Is this how the theater kids show their love?

Jesus.

I finally corner Milo when everyone's exited the stage after
our final bow. I wouldn't have even managed to make that happen except that I don't get changed first, like we're supposed
to. I just march straight back to the boys' dressing room and
wait outside. Milo flies out of it within moments, which I know
means I wouldn't have caught him had I not come straight here.
He shakes his head when he sees me. "This is not a thing we do,

okay? This is not our tradition, where you suck and then ambush me to try to explain why you don't suck."

"Fine, I suck," I tell him, except that it immediately rubs me the wrong way. Maybe I've been confused, but that doesn't make me suck. "You could have told me, you know that?"

"Told you what?" Milo's eyes are darker than usual. "Told you to stop using me? Maybe thanked you for making me your truck stop on the way to Tuck Town?"

"Gross, that's not a thing. Tuck Town is not a thing." Speaking of which, the absolute last thing I want is for Tuck to come out and see us fighting about him. "Milo, can we go somewhere else and talk?"

"No." He folds his arms, glaring down at me. "I'm not mad that you like him. You're allowed to like whoever you want. What sucks is that at the beginning, I thought I was reading the signs wrong. That there were hidden codes, that still waters run deep and all that bullshit." A short, harsh laugh escapes his lips. "Nope. Nothing hidden. Everything about you was in plain sight all along. You pulled strings to get here, you didn't know what you were doing, you didn't give a crap about any of it."

"Yes I did!" Right now, I give a crap so hard it hurts. "I got confused. I don't even want to be with Tuck."

"Congratulations." Milo's smile is brittle. "How lovely for him. We are two lucky guys."

"If you had told me how you felt—"

"What." He interrupts me, taking a step backward. "We could have screwed around a couple times? Hooked up at a party or two? I've done that, Rainie. I always do that. This time

- 267 -

I wasn't going to. This time I was going to wait—" He stops. Glaring at me. "Do you even get how cliché you are? Chasing the lead. It's just so . . . obvious."

Of course it is.

Because that's me.

Obvious and uninteresting.

Like always.

I watch Milo stalk away onto the trail, and then, as Tuck comes out of the dressing room and swings his head in my direction, I duck back onto the deck. I lose myself in the crowd, circling back behind the railing to the trees beyond. Waiting there in the darkness alone until Ella texts, asking where the hell I am.

• • •

I don't think I sleep at all, at least during the night; I'm still awake when the sun rises. But I must fall asleep at some point after that, because when I wake up, Ella's gone and the wall clock says it's midafternoon. I hear murmurs, so I stumble into the living room to find Ella and Annette sitting on the couch together. Ella flutters her hands at me. Her fingernails have been newly painted a sunny yellow. "Annette did my left hand," she tells me.

"Ella did mine." Annette shows me her fingers, which match Ella's.

Ella hops off the couch and walks over to me. "Get dressed," she orders. "I want to show you something."

"Is it the entrance to hell?" I ask her. "Because I've already seen that. It's my life now."

"God, overdramatic much?" She rolls her eyes. "What are you, a theater kid or something?"

Thirty minutes later, Ella is leading me down Nine Muses. "Annette quit Bel Giardino," she says as we walk past McKay's green awning. "She already turned in her apron, and the only thing she has to do now is pick up her paycheck. The campus librarian offered her a job and she's taking it. She won't make as much money, but it'll be more conducive to getting good grades."

"And less conducive to needing rescue from parties?"

"Yeah." Ella shakes her head. "I think she just went bananas for a while. People do that sometimes, you know? I think my mom did, back when everything happened with her and Dad."

I nod. Maybe that's what I did this summer.

Maybe I'm still doing it.

I give Ella a tiny nudge. "Better hope the bananas aren't a genetic thing."

"Yeah, right?" We go past a parking lot and an art store before Ella takes my elbow. "This way." She pulls me toward the mouth of an alley, right off the sidewalk.

"Um . . ." I let her guide me past a rusty blue dumpster that lists to one side. "Is this safe?"

"It's Olympus," she tells me. "Everything here is safe."

Not in my experience.

We walk past a fire escape, stepping over an old blanket and someone's fast-food remnants before Ella pulls me to a stop. "Behold." She sets her hands on my shoulders and turns me ninety degrees. "The best graffiti in all of Olympus."

I look up at the wall. There, spray-painted across the bricks in giant red letters, are four words:

HAROLD, I'M NOT PREGNANT.

Below them, there's a huge happy face.

I stare at the message for a long moment—at the blatant, basic, obvious nature of the message—and then I burst out laughing. Ella joins me. I raise my arms in a gesture of appreciation. "That . . . is brilliant."

"Says it all, doesn't it?"

"It certainly tells a story."

"Nothing confusing." Ella turns back to me. "And speaking of which, I need to clear up some potential confusion about Milo." She tilts her head, gazing into my eyes. "You don't need my permission to be with him. But just so you know, you have it."

"Thanks." My smile must look as sad on the outside as it feels on the inside. "But I think that train has left the station."

"Trains can't leave unless someone is driving them." Ella makes a motion like she's pulling a horn. "Toot toot."

"That doesn't make any sense," I tell her.

"I know." She offers me a half grin. "I thought I'd try."

"Thanks."

• • •

Ella stays at the apartment while I go to Bel Giardino. She says she's afraid she'll stab Vic with a steak knife. I agree it's better for everyone concerned if I go alone. A light sprinkle of rain starts as I pull past the restaurant and into the gravel parking lot behind it. On weekdays Bel Giardino closes between lunch and dinner, and right now it's not open yet for the evening.

When I trot up the back steps, Cute Cory is just opening the adjacent wide double doors that lead to a covered metal ramp. I wave at him and—after a second of recognition—he beckons to me. Rain mists onto my face as I make my way to him. "Annette's friend, right?"

"Yeah. I need to pick up her paycheck."

"I can get it for you," he says. "How is she?"

"Good," I tell him. "She's got a cool new job at the library."

"Awesome." Cory's smile widens. "I'll go see her when school starts."

"You should do that." I watch him head into the restaurant, then turn back to watch the rain spatter across my car. Not enough water to clean it, not enough to cancel the show. Only enough to make things damp and uncomfortable.

A moment later there's a scraping on the metal ramp behind me. I look back to find not Cute Cory but Vic. He's holding an envelope with Annette's name scribbled across it. My immediate surge of contempt must be visible, because he looks properly cowed. "You think I'm a jerk."

"Only because you *are* a jerk," I tell him.

"Maybe you're too young to get it." Vic looks thoughtful. "Maybe Annette's even too young. But it was actually better that it happened like this. No long, drawn-out conversations. No waiting around for the ax to fall. No one got really hurt, you know?"

I stare at him. "Annette got hurt." I leave out the end of the sentence: *you dumb shit.*

"I know, but she's the victim. In a way, that's easier for her. She's free. I'm the one who has to live with what we did. She gets to go on with her life." He peers down at me. "You want to know a secret?"

"Not particularly." But because he's still holding Annette's paycheck, I fold my arms and wait.

"You're still young enough to think you'll have all the answers someday." Vic shakes his head. "Here's the secret: you won't. There's no magical age when you understand everything. Don't expect magic. There isn't any."

"Thanks." I reach out and pluck the envelope from his hand. "You're a lying cheater *and* a philosopher. Your fiancée is a lucky woman."

I turn and walk away from Vic, down the ramp and into the mist. Although—no doubt about it—he's a disgusting toad, I'm reminded of the thing Milo always said. Villains don't know they're villains. So even though this guy—this shitty college-town assistant restaurant manager who screwed over two women— even though he is the villain in the story of my summer, he doesn't get it. He can't possibly.

But as I pull my seat belt over my body and click it into place, another thought crosses my mind. Milo also said that villains have one redeeming quality. Maybe Vic's redeeming quality is a secret he told me. Not the message he *thought* he was giving me, but rather something he said earlier in the conversation. Something about victims. Something about freedom.

• • •

I'm back with just enough time to pick up Ella from our apartment and drive to the theater. When we arrive in the parking lot, I don't open my door. She's digging through her purse for something but stops when she realizes I'm looking at her. "What?"

"Thank you."

"For what?"

"For all the things. For the summer."

"Whatever, you weirdo." But she's smiling. "You're welcome."

I swing from the car and put my plan into motion. The plan I came up with in the last hour, that is.

Ella and I walk down the long cement stairs of the theater, past the rows and rows of aluminum bench seats. We take the dirt pathway to the backstage area, where Ella heads for the dressing room. "I'm going to grab a grilled cheese," I call after her, but then I keep standing there, watching her walk away. If nothing else, I think I got my friend Ella back this summer. That's pretty cool.

I turn and head down the wooden deck, which is not empty but not yet crowded with people. I stop at the corkboard, where a new poster hangs for the night, and scribble a quick *happy birthday* to Bianca. I take a few steps away, then stop and go back, grabbing the marker again to add a word to my greeting: *sexy*. If Gretchen can endeavor to make everyone feel good about themselves, why can't I?

From the kitchen comes the greasy smell of grilled cheese.

I head in that direction but pass right by it. I turn at the boys' dressing room, shift onto the trail by the side of the theater, and walk all the way back up to the parking lot. Thankfully, I don't pass either Tuck or Milo before I can reach my car, turn off my phone, and drive away.

Chapter 28

On my way back to the apartment, I stop by the 7-Eleven so I can stock Annette's freezer with three cartons of strawberry ice cream and the refrigerator with a dozen strawberry yogurts. I pack up the contents of my side of the bedroom and my bathroom shelf and then make four trips down to my car with duffel bags and suitcases. I put the rest of my cash on Ella's pillow—it's more than enough to cover my portion of the rent and the last power bill—and slide the apartment key off my key chain. The last thing I do is set it on the coffee table alongside my bottle of bright blue nail polish. Then I open the front door, turn the lock on the knob, and pull it closed behind me.

Down in my car, I finally turn my phone back on. Predictably, there are several texts from Ella, two from Tuck, and a missed phone call from the production office. But I'm only returning one of the messages tonight, and that's because I know where the recipient will be at this moment: in a Grecian garden, kissing Gretchen. I plug my headset into my phone so I can talk while I drive.

"You were right," I tell Tuck's voice mail as I wind out of

Olympus. "You said this summer would be a risk, and it was. Everything: the show, living with Ella, you. But I'm done now. You are so cute and so nice and I know I am chickenshit to be doing this over the phone, but I don't think we're a thing. And I don't want to go back to Dobbs pretending that we are. I came here because of your monologue. Which was awesome, by the way, and totally changed my life . . ." I pause, trying to figure out what I need to say to him. "But it was the words that made me come, not really you. So thank you for saying those words." I take the turn onto the road heading out of town. I'm really doing this. My thumb is almost to the button when I pause. I leave a final comment. "Sorry again."

I hang up my phone and turn up my music. It's hard to drive down a mountain at night while you're blinded by tears, but—somehow—I manage to do it.

• • •

A rapping sound awakens me. I straighten in my seat and gingerly try to tilt my head upright with my eyes still closed. It's tough because I've apparently acquired the world's sharpest neck crick during the few hours I've been sleeping here. I yawn and stretch my arms forward, accidentally hitting the center of my steering wheel. The loud horn blast startles my body upright and my eyes open. I shake my head, blearily focusing on the source of the sound.

It's Marin. She's standing by the side of my car—which is right where I parked it, at the curb in front of her house—and staring at me. I open my door. "Hi."

"What are you doing?" Marin's wearing tight orange running gear and a headband. "Have you been here all night?"

"No." I roll my neck and dig my fingers into the side of it, trying to work out the kinks. "I drove around Dobbs until I was almost out of gas."

Marin pulls my door open wider. "Inside," she tells me. "Now."

• • •

When I wake up again, hours and hours later, I'm burrowed into the center of Marin's bed. Sarah showed up not long after Marin found me. They gave me toaster waffles and made me take a shower, possibly because I couldn't stop crying, and at some point they didn't know what to do with me anymore. Marin gave me a pair of hot-pink shorts, a matching midriff top, and a small white pill. "It's herbal," she told me. "Melatonin. Over the counter." I don't know if it was that pill or the fact that I hadn't slept well in days, but now as I'm looking at Marin's clock, it's almost call time in Olympus. I've slept the entire day.

I scramble out of bed and pick my dirty jeans off the floor so I can yank them over Marin's shorts before going to the living room. There, I find Marin and Sarah curled up next to each other on the couch, thumbing through trashy magazines.

"Finally," Sarah says when she sees me.

"We were going to wake you up in twenty minutes," Marin informs me. "How do you feel?"

"Better." But then my eyes well with tears. "Maybe not that much better."

My friends hop up. They each grab one of my arms, pulling me to sit between them. "What happened?" Marin asks.

"Do we need to kick someone's ass?" Sarah says.

"No." I smile through my tears. "I like a boy, that's all."

"Well, duh." Sarah squeezes my hand.

"Not Tuck." I pull away from her. "The other boy. He's sweet and funny and smart and so, so hot and . . ." I trail off, dropping my head into my hands. "And I ruined everything."

Sarah and Marin immediately turn into two chickens, clucking and cooing over me. "No," Marin says. "I'm sure you didn't ruin everything."

"He's a dumbass if he doesn't like you," Sarah says. "The stupidest boy on the planet."

"No, he *did* like me," I tell her. "But I screwed everything up and . . ." I pause, trying to sort through how to explain it, how to give words to the summer. "I think my heart is broken. Is this what it feels like when you follow through on a thing to the end? When you actually let yourself like a person? They can mess you all up and make everything hurt?"

I see Marin and Sarah exchange a look. Marin peers into my eyes. "I mean . . . sometimes."

Sarah shakes her head. "I'm telling you, we're happy to kick someone's ass."

"This sucks," I tell them both.

"Do your parents know you're home?" Marin asks me.

"God no." I run my fingers through my tangled hair. "They're going to be so pissed. Can I just hide out here for a while? They won't even know. They think I'm still up in Olympus."

"Until Sunday, yeah." Marin glances at Sarah. "Then mine will be back from Vegas. We can probably still swing a night or two, but then we'll have some explaining. Sarah?"

"Mine won't give a shit." Sarah shrugs. "What do you need, like a week?"

"Yes," I tell her. "Then I can just arrive like I'm coming home from Olympus."

"That's messed up," Marin says.

"I know," I tell her.

Sarah abruptly stands and leaves the room. She comes back with my backpack. "You should check your phone," she says. "It's been blowing up all day. We finally put it in the kitchen because the buzzing was getting on our nerves."

Reluctantly, I take out my phone and look at it. It's the same two names over and over: Tuck and Ella. Milo hasn't texted once.

"Maybe you should call one of them back," Marin says.

"No." The sigh comes out of me accidentally. "Nothing I have to say is going to change anything."

"I'll be the judge of that." Sarah grabs the phone out of my hands and scrolls through my messages. "Tuck has literally texted you twenty-six times."

"Weird," says Marin.

I don't say anything.

Sarah keeps looking at my screen. "He says he needs to tell you something important."

"He *is* really cute," Marin says.

Sarah flicks her in the arm. "Cute isn't everything."

"I know, but he *is*." Marin grabs the phone out of Sarah's hand. She looks at the messages. "Rainie, seriously."

"Stop," I tell her. "I broke up with him, okay?"

But Marin's still looking at the screen. "I don't think that's what this is about. I'm going to answer him." She starts typing on my phone.

"No!" I make a grab for it, but Sarah catches my hands in midair.

"Two to one," she tells me. "You're overruled."

"You can't do that!" I try to tug away, but Sarah is strong. "Marin, what are you saying to him?"

Marin holds up my phone so I can see the one word she typed in response:

What?

Immediately, an ellipsis pops up on my phone's screen. Tuck is writing back. A second later, his words arrive:

At school
On the stage

Marin looks up at me. "What is he talking about?"

"His monologue," Sarah reminds her. "When he got all weird and stared at Rainie."

"What about it?" Marin asks.

"Shush," Sarah says, pointing back to my phone screen. Another ellipsis, then . . .

I said the words. I didn't write them.

Marin's thumbs immediately start moving over my screen:

Who did?

But her question is unnecessary. As I stare at my phone, at the tiny ellipsis, I already know. I know what Tuck is typing before the bubble pops up on my screen. I know what he *has* to be typing, because it's the only thing that makes any sense.

Milo.

Chapter 29

The only thing more stressful than driving *down* a mountain in the middle of the night when you're exhausted is driving *up* a mountain at the beginning of the next night when you're in a massive hurry and you're stressed and heartbroken. Which is why, in this particular scenario, Sarah is the one behind the wheel.

Also, I know better than to text and drive, and right now I am sending text after text after text. As we wind up the mountain, moving in and out of cell-service range, I receive messages back, out of order in scattered bursts.

From Tuck:

> You're welcome.

From Ella:

> Did the bananas rub off on you? Okay, forgiven.
> See you soon.

And then:

But I'm keeping the blue nail polish.

From Milo:

Trying to work. Rainie, stop. Please.

Of course I had anticipated Milo's reaction, but seeing it on my phone screen made it even more real. And even more painful.

We squeal into Olympus after the end of intermission, which is easy to ascertain, as the Act II opening strains are already piping from the speakers, echoing up to us. There are a few stragglers in the parking lot, still eating hot dogs or finishing cigarettes or coming out of the bathrooms. I point Marin and Sarah in the direction of the box office and race for the trail that runs along the outer edge of the amphitheater. It's the long way to get there, but since we're mid-performance, I can hardly trample down through the seats and across the stage.

The wooden deck is mostly empty when I pound onto it, breathing hard from my run. Gretchen and Brilliant Master Thespian Hugh Hadley are in the center, near the corkboard. When they see me, Gretchen waves and hands something small to Hugh. The object glints under the backstage lights. I head in her direction, stopping about halfway at the location of the best place we have to watch the show from back here. I step onto the wooden bench attached to the floor and peer through a hole in the wall. The audience can't see me because I'm hidden by leaves and fake boulders and the darkness of the upstage area, but I can see what's happening out there. It's the big group polka number, which happens as the Greeks and Trojans fight. I see my usual dance partner—Jon the lipstick thief—miming that he's dancing with an invisible person. Ugh, awkward.

I'm scanning the stage for Milo when Gretchen and Mandy arrive from opposite directions. "Where have you been?" Mandy whispers.

"They forgot to give away your line," Gretchen says. "It was real weird in the 'who's the prettiest' scene."

"The whole show is a mess," Mandy tells me. "The first light cue didn't go on time, and everything's been screwed up ever since."

"Tuck tried to ad-lib," Gretchen says. "Tuck sucks at ad-libbing." She brightens. "Hey, 'Tuck' rhymes with 'suck'! How did I never notice that before?"

"I don't know," I tell her. To Mandy, I say, "Sorry I wasn't here yesterday. Or part of today."

Gretchen giggles. "I guess I was too focused on another word that rhymes with 'Tuck.'"

This time, Mandy and I both turn to stare at her. "Are you *drunk*?" Mandy asks.

"Hey." Gretchen holds up a hand like she's being sworn in at court. "Hugh was knocking it back, like, more than usual. I took a little for the team."

"Crap," Mandy says.

"You should thank me. I am a sacrificial lamb." Gretchen giggles again.

"Let's get you some coffee." Mandy grabs her hand. "You're about to go back on."

Mandy pulls Gretchen away toward the kitchen counter, and I turn back to the hole in the knotty wood of the deck. Onstage, they're still fighting. Swords clash against shields. Trojans and Greeks wheel around each other, ducking and lunging. I finally locate Milo in the midst of it all. He's wearing his armor—emerald green against the mossy color of the other Trojans, to differentiate him as a principal character—and brandishing his sword at Paul, who in this scene is Grecian. Finally, now that I've divested myself of all Tuck-related confusion and guilt and misplaced feelings, I'm free to just appreciate Milo. The way his arms tense when he swings the sword, and how he dodges to the side when he's swung upon. His hair, damp with sweat, clinging to the edges of his angled face, and his heaving chest as—

Hold on a minute.

I squint, pushing my forehead right to the wood above the peephole. There's a *lot* of clinging and heaving out there. Milo looks exhausted. . . .

I jerk back from the peephole and whip around to see Hugh, still standing in the center of the deck, tipping back his flask. Because it's faster than racing over there, I reach down to pull off a sneaker and throw it at him. It hits him in the lower leg, and Hugh jumps, startled. His flask clangs to the ground, and he shoots me a look of accusation. I point toward the stage. *"You're on,"* I whisper as loudly as I dare.

Hugh starts and then heads for the stage entrance as fast as he can wobble. A second later, I hear his raspy, microphoned voice. "Enough!"

A second after *that,* a cannon booms. I drop my head into my hands. The pyro crew must have decided to try to improv their way to the end of the scene by shooting off some weaponry.

I clamber back onto the bench and look through the hole as the Greeks and Trojans all come to a weary halt and trudge offstage, much later than they should have.

I jump off the bench and charge along the deck, which is quickly filling with tired warriors, to the entrance where I know Milo comes offstage. Sure enough, there he is, swinging through the crowd, sliding his sword into the scabbard at his waist. He's still breathing heavily, and his skin is glistening with sweat. When he sees me, his eyes flash dark. "I thought you were gone."

"I came back." *For you.*

I don't say the last words, but I don't think it would have mattered, because Milo is striding across the deck to cue up for the Trojan horse scene. From onstage, the sound of Helen and Pollux's duet floats through the night air. Helen's part—which is mildly slurred—is all about how much she loves Paris. Pollux's side is the same, but it reframes the emotion as bro-love instead of romance. The crux of the song is about how a relationship can start in deception but end in everlasting happiness. Helen's final line—"Look how happy everyone is now!"—is undercut by Pollux's (supposedly) humorous last words:

"Except for all the deaaaaaaaaad people!"

Laughter erupts from the audience, so maybe they can't tell

how insane the show is tonight. Maybe they think slurred words and long battles and inappropriate cannon shots are all part of the program.

As the onstage Greeks—led by Milo-as-Achilles—inform the audience that they're leaving because they've been beaten by Troy, I take off running. I might be late, I might be doing it all wrong, but the very least I can do is show up. I sprint down the deck, weaving in and out of armored Trojans and toga-clad Muses, tearing into the girls' dressing room. Ella looks up from where she's adjusting her leather sandals, crisscrossing the straps around her shins. She scans my body—"You're a hot mess"—and I remember I'm wearing Marin's pink half shirt, my own dirty jeans, and one shoe.

"He won't stand still long enough to let me tell him," I say.

"Milo?"

"Yes."

"Tell him what?"

"That I'm sorry and I was stupid and I love him." The words come out before I can edit them, and now that they've been said, they're real. "Crap, I love him."

Ella stares at me for a long moment, during which I can't tell what she's thinking. Then she jumps up and grabs my toga from my hook. "Then you have to make him hear you. After the show, make him hear you."

I start undressing at the speed of light, grabbing my toga from Ella and jerking it over my head. "What do I do *during* the show?"

"During the show, just enjoy the way he looks in that armor." She grins at me. "It's kind of spectacular."

Several minutes later, I'm in the wings with Ella and Paul and Jon and all the other actor-techs in our chorus robes as onstage the final scene rages on. The sounds of war are enhanced and amplified through the speakers, making the battle seem worse and louder and scarier than it really is. Tonight it looks like the makeup team went a little overboard, because red goo is everywhere. When Paris kills Achilles—which, as always, makes my heart clench—the blood bag beneath Milo's armor explodes dramatically and they're both sprayed with crimson. Milo slides slowly down the length of Tuck's sword, crumpling to the ground, and it's all I can do not to rush out there and curl my own body around his.

But there are only a few minutes left in the show. I can wait.

Tuck-as-Paris sheaths his sword while, across the stage, Logan-as-Pollux makes a final kill. They stand amid the glory and the ravages of the battle, everyone else either a corpse or too wounded to rise. Then Pollux also slides his sword away. He starts striding slowly toward Paris, exuding the air of tragic victory he has maintained all summer, as Paris gazes at the horrible aftermath of what he began when he stole Helen. "Paris. Brother." Pollux indicates the carnage littering the stage. "Look what we have wrought."

Paris sighs heavily and takes off his helmet. "We have won the war."

"But at what cost?" Pollux lifts his eyes skyward, as if to entreat the gods. "We should never have come here, Helen and I. The reason was false. It was a trick—"

"That turned into love!" Paris interrupts in a shout.

"That turned into war!" Pollux yells right back.

They stare at each other like they've been doing since the first rehearsals, all tragic and furious. From the wings where I stand, Milo's face is visible. His helmet came off in the battle, and because of the way he's fallen, his head is turned away from the audience. His eyes are open so he can watch Paris and Pollux's final fight.

Someone backstage must be prompting drunk Hugh, because this time Zeus makes his entrance right when he's supposed to. A spotlight appears on him, standing in Olympus above the battlefield. "For Achilles!" he thunders, just as he thunders every night . . .

Which is when a lightning bolt is supposed to crash and a bright flame should split the stage and kill Paris. Pollux, who's already heading toward him, will speed up in order to catch him as he falls to the ground. Then Pollux will lower Paris's dead body before standing again to give the travesties-of-war monologue right before Eros and Eris lead us all out for the mournful dirge. That's how the order of events is supposed to go: lightning, death, travesties, dirge.

Except that tonight, there's no lightning bolt. There's only Zeus yelling . . . and then a frozen pause. The pyro effect doesn't go off with his line. It *should* be fixable, because there are backup bolts in place for just such an emergency . . . but those don't go off either. Which is unfortunate because Tuck has already started his slow collapse to the ground in anticipation of his imminent death.

But his death hasn't happened, because he hasn't been shot

with lightning, which means that Pollux, who has rushed across the stage to catch him, instead catches him in a weird hug, mid-fall. In the wings, I hear my gasp echoed by those around me as Paris and Pollux wobble there in a half-crouch for a few seconds before Pollux pulls Paris back to his feet. Gretchen was right about Tuck not being great at ad-libbing, because he doesn't say or do a thing to rectify the situation. He just stands there. Frozen. Staring out at the crowd.

"What is he doing?" Ella whispers.

"What can he do?" Paul whispers back. "He's not dead."

"Then he should say something," Ella says. "When you're not dead, you say things."

When you're not dead, you say things.

The assistant stage manager rushes into our midst, loud-whispering to Nikki through his headset. "I don't know. Do you want me to start the dirge?"

As he waits for an answer, as everyone else watches the train wreck onstage, I suddenly turn to Ella. I grab her by the shoulders and repeat her own words back to her. "When you're not dead, you say things."

Ella looks confused. "That's what I just—"

But I've already pulled away and am walking toward the stage. From behind me, I hear her whispered "Oh shit," but it's too late.

I'm already in the light.

Chapter 30

Both Tuck's and Logan's eyes get really big when I appear onstage in my white toga robes. I would go so far as to say that Tuck looks legitimately panic-stricken. But I only give them a half second of attention before turning to Milo. He's staring up at me from the ground, and although he doesn't look terrified like Tuck, he is certainly surprised.

Almost as surprised as I am.

I turn toward the stadium seating of the amphitheater, which—of course, with my luck—is packed. I have no idea where Marin and Sarah are in the blur of faces, but I'm sure that wherever they are, they're shocked as hell to see me march out here. I put one fist on my hip and use my other hand to point at Logan. "You are right, Pollux," I call out loudly, like the principal actors do when they're saying their lines. "You should not have come here."

In my peripheral vision, the other actor-technicians huddle together, watching me. Stunned.

"But since you have done that," I continue, "now you must ..." *Deal with it, deal with it, deal with it ... what's*

Grecian for "deal with it"? I glance up at the production booth for inspiration, but there's none to be had, since, even from here, I can see that Nikki is looking down at me with a face of fury. "Reap what you have sown!" I spit it out really fast, and then slow myself down for a second crack at the improvised line. This time, I intone it all deep and solemn. "Now you must reap what you have sown."

Logan takes a step toward me. "How so . . . Olympian Muse?" He winks. Thank Zeus and the rest of the gods, mythological or otherwise, Logan—of all people—is playing along.

"I too have lost someone today," I tell him, with a glance down at Milo, who *has* to listen to me this time, since he's all dead and crap. "I lost him because I—like you—was fighting the wrong war."

I jerk my gaze back to Logan, who tilts his head so the audience can tell he's asking me for answers. "Pray tell, oh Muse."

"Yeah." Tuck finally manages to spit out some words. "Pray tell?"

"That warrior." I point dramatically at Milo. I think I can detect the tiniest twitch in the corners of his lips. Like he's trying not to smile. I manage to find enough self-control so that I don't fling myself on top of him. Instead, I stay right where I am, one finger poised in his direction.

"Achilles?" Logan asks helpfully.

"Yes." I nod, and then—because I don't think it was visible to the audience—I do it again, more emphatically. "I have lost my chance to tell him . . ." I trail off, my heart thudding wildly against my chest. Milo's upstage hand, the one hidden from the audience by his body, is moving. Although the rest of him stays still, that hand slides toward me. Just a tiny bit. And his fingers splay open in the dirt. He wants me to come closer.

I take two steps toward Milo's fake-dead body, and then glance up into the production booth again. Nikki is leaning over the controls, watching me intently. I'm sure if this was a regular stage—the kind that's indoors and not carved into the side of a mountain—she'd have brought the curtain down on me already. But here . . . she's kind of stuck.

I take another step . . . and another. Until I'm close enough that I could kick Milo with a sandaled foot if I wanted to. I turn back to Logan and say the words I should have said weeks ago. "I have lost the chance to tell him that I love him."

"You love him, huh?" Logan looks totally amused. He's getting a kick out of this. "Speak more, Muse."

I narrow my eyes at him. "I love him, all right, Pollux?"
Oops, doesn't sound very Grecian.

I turn back to look at Milo just as I feel his fingers slide around my ankle, caressing it gently. "I love you," I tell him. Then I glance up at the audience. "I love you, Achilles," I say louder. "I only wish we could have had more time together."

Then, from behind us all, there's a thunderous roar that makes me jump. "Your wish is granted!"

Milo's eyes widen, and I—along with the audience—turn to see Hugh . . . I mean, Zeus. He's standing on the upstage boulder, pointing down at us. "War is bad," he bellows. "Love is good."

Aaaaand . . . this is why actors need writers. Still, I appreciate the sentiment.

"Rise!" Zeus's command is deep and deafening. It's the most godlike he's sounded all summer. "Rise, Achilles!" He points at Milo. "Live for love!"

Holy shit.

Nikki is going to kill us all.

As I whirl frontward, I catch a glimpse of Tuck and Logan. Tuck looks horrified, but Logan has a huge grin plastered across his face. Who knew that Logan's redeeming quality would end up being his willingness to improv along with me?

I squint against the stage lights that seem to be blazing brighter than ever. It takes me a few seconds to recognize it's not just my fevered brain. Up in her booth, Nikki has gone along for the ride. She's decided that if we're going to force ourselves into the spotlight, we might as well get the actual spotlight. The audience is a giant indistinct shadow somewhere before me as my section of the stage flares and something brushes against my shins.

I don't have to look down. It's Milo. He's rising at Zeus's command and at my impassioned declaration. He stands there, inches from me, all dark eyes and angles and perfect mouth, and we just stare at each other for a moment. Then he reaches out and sets his hands on my shoulders. I raise them just slightly under his touch, wanting to feel more of his warm palms against my skin. His gaze leaves my eyes, skimming up to my hairline before plunging back down to my lips. I feel pressure against my shoulders. He's turning me, cheating out for the audience so he's not blocking me.

"Thanks for raising me from the dead." He says it quietly

so there's no way anyone on the aluminum bench seats can hear him. From where they sit, we'll look like two reunited lovers sharing a private moment.

Which—maybe—is what we are.

"I want you to kiss me," I whisper, and watch the smile spread over his face.

"That would be a very obvious move," he says. "The message is not hidden at all."

"Good." I rise up on tiptoe and slide my hands up his arms, linking them together behind his neck so I can pull his head down to mine. His mouth is warm and firm, and, from the way he kisses me, I can tell he's been wanting to do this for a long time. Maybe as long as I have.

As the opening strains of the mournful dirge start blaring from the speakers, it takes me a second to recognize that the sound underneath it is applause. Two thousand people out there are clapping for us. For our kiss. For the surprising ending to this uniquely inaccurate play.

Even though the very last thing I want is to lose contact with the deliciousness of Milo's mouth, I pull back so I can look up at him. His pupils are huge and liquid, his brown irises a soft line around them. He touches my temple with one finger, tracing it down the side of my face to my chin. "When I was taking pictures of you, I probably should have mentioned that I find you very beautiful."

"It was implied," I tell him, and stretch for another kiss. It's a really good one.

Behind us, the other cast members are making their way

across the stage. This time, there's nothing mournful or dirge-like about their singing. In fact, it sounds almost like a song of victory. As Milo and I pull apart, I catch a flash of Ella. She's grinning and practically doing a high step as she marches along.

Milo jerks his chin toward the line of our coworkers. "Think we should join them?"

"Eh." I shake my head. "We're kinda doing our own thing over here."

"You are crazy," he murmurs.

"I caught the crazy this summer."

He laughs and leans forward to nuzzle my nose with his own. "Must be contagious."

"Kiss me again, please," I tell him.

And he does.

A lot.

Epilogue

I walk across the bedroom floor, my black boots echoing loudly against the wood. Yep, just like I figured. There it is: a jacket at the foot of the bed.

Again.

I snag the jacket and take three steps past it to the rug, where there's a crumpled shirt lying. Next to it, a pair of pants. I roll my eyes.

Tuck Brady.

I grab up all the clothing and stalk out past the heavy red curtain and down the stairs to the backstage area. I barge right into the boys' dressing room, which makes Wendell squeal and leap to cover his underwear-clad self with a towel. I ignore him, dropping the jacket, shirt, and pants onto the lap of their rightful owner. I fold my arms, glaring down at him.

Tuck gives me a look of apology. "Sorry . . ."

"You are very pretty when you're not wearing most of your clothes," I tell him. "But if you don't put your costume away after one-act rehearsals, I will make it my personal mission to screw up your light cues so drastically that the audience will never have a chance to see any of"—I gesture to his body—"that. Got it?"

"You're kind of a hard-ass when you're on the crew," Tuck says.

"You're kind of a doink when you're one of my cast," I retort, shaking my head.

And yet we smile at each other.

Actors.

I'm all the way to the door when he calls me back. "Hey, Rain. Are you bringing Sarah to the party?"

"I don't know." I lean against the doorjamb, regarding him. "Are you still smoking?"

"No." He says it immediately but then follows it up with: "*Mostly* no."

"Then yes. *Maybe* yes."

"C'mon, Rain." He looks pleading. "She's killing me."

"Sarah doesn't like boys who smoke." I give him a pointed look and head out. I don't have time for Tuck's romantic troubles tonight. I'm already late.

Outside the school, I join the stream of students and parents making their way toward the entrance to the football field. I scan the crowd, searching . . . searching . . .

There he is.

Milo leans against a post at the main gate, his legs crossed at the ankle. He raises a hand in greeting, and my heart swells. It's only been five days since we last saw each other, but still. Apparently, this is just how it is now.

I trot toward him, and he swings away from the gate to meet

me, enfolding me in his arms. I run my hands beneath his jacket, sliding around his rib cage to link behind his back, and tilt my face up for a kiss. He obliges, and—as always—it's so damn good.

When, after a moment, Milo pulls away, I yank him back into me. "One more," I tell him.

"You're bossy when you're in rehearsals." He clocks my grin. "What's so funny?"

"Nothing. Just kiss me," I order.

And he does.

Finally, we come up for air again, but only after a freshman tells us to get a room. Milo checks out what I'm wearing: black jeans and a matching sweatshirt. "Are you going to be warm enough?"

He has a point. It's mid-October, which means it'll be chilly by the end of the game. "We might have to cuddle."

"Approved." He laces his fingers through mine and we head through the main gate, stopping long enough for me to fork over a pair of tickets. "Your side or mine?"

"My home game, my side," I inform him.

"Ugh." Milo pulls a look of mock horror. "I'll get killed over there."

"So don't cheer for the marching apples, whatever." I grin up at him. "I'll make it up to you at intermission."

"How?"

"Oh, I don't know. . . ." I shoot him a sideways glance. "But it might involve us alone, under the bleachers."

"Tempting." He runs his fingers through his crow-black hair, pretending to consider my offer. "You know it's called halftime, you theater nerd."

"I know that." I stop walking so I can pull him in for another kiss. This time, his fingers tease under the lower edge of my sweatshirt. Goose bumps rise along my waist, and all I want is to stay there forever, but we have an audience, so I pull away. After all, this isn't *Zeus!* "Intermission," I tell him.

"Fine." He takes my hand again. "Where do you want to sit?"

"The thirty-yard line," I tell him, and watch his eyebrows wing upward.

"Are you always so specific about football?"

"Ella and Bradley are saving us seats."

"Ah." Milo smiles at me. It makes me wish that intermission— I mean, halftime—would hurry up and get here. "Then we'll sit with Ella and Bradley," he says.

"Don't forget about the cuddling," I remind him.

"Oh, I haven't." That smile again. He's killing me. "Don't worry."

The great thing about it is this: I wasn't actually worried.

Not at all.

Zeus!

♡ ⚡ ♡   ⚡ ♡ ⚡ ♡

RAINIE'S CHEAT SHEET

ACT I

SCENE 1

Eros and Eris (subpar gods) tell about ancient Greece. Greek chorus (me!) explains story for audience. Zeus falls in love with Leda during her ballet solo, turns himself into swan. Swan Zeus woos Leda via dance, carries her offstage for hot poultry love.

SCENE 2

Chorus sings while Helen and Pollux (not chickens) hatch from giant eggs. She is most beautiful woman on earth (gag), he is not. Plan: Helen will be given in matrimony to King Menelaus of Sparta. Pollux: "Wait, what about me? (squawk!)"

SCENE 3

Greek forest. Goddesses Hera, Aphrodite, Athena waltz. Fine until Eris (subpar god of discord) crashes party, tosses golden apple of ~~plaster~~ discord, and says prettiest goddess gets it. Commence goddess throwdown. Zeus doesn't like fighting and says he'll get the most handsome man to choose the prettiest goddess (WHATEVER!).

SCENE 4

Paris looks in mirror and practices special self-talk about own handsomeness. Greek chorus agrees. Hera, Aphrodite, Athena show up: "Which of us is the prettiest?" Each promises a gift if Paris picks her. Aphrodite's gift is most beautiful woman on earth. Paris is into that, so he picks her.

SCENE 5

Paris and army sail across Aegean Sea to Sparta. ("Sea" made of blue cloth ... v. heavy.) Lights up on Menelaus garden, where Helen chills with friends. Eros (subpar god of love) shows up with plans to upset the apple cart: "Get it, APPLE cart, like the golden apple of discord?!" Eros shoots Helen in boob with love arrow. SO IN LOVE. Paris taking her back to Troy. At the last second, Pollux decides to come too: "Sounds like fun!"

SCENE 6

Greeks (green togas) prepare for war against Trojans (white togas). Four Greek maidens carry flaming arrows, dance around fire pits. King Menelaus (big green outfit, big green headdress, biggest flaming arrow) screams, dances, screams more. Chorus: "THIS IS WAR." Stage goes black.

INTERMISSION

ACT II

SCENE 1

Chorus tells everyone that ten years of war have passed. Big polka number. Even gods take sides and fight. Zeus finally sick of it: "Enough!" Gods stop fighting, but Greeks and Trojans do not.

SCENE 2

Helen and Paris hold hands in Trojan garden (gross). Pollux happily watches sister and bromance-bro. Battle sounds in distance. Helen/Pollux duet. Helen's part is about how much she loves Paris. Pollux's part is the same, but it's all about their bro-love. Paris apparently can't hear them singing right next to him. Crux of duet: relationships can start in deception but end in love because "look how happy everyone is now." Pollux: "Except for all the deaaaaaaad people!"

SCENE 3

Greeks (loud stage whispers) say they're leaving because they've been beaten—"But there's no room for THIS"—and exit stage. Two Trojans: "No room for WHAT?" Trojans go offstage and come back pulling giant wooden horse. Trojans think it's their new trophy (stupid Trojans) and have victory dance.

SCENE 4

Fake moon rises, spotlight on horse. It OPENS, and Greeks sneak out. Chorus (helpfully): "The horse is hollow!" Greeks open city gates and run inside. Sun rises.

SCENE 5

Battle: swords, punching, cannons. Blood galore. Tide turns toward Trojans. Paris kills Greeks' greatest hero, Achilles (hate it). Battle seems to be over. Most Greeks dead. Pollux goes to high-five Paris, all tired after war, when Zeus shows up. He's pissed again. Zeus: "For Achilles!" Zeus throws lightning at Paris, kills him super dead. Pollux catches Paris. Pollux: stirring monologue about travesties of war. Eros and Eris lead trudging march and mournful dirge.

CURTAINS
(except there's no curtain)

Acknowledgments

Much and many thanks to the following army of awesome . . .

My Carol-Carol Used-To-Be-Barlow Sigmon, for making me go to that first audition.

Maria "Maris" Moore, who grew up to teach theatre and is damn good at it.

David Furr, who is now a star.

Chet Longley, for helping me figure out why I wanted to write about this "fading institution" and why it hasn't really faded at all.

Noelle McKay, with whom I got lost in the woods, the story of which is now a thing of legend.

Sarah Horstman, for keeping the world spinning in the correct direction.

Nina Berry, for always reading proposals when I'm on deadline and desperate.

Chelsea Eberly, for gentle guidance and extraordinary vision.

Lisa Gallagher, my champion as always.

Mallory Loehr, Michelle Nagler, Elizabeth Tardiff, Barbara Bakowski, Jocelyn Lange, Josh Redlich, and the entire sparkling Random House world.

My big, nutty, chaotic extended family—parents, grandparents, sisters, cousins, aunts, uncles, everyone—for the inspiration, the support, and sometimes the names.

Everyone involved in the thirteenth season of *Grey's Anatomy*. I have the best job in the whole world. And, sure, the show is fantastic . . . but it's the people who knock my socks off.

But most of all—if you're reading this—you. You're the reason. Thank you.

About the Author

JEN KLEIN is the author of *Shuffle, Repeat*. When she's not writing YA novels, Jen is an Emmy-nominated television writer, currently writing on the series *Grey's Anatomy*. She lives in Los Angeles. Visit her online at jenkleinbooks.com and follow her on Twitter at @jenkleintweets.